'The Norwegian Arctic of Dinerstein's imagination is a strange and wonderful place, half stark wilderness and half Scandi-kitsch paradise. The constant sunlight of midsummer feeds the book's dreamy, surreal quality' *New York Times*

'A richly imagined and darkly comic story about loneliness and love at the top of the world' Jenny Offill, author of *Dept. of Speculation*

'A luminous story about love, family and the bewilderment of being young. Enchanting in every way' Maggie Shipstead, author of *Astonish Me*

'By turns ravishing and hilarious, *The Sunlit Night* is more than a shining debut – it's the work of a young master. Dinerstein writes of her two lovers with sensitivity and chutzpah … Here's an exciting new voice that sings perfectly in key' Darin Strauss, author of *Half a Life*

'Exhilarating and undeniably wise. Funny, straightforward, heartbreaking and startling, this book gets our appetites up – for more life lived … It's a book you'll be thankful for reading' Jenny Slate

'The oddball humour and pensive lyricism of Frances's narrative, as well as Yasha's poignant quest, feel alive and engaging … *The Sunlit Night* heralds the beginning of an intriguing career in fiction during which Dinerstein will hopefully continue to take us off the beaten path' *Huffington Post*

'A poetically writ_____'s more important than g____

'Dinerstein's special blend of melancholy and hope renders a character-rich, multifaceted story' *ELLE*

'*The Sunlit Night* is an original work of gentle irony counterpoised by delightful sincerity, which offers distinct turns of phrase with precision and beauty ... A novel about grief, separation and disruption – and the curative qualities of love and landscape' *Wall Street Journal*

'Well-crafted ... Perfectly rendered' *Conde Nast Traveler*

'This darkly charming debut novel takes a thoughtful look at the uncertainty of young adulthood ... Dinerstein's prose is detailed, and keeps the novel grounded as the characters face the arctic summer's end' *New Yorker*

'Two broken strangers meet by chance on a stark, sun-blasted Norwegian archipelago above the Arctic Circle; each has come in search of solitude among the mountains and fjords, but in Dinerstein's poetic debut novel, something else unexpectedly blooms' *National Geographic Traveller*

'Dinerstein's writing is light and lyrical, and her descriptions of the far north are intoxicating. Yasha and Frances and the cast of sitcom-ready Norwegian misfits who staff the museum are engaging and sad and quirky ... A poetic premise with language to match' *Kirkus*

'I curled around *The Sunlit Night* as I read, cradling it like a secret. After, I raced to share it with everyone I love' Zoe Kazan

A NOTE ON THE AUTHOR

REBECCA DINERSTEIN is the author of *Lofoten* (Aschehoug, 2012), a bilingual English–Norwegian collection of poems. She received her BA from Yale and her MFA in fiction from New York University, where she was a Rona Jaffe Graduate Fellow. She lives in Brooklyn.

rebeccadinerstein.com
@beckydinerstein

The
SUNLIT
NIGHT

REBECCA DINERSTEIN

BLOOMSBURY

LONDON · OXFORD · NEW YORK · NEW DELHI · SYDNEY

Bloomsbury Paperbacks
An imprint of Bloomsbury Publishing Plc

50 Bedford Square
London
WC1B 3DP
UK

1385 Broadway
New York
NY 10018
USA

www.bloomsbury.com

BLOOMSBURY and the Diana logo are trademarks of Bloomsbury Publishing Plc

First published in Great Britain 2015
This paperback edition first published in 2016

British Library Cataloguing-in-Publication Data
A catalogue record for this book is available from the British Library.

ISBN: HB: 978-1-4088-6303-9
         TPB: 978-1-4088-6304-6
         PB: 978-1-4088-6305-3
         ePub: 978-1-4088-6306-0

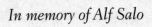

In memory of Alf Salo

CONTENTS

CONTENTS

Coda

PART ONE

. . .

The Mason Estate

In the moment after Robert Mason's condom broke he rolled off me, propped himself on his elbow, and said, "What you do doesn't help anybody." He was a four-time All-American diving champion with political aspirations, Jewish, proficient in Japanese, and a recent head page to the Department of Justice. We were both twenty-one years old. When I didn't answer, distracted by feelings of pregnancy and damnation, Robert got out of bed. He covered his magnificence with a shirt and went out to sleep in another room.

We were spending a weekend at the Mason estate, a compound in northern New England where his father, a tycoon in the tire industry, exercised his dogs. The house had many bedrooms—I was in one, Robert in another, his sister and her fiancé in a third, seven more going empty—and a large back territory, full of trees and a small body of water where one could see that summer had come. I had the impression that the summer I saw here over the lake was just a corner of a larger summer, one that stretched over the entire hemisphere, and that it was possible for me to float freely through it, riding the light wherever.

It was May, and I was interested in getting all my light in one nightless season. Then hanging on to it. That's what I needed, I

3

thought, a lesson in either light-making, or light-keeping. To fulfill graduation requirements for the art major, I had submitted a paper on urban landscapes and a few paintings of buildings. The buildings I painted were gray and wintry, pocked by rows of black windows. I had read of a man who was painting with only the color yellow—he lived in the north of Norway. The artist colony where he worked had offered me a room for the summer, as part of a painting apprenticeship program. That same week, Robert had asked me to join him in Japan after graduation. I had promptly turned Norway down. The Arctic Apprenticeship Committee argued that the master painter would accept assistants for this summer only, that I was missing a rare opportunity. I felt it was a rarer opportunity to spend the summer in love, in Shinjuku.

Now that Robert had dismissed me, I had no reason to go to Shinjuku. Robert had been invited by JANIC, the Japan NGO Center for International Cooperation; I had been invited by Robert. I scrambled for alternatives. Maybe I could go north, maybe they'd still have me. Maybe I could learn something about the world's brightness from that man and his yellow paint. Maybe I could learn to be alone.

The pharmaceutical attendant who sold us Plan B heard more of Robert's voice than I had over the course of the weekend. His silence confused his sister, who was soon to be married, and was very much in love with Timothy, her patient, bug-eyed life partner. Back at the estate, I helped myself to fruit salad. Janet and Timothy offered me napkins, water. They tilted their heads at me, looking confused and a little like Colombian lovebirds. I shrugged back, admitting that I did not know why I had been brought to their house or why I was still in it.

We heard the sound of Robert diving into the lake. He was in the habit of diving twice a day, once for form and once for breath-control drills, before and after lunch. I'd had enough silence and fruit salad and wanted to make him talk. I folded my napkin, walked out to the water, and jumped in.

He really did look happy to see me when he came up, gasping and shooting snot from his nose into his hands, and then grabbing me by the shoulders. It looked like he was about to say something. He changed his mind and went under again. He came up with a distant expression that was half Rembrandt and half Marine, shook the water out of his buzz cut, and told me we were heading inside.

His blond leg hair was tangled with weeds and algae. As we walked across the backyard, I wanted to pin him down and shave his legs, especially as we passed the outgrown family sandbox with its rakes that looked like big razors. We got to the back door and he took off his shorts. Keeping both parts of my bathing suit on, I joined him under the outdoor shower. Robert Mason Sr. had installed the stone floor himself in a little ring just big enough for two right and two left feet. Robert Jr. took it upon himself to soap us both down.

He and I had been dating for three months, during which we'd had sex infinity times and imagined a Jewish wedding. We would graduate in a month, and I'd believed that we would go out into the world as partners and live in it until we died. Japan, marriage, brises, bar mitzvai. Gradually, over the last three weeks, the fact of our being not merely incompatible, but enemies, had snuck up on this dream.

There, in my dreamy, birth-controlled stupor, as I watched the shower stream down the length of him, it was mystifying to me—the way he was essentially unkind, in the way only heroes can be; the insane thing he'd said, and the insane moment he'd said it. The shower water was warmer than the lake, and I began to feel blood again, and I began to shiver with anger, which he interpreted as a chill, turning off the water, rubbing us both with one big white towel, and leading us up to the patio where we could dry in deck chairs in the sun.

"Don't be angry, Frances," he said, finally looking at me, and meaning it. "I'm sorry about last night. What can I do?"

"You help people."

"All Masons do," he said. "It's in my blood."

Robert was an exceptionally pale young man whose veins showed at his temples. I wondered how much blood he had.

"That's the real problem here," he continued. I sat up from the leaning deck chair, wanting very much to hear the real problem. "It's where we come from. If your mother decorated, let's say, the interiors of *hospitals*, we might have more to say to each other. If your father—"

"Who said I was going to help people?" I said, leaving my parents out of it. "I am going to make paintings using the color yellow, *Bob*."

I had never called him Bob before.

"That looney tunes gig up in Lapland?" he asked.

"I'm not coming to Japan."

"In that case"—he paused—"I can't help you." He squinted at the trees in the distance, as if keeping his eyes on the future.

. . .

Janet drove us down from the house at the end of the weekend. Being from Manhattan, I had never learned to drive a car. She said we would be stopping in Providence for burritos and adjusted her rearview mirror. We drove down the interstate.

I drew up a map in my mind. Robert and I held separate tickets to Japan: the Masons' frequent-flyer miles had put Robert on a direct flight, and I had assembled a discounted multi-leg itinerary through the backlogs of the Student Travel Association. It didn't seem likely that the STA would offer flights to the Bodø Airport of Arctic Norway. And even the most inventive flight path wouldn't help: in the weeks since I'd turned it down, the apprenticeship had surely been filled. I was going home now, apparently indefinitely, and wherever I went next, there would be no more Robert Masons. I saw how everything that was about to happen would be controlled by its own door. The car door would open and let me out, the car door would shut behind me, the door to my parents' apartment would open and let me in, I would sleep there, and in the morning, as soon as I opened the door and went out, Robert would no longer be anywhere in the world. I was about to cry. I bit the skin of my inner cheek and tried to think about rocks and lizards.

We parked the car at a meter. Timothy was rubbing his hands together and saying, "Gonna get chicken." Crossing the road to the Burrito Barn, I watched Robert ahead of me in the intersection, performing his slow, weekend swagger for the cars at the next red light.

The Burrito Barn had no seating, so we ate on the road. Janet steered with one hand. I hadn't noticed the pill's aftertaste until it clashed with my chipotle sauce. When the burritos were finished and the tinfoil was bunched up and collected in the gross paper bags, there, in the backseat of the Land Rover, I let myself fall against him. I wanted to feel his solid shoulder one more time.

Robert petted my hair. He stroked my cheek, and when his fingers dragged down to my chin he pinched it. We nuzzled our heads together, in the spirit of being ex–true loves. I missed our true love. I hated him for his shoulders. My stomach burned and kept burning down I-95. Half an hour later, somewhere in New Jersey, Janet pulled over to the side of the road. Robert opened the door, carried my bag to the bus stop, and dropped it onto the curb. He pointed to one end of the road and said the bus would be coming from that way. He thanked me for coming, got back in the car, kicked the trash bag to the side where I had been sitting, shut the door, waved through the window, and went.

· · ·

I looked down the road.

After an hour, a bus came.

· · ·

I got home to find my sister climbing out the window. She had my mother's long legs—half a foot longer than mine. I climbed out after her. The fire escape had always been our only hope for a tree house, but now we hardly fit. We sat with our legs tangled, on slats just over the tops of the sidewalk trees. We took off our shoes, squeezed our calves through the slats, and let our feet hang between the branches. We were six stories high.

My sister was grinning at her toes. I assumed she would explain her delight, but she let out only a long, lazy sigh. I wanted to tell her that it was over. I wanted to tell her that I felt jilted, half pregnant, heartbroken—but Sarah was preoccupied. She looked out over the trees. I saw her eyes following each passing car, as if she

8

were counting them, lulling herself into a daze. There was no point in spoiling her lullaby with the Mason nightmare.

I left her to her joy and climbed back through the window to see my parents, who tended to be as miserable as I felt that night.

My mother wanted to know how the weekend had gone. I never gossiped with my mother, she never knew anything about whom I kissed or when I kissed them. When she asked me how things were going, I generally answered, "Good."

"Not that well," I said. My father burst out from the kitchen. "I knew it!" he said. "I knew he was no good from the night we were standing on Harrison Street, and we'd all just seen *How to Succeed in Business*, and I asked him how he liked it, and he said, 'Your daughter has very talented friends.' I should have told him, 'Go blow,'" my father said.

My father grew up on Flatbush Avenue, in a Brooklyn from another time, where his parents dressed gorgeously and drank unapologetically. My mother grew up on the only Jewish cow farm in Vermont.

"Thanks, Dad," I said.

My mother asked again what had happened. I didn't think I could answer fully, though for the first time I wanted to, because when she was my age she wasn't having sex, she was milking cows.

The most I could say was, "I don't want to see him again," which was true.

And then it was time for bed. Our apartment unfurled itself. It was a night-blooming plant of some kind—the sofa bed opening up for my parents, filling the living room until it was nothing but a man and a woman in bed, with no room left, the foot of the mattress reaching just to the knob of the front door. In the bedroom, I crawled into my bottom bunk. The top belonged to my sister, who attended New York University and lived at home, but rarely slept there. She was a year younger than me, and in love.

There was no question that her boyfriend's bed was more comfortable. It was simply larger. Everything about my family was small. It was just the four of us. We had no first cousins, no living grandparents. Physically, I had always been small. My father had been chubby as a child, had been teased for it, and now ate almost only ketchup. My mother had been long-haired and go-go-boot-wearing in the sixties, but was now short-haired and flat-shoed and ate almost only apples. We crawled into our beds like mice into holes, holes just our size. All night long, my mother would wake up and pee. My parents' pajamas were stored in the one bedroom, the one they had given to their daughters, and my father would fall asleep in his clothes on the sofa bed before coming in, middle of the night, to change. I pretended to sleep and not look at his legs when he took off his pants. Then we would all fall asleep again, in our nearby holes, and the apartment would accommodate us though we asked too much of it.

· · ·

As a child, my father had wanted to be a doctor. He followed the track faithfully: Brooklyn Borough Science Fair, AP chemistry, pre-med major. Nothing deterred his interest, until at nineteen he received a sudden rush of praise. His molecular genetics professor raved about the precision of his double helix illustrations. His organic chemistry professor photocopied my father's line-angle representations to distribute as study materials. My father started to understand his passions as distinct from his classmates', from the sea of students pursuing identical paths. He loved the way the gallbladder had the shape and color of a cactus leaf. He hated the way his course textbooks depicted the esophagus as a rigatoni noodle. He discovered that he had a talent for drawing organs the way he wanted to see them, focusing on their harsh complexity. He discovered the Association of Medical Illustrators. He believed he'd found a way to contribute his best to the medical world.

His friends progressed from pre-med to medical school. He entered a biological illustration graduate program for CAAHEP accreditation. His friends called him "lucky" with affection and disapproval: his program would take only two years. He earned his first paycheck illustrating a cross section of the human palm. His illustrations were bold. He never redrew a line. His friends, having completed their studies, and over the years having completed their residencies and having started their practices, didn't need to consult his good work. They had long since put their textbooks aside. He'd never met anyone who'd seen his illustrations. Thirty years into his work, my father couldn't say what his excellence had earned him.

His drafting desk was a slab of wood resting over his clothes drawers, in my bedroom. Scattered over the desktop lay the empty cardboard cartons of graphite crayon sets—the crayons themselves lying out one by one with broken tips—an X-Acto knife and its gleaming spare blades, stacks of sketchbooks, rolls of masking tape, a half dozen mugs. My father, his sixty-year-old head full of eternally growing hair, liked to stand at his desk with all his drawings out, smiling, talking about how miserable they made him.

How miserable they made him. How many cups of coffee he drank a day. How mad he made other men with his full head of blond hair. I believed my father's love of life was demonstrated by the coffee he drank—rabid, charged, sickening, acidic, addictive. Nobody had a bigger built-in smile than my father, though his mouth lent itself equally to extraordinary rage. At breakfast every Sunday, he asked me if his pictures were still good.

A diner we found one such morning was playing Ella Fitzgerald, so he wanted to stay. He spread ketchup over the omelet we were sharing, put his knife down, gazed out the window, then turned back, picked up his fork, scraped the ketchup off the top, and ate it alone, without egg.

"The sound is especially good in here," he said. "It sounds like they're playing live music."

Ella was singing "Cheek to Cheek" in 1956.

Nowhere was my father more at home than in a diner, in the company of waitresses and condiments. He was the most American person I knew. Perhaps my mother was the least, with her specific intelligences, her tininess, her incredible talent for self-restraint.

A toddler ran past our table waving a bendy straw. We laughed, and then my father got wretched. His flaring nostrils signaled the turn.

"No solution," he began.

I ate and let him go on.

"I did it to myself," he said. "I could have been a podiatrist. Instead, I draw feet. It's not science, and it's not art. It's just pictures. Students don't look at them. Doctors *definitely* don't look at them. How am I supposed to keep making these things when nobody cares if they exist?"

"They're gorgeous," I said. They were.

"What does it matter if you do what you love, if what you love doesn't matter?"

The waitress wanted to know if the coffee should be refilled.

He said to her, "What I do doesn't matter."

She asked, "What?"

I said, "Yes, please."

"I am sixty years old," he said to me, while she leaned, patient, voluptuous, over our table, her pot filling his cup, her hair like mine—thin, curly, getting long—and it was such a relief to have three of us at the table for a moment, another innocent party, allowing us to pause, while a French family at the next table consulted their maps.

I wanted to be able to speak to him happily, to show him the way I was when I was away from him, which was happy, which was how he wanted me to be. I had a copy of Dostoyevsky's *The Eternal Husband* with me and showed him its bright pink cover, to change the subject.

"Bought it for the title?" was his first joke. He flipped the book over. There was only a single line of text on the back: "The most monstrous monster is the monster with noble feelings." We looked at the quote together from opposite sides of the table.

. . .

My mother keeps a sea monster in five porcelain parts (\ ^ ^ ^ /) on her office desk, beside a row of long-living orchids. She works at a small interior design company. On a shelf beside her upholstery samples, she keeps a photograph of my father making a duck face with his lips, a photograph of me as an eight-year-old in a purple summer camp T-shirt, and one of my sister, age eleven, holding a pizza box on Lexington Avenue. The photos are displayed in reversible, clear-plastic frames that hold four images but take up the counter space of two. The thing that my mother likes most, personally and professionally, is the efficient use of space.

An example of which is the sofa bed. If the pillows are hidden in the chest-bottom of the Oriental side table with the remote controls on top; if the blankets are folded up into the groove between the piano and the wall; if the pajamas are in the children's room; if the kitchen bowls and cookie tins fit concentrically inside one another, inside the cabinets with their clever wire separators; if the children sleep on top of each other; if the sofa bed pulls out to the door—

My mother apologized to every person who entered our home for its size. She told strangers her dream of a bedroom with a door. She designed duplex apartments, four-bed, three-bath; she made pillow recommendations to the owners of five-story brownstones; she was responsible for the strippable, nonwoven wallpaper of Connecticut summer homes. Two healthy daughters and one city-priced bedroom later, her salary was spent. She did what she could to make our space count.

· · ·

I don't remember why they fought. Why was my father always, *always* screaming? I can't remember it ever having to do with my mother herself. It was a performance *for* her, as she was his best audience. "He's an actor," his mother had said. He was, with his wildness, showing my mother how genuinely angry he was: a good and smart man who worked hard at what he loved, in the field where he had become at last excellent, making work that he knew was beautiful and useful, but that nobody ever used.

He bellowed. He never struck her. It was not that kind of attack. My father was only screaming a version of Love me, because I love you, because you allow me to suffer, because it feels good when we suffer near each other.

Other fights were fights about fighting.

"You only know how to bark," she would say.

He would shout something unintelligible.

"Bark! Bark!" would be her retort.

Sick of her barking, he would storm out.

Whose problem was it? Mine, or hers, or his? In the chain of things, it became mine: my father was an innocent victim of the medical community; my mother was an innocent victim of my father; I was an innocent child. If it wasn't our apartment's door that he slammed, it was the diner's door. If it wasn't my problem, it was nobody's, and then what? Innocence felt so much like inertia to me, I wanted conviction. This desire coincided with high school. I wore my pants baggier and baggier, my shirts tighter and tighter, my headphones the size of my head.

My parents were older than all of my friends' parents. They had been college seniors in 1969 and lived in Greenwich Village in the seventies, but I knew that my parents had never been involved in any kind of free love, that they hadn't bothered over Dylan or Mitchell, that they listened to the same Bach partitas then as now. I don't know what they were doing while their classmates were stringing flowers. I pictured them climbing concrete staircases.

The way my parents weren't cool was timeless, as if all the bands and pant shapes and shoe heights of all the ages had passed right by them, leaving their good sense intact.

With pride, my father always said I was born a "dark, serious" baby. He always followed that, sadly, with the fact that I had become "a blabbermouth." It was difficult to be nearly as serious, as Bach-like, as my parents liked things to be. When my younger sister turned eighteen, she began dating Scott Glenny, a boy who had been allowed to play video games all his life. He would turn out to be a gifted computer programmer, but my parents couldn't have known that. Scott's talent bred in him a rude form of confidence, one that led him to mock my father's "doodles," and even on occasion to belittle Sarah's veterinary studies—her "girlie" love of animals. My parents suspected him of being a jerk and a moron. When my sister came home from his big messy bedroom, she would beg for the radio station to be switched, for something other than Chopin to be played in our house. It never happened.

We all lived together in our one-bedroom over the Crane, a classic American restaurant whose classic American roaches scared me when I turned on the bathroom light. I went out and could not come home at night without opening the front door right into the sofa bed and my parents' open-mouthed sleeping. The only way we knew how to be was in each other's way.

I could not call it a loveless marriage. There was this certain, occasional thing that happened where my mother held my father's head in her hand and brushed his hair off his forehead. I knew their tenderness when I saw it. But was it the luminous partnership I wished for myself, and for my sister?

. . .

My father and I were at the kitchen table for breakfast. I had woken up early from a night full of Robert nightmares, but my sister was still sleeping deeply, her taxicab lullaby evidently a success. My mother was in the kitchen, scrambling eggs.

When the eggs were hard, and the juice poured, and the napkins folded perfectly, my mother sat down. I moved the toast and the Nutella from the kitchen counter to the table. Morning light bounced off the back of Sarah's chair.

"Sleeping Beauty," my father called to the bedroom.

And then the bedroom door opened, and Sarah and her left hand came to the table.

Had it been there the night before? She sat down and we stared. Had I failed to see the sparkle in the dark, on the fire escape? Sarah rested her adorned hand on the lid of the Nutella jar.

She looked around the table, pausing at each of our faces, but none of us spoke, so she opened the jar, dipped her knife to the bottom, and spread a piece of toast over until it was completely brown. She bit and chewed with her lips closed, smiling.

"How did he propose?" I asked. My sister began her answer, which to my embarrassment I could not fully recall when Yasha asked me about it months later. They had taken a ride on the Staten Island Ferry. I think Sarah had been posing as the Statue of Liberty when Scott got down on his knee. While she told the story, I was distracted by my mother's enormous eyes, which were full of agony. My father was ready to speak. I saw something on his mind gaining momentum. When my sister ended her story, my father said, "Good, because your mother and I are separating." He added, "Good you'll be out of the house." He looked at my sister, then at me. He concluded, "There won't be a house for you anyway."

My mother said, "Saul."

He said, "Cat's out."

She said, "Saul."

My sister said, "Mom?"

My mother said, "Congratulations."

"He's a schmo, Scott Glenny," my father said. "You're marrying a schmo."

. . .

I went as quickly as possible to Grand Central Station. Without a ticket, I boarded the train and lay flat across three seats.

My sister was at Scott's dorm by now, being consoled. I wondered if she would tell him what my parents had said. Schmo. Putz. All the Yiddish words for *not this guy*. The wedding was scheduled for September. Mrs. Glenny was hosting. Mr. Glenny would spend the summer repainting the Glenny house; they could marry in the Glenny garden. Summer didn't come to San Francisco until September, Scott's mother told Sarah, and when it came, it was glorious. In explaining the arrangements, Sarah repeated the word *glorious*. My father repeated the word *schmuck*.

Scott was my year, graduating. Sarah intended to take a year off before her senior year, move to California, and then see about graduating with work-credit transfers. Dropbox had offered Scott a staggering entry salary. Sarah would have plenty of time before she needed her own income. I knew this would only encourage Scott to call Sarah's work "superfluous." My mother wanted to know what she had done to drive Sarah to this marriage. My sister wanted to know what she had done to drive our parents to this separation. None of us could fathom one another.

The jig is up, I thought, riding the front car of the 11:07 train. We'd finally canceled one another out. It was a two-hour ride back to school. I had one more week of exams. Two months until Robert left for Japan. Four months until the wedding, if there was going to be a wedding. All the sailboats in New England were mounted, dry, along the shore that curved in the train's eastern windows—boats that would soon be waxed for summer.

I wanted to steal a boat. Preferably a houseboat. Someplace where I could live for a while, while my family adjusted.

I wanted to know whose idea all this had been. I wanted to know if my father had been a good kisser. I wanted to know how many men had kissed my mother, and how well. I wanted to know if she planned on kissing new men now. I wanted to know if my mother was a good kisser. I had been told that I was a good kisser, and I wanted to kiss my mother and talk to her about romance.

Sarah and Scott had gone on their first date in October of Sarah's freshman year. My parents, from the start, found Scott unforgivably un-Jewish, unimaginative, tasteless, sporty, and dull. My sister found his talent for leisure and his lack of anxiety breathtaking (our family loved work, loved anxiety) and spoke to me about his being a "liberated man." I think it was this very liberation my parents resented. And was my sister liberating herself, then, via marriage?

The conductor came and asked for my ticket. It was a young conductor, his uniform too large for him, and I was crying, and this frightened him. He apologized for asking, waited a second, then asked again. I wanted to make him comfortable—I sat up straight and slapped myself on the cheeks a little and gave him my debit card. He charged me the station price. He apologized again and said that I had saved four dollars. I thanked him and blew my nose in my ticket and turned back to the window. More boats, more houses.

I hadn't ever made a decision as large as getting married, or getting divorced. I liked to move alone through vast fields or pastures. Throughout college, during the summers, I would find ways for the university to send me somewhere, wherever they were sending people. I went with a small suitcase, to stare intensely at the livestock—Irish sheep, English sheep—paint the animals, and find somebody with a funny foreign name to make love to on a foreign kitchen floor before coming home to my parents' empty refrigerator.

There would be two refrigerators, surely still empty, humming in the corners of my parents' separate apartments. They were taking the summer to move out of our old place and find new ones. I wondered if they would eat more without each other. Whether they would grow fatter and happier, or waste away. And why they were doing this, doing it now, after not doing it for so long. An announcement said, "Please take all your belongings with you." The train pulled into the station with a screech and a thump, marking the last time I would come back to school before it too ended.

. . .

I shared a dorm with four girls, most of whom had made some kind of plan. One was accepted into the Yale School of Drama. Another was accepted, together with her high school sweetheart, into the University of Chicago Law School. A third got a job in the offices of Kaiser Consulting.

My father had never worked in an office. In his post-college youth in New York, he ate toasted bagels with his friend Carl at Fanelli's on Prince and Mercer, got drunk on spiked milk, and occasionally helped his mother package blush behind her makeup counter. His proudest commercial achievement was "making change" ("Do you have to make change?" he asked brightly when I got a high school waitressing job) on his parents' noncalculating cash register. New York no longer had room for this particular, charming kind of bum.

My friend Igor wrote code for Google. I had recently visited his office for lunch. We'd jumped in ball pits and cruised down the halls on Razor scooters to reach the cafeteria. In the first draft of my cover letter to Google Marketing, I had written about my enjoyable visit to the Google office and "the jazz of the ball pit." My cousin, a software engineer, suggested I cut this phrase. I rewrote the letter to include the terms *product, content*, and *enable*. My interview gave me an excuse to wear a magenta blazer, but I didn't get the job.

At the open information session for private equity jobs, I had gotten as far as a pair of giveaway rubber flip-flops and a Rubik's cube. I had a preliminary interview with the Boston Consulting Group, but I couldn't say how many dentists there were in America. The interviewer suggested I begin my calculations, next time, with the number three hundred million.

I wasn't cut out for these jobs. I had been born, as Robert Mason had pointed out, into a desperately artistic family.

Perhaps there were other parts of the world, I thought, where one could make a living as an artist. I sat by the window of the pizza parlor nearest the train station and ate a Grandma slice, trying to imagine the Arctic. Was it yellow up there? Was that what this man's paintings were all about? I didn't know what it meant to live in an "artist colony," and I wondered how many artists there would be. If they were local artists, they would be very good, by now, at painting wide-open spaces. Maybe they could teach me how to paint light. Maybe I could teach them how to paint buildings. Maybe they knew of whole new un-American colors. Colors New Yorkers would want to buy. Colors that came out of that thin northern air. A breeze blew in through the pizza shop's windows. I put back the oregano. In the computer lab down the street, I found the colony's invitation halfway down my Gmail trash folder.

It promised to be solitary, and terribly far away. The directions described an eighteen-hour train ride that started in Oslo and connected to a four-hour ferry across a major fjord. It was recommended that I bring gear for heavy storms. The colony denied responsibility for the health and well-being of its tenants. The master painter was not to be held accountable for the artistic progress of apprentice painters. The Norwegian government requested that all international tenants state their purpose to the local police upon arrival. Leaving the colony was possible only when the fjord proved crossable, on select and unforeseeable days.

I asked the Arctic if it would still have me.

A girl named Ingeborg had taken the apprenticeship. The committee did not fail to describe her talent, her cordial personality, and their excitement at the prospect of her joining the Yellow Room project before explaining that she had subsequently declined the position and instead taken an internship at the Norwegian National Gallery.

In the morning, our last roommate, the one who kept track of job offers by sticking Post-it announcements to our suite's front door, who herself had not yet found a job but would soon become the cactus expert for the Natural Gardener in Austin, Texas, posted a note on the wall with my name and the words *Far North*.

. . .

On Graduation Day, my parents arrived with Sarah, who'd flown in from a hiking vacation with Scott's family. I had never seen either of my parents put their feet into water. I had never seen my father's calves. My parents liked to be clothed, indoors, and in Manhattan. To the graduation ceremony, my mother wore a royal blue dress with large buttons and black rubber-soled shoes. My father's tie was brown-red, the color of scabs. I was wearing a cowboy hat with small red berries embroidered around the brim.

I don't remember the origin of the hat tradition, but all of us graduating had our heads covered: with straw, crowns, helmets, plain yarmulkes, open books tied to the head with ribbon and worn as bonnets. We filled the yard in our folding chairs. My friend Emily was called up onstage to accept the George Andrus Prize for intellectual achievement, character, and personality. Robert Mason was called up onstage to accept the Hart Boell Award for qualities of courage, strength of character, and high moral purpose.

I recalled the bus station where he'd left me. I thought of highways, superbridges, stretched lines, my father's pencils, my future canvas. All I had was a direction, north.

What did my father have? Saul had the American songbook, the Brooklyn Bridge, his love of babies, and Catherine Deneuve's chocolate cookie recipe.

My mother, though this was perhaps not a blessing, had a new interior to design. As the honorary degrees were conferred, I pictured my mother living alone. It looked queenly. When I turned around to look for her in the crowd, I saw she had taken a seat behind my father. My mother looked like she could see the whole world from where she sat. My sister sat in the row behind my mother, looking just like her, except pinker in the cheeks. My sister's focus was narrowing steadily on a single point: Scott Glenny. She and my parents were still barely speaking to one another, overwhelmed by what all three called *disgust*.

Robert came down from the stage and retook his chair, not far from mine. We too looked straight ahead. All the graduates rose and were recognized.

After the ceremony, I packed up my room, keeping only what I'd take north. How hot was an arctic summer? I took both sandals and wool sweaters. I gave shoes and dresses to my sister. I took my necklaces, my brushes, and all my socks. My room-mates picked from among my books, and the rest were left outside the library in a cardboard box. It took a long time to make the room really empty. I didn't know then that I was practicing for a greater emptying, the one I'd perform four months later, when the entire Gregoriov Bakery would need to be closed and cleared. Once my dorm room looked ready for someone else to move in, it was time to go.

We got home and found the sofa bed unmade. My mother, in our previous life, would never have left it this way. Now she flung her handbag onto the heap of blankets, removed her shiny black shoes, and sat on the corner of the bed nearest the window. She leaned her head back, as if in meditation. My sister moved her bag and sat atop the blanket heap. My father sat on the corner of the bed nearest the door. I was left the fourth corner, the one canopied by my mother's collection of orchids. I slouched under the flowers and found they had no smell. None of us faced each other. For the first time, the thin pull-out mattress seemed large, seemed adequate.

. . .

Early in the morning on the first of June, I rode the A train from West 4th Street to JFK. It took an hour and a half; the city's population boarded and exited the train along the way, and I focused on the presence of so many people, soon to be replaced by artists, mountains, animals. I entered the departures terminal and checked in.

Some people claim that life is not making love to them. My father claimed this. Some people have never been made good love to, or don't remember, or haven't been taught how, and cheat their lives out of the pleasure we each can make in one another.

I thought: one must want to make love to life.

From my father, I had inherited a certain amount of discipline. We both could wake early and work intensely for hours. We were both comfortable in our own company. We were not lonely, or lazy. But discipline, I felt certain, had to be paired with joy. Otherwise it went to waste. Waste, like pictures that nobody sees, or waking up early without then slicing your bread, nodding to the weather, and relishing the fabric of your sleeves as you push your arms through.

Lofoten lay some ninety-five miles above the Arctic Circle, a string of six islands in the Norwegian Sea.

I was looking for a love unlike my parents' love or my sister's love or the love on a foreign kitchen floor. I wanted my own kitchen to keep clean and full of bread and milk and hot sauce and a big clean empty sink where I could wash my dishes. I wanted to forgive my mother and father for their misery and find myself a light man who lived buoyantly and to be both his light and his dark, serious baby.

PART TWO

. . .

The Gregoriov Bakery

Yasha had begun to measure time in bread. The Gregoriov Bakery was in its tenth year. His father had propped up in the store window a "10" made out of a cruller twist and an everything bagel, which he replaced on the first of each month. The stale twists were fed to Septimos, their Brooklyn cat, named after Septimos, their Russian cat. Both cats were black. Yasha's mother, a piano teacher, had chosen the name in honor of their first cat's unusual purring: precise musical sevenths. Brooklyn Septimos purred like a normal cat. Yasha had taken to calling him Sam. Yasha could no longer recall, even when he tried, the sound of his first cat's sevenths. He could recall only the image of Russian Septimos licking his mother's hands as she played piano. This anniversary would also mark the tenth year since Yasha had seen his mother.

They had been doing all the work without her. Yasha's primary responsibilities were maintaining the window displays and "customer seduction," as his father Vassily called it. Vassily knew what he had working in his favor: his son's natural handsome-ness, his store's plot on central Oriental Boulevard, the age-old significance of bread, the fact that bread went stale and needed replenishing. These were the forces driving his business. He was not driven, himself, to increase the bakery's sales, especially in this tenth year. Aside from the special window display, the anniversary went uncelebrated. He no longer wanted the bakery; he no longer wanted America. He wanted his wife.

The two Gregoriov men woke each morning, did stretching exercises—Vassily was a proponent of stretching in the morning— and baked. It was Yasha's senior year of high school and he was the only kid he knew who woke up before five. There was, because of that necessary principle of replenishing, a great amount to bake each morning. Yasha moved the loaves in pairs, from the cooling rack to the window display. The window became a kind of ark, and Yasha sometimes tried to make the twin babkas and Danishes look like mating animals. It was hard to make bread look alive—it had no legs, no face. Yasha had once tried carving a smiley face into a particularly yellow challah. His father had slapped him for making the bread look cheap. Sudden movements, like slaps, or a loaf slipping from Yasha's hands to the floor, lifted the thin coat of cornmeal from the bakery's every surface into a brief fog.

· · ·

One June Friday, Yasha made a window display out of fresh cheese Danishes. It was his favorite kind of Friday—dark, warm, and foggy. This fog, unlike the sour air of the bakery, was thick and odorless. He liked to move through it, feeling it part for him and cling to his sides. He went to school feeling unusu- ally relaxed. There were only three more days of school. He had American government, gym, and comparative economics, followed by a lunch of three plain pizza slices. In senior workshop, his teacher asked him to write a story that revolved around one central problem. Yasha was astounded by how little came to mind. It should be easy, he thought. He started a list.

A problem:

Cat scratched customer
Out of bialys
Hypertrophic cardiomyopathy
Friday night oven cleaning

He erased the whole list. He looked at the blank page, and then wrote his name in the upper right-hand corner.

YAKOV VASSILIOVICH GREGORIOV

It was a long name. Too long. He leaned his chair onto its two back legs. Americans didn't have such long names. They were economical with their syllables. If he was going to have such a long name, Yasha thought, he might as well get more bang out of his syllables. Under his name, he wrote:

YASHA: THE SUBHARMONIC
THUNDERGROWL OF THE WEST

"Five minutes," his teacher said.

Yasha tried to focus on his problems. He imagined his father at the bakery, alone, eating a bialy. It was too hot to eat soup. He could see his father sitting with a quarter-pound tub of cream cheese, dipping his bialy into it. High school would end next week. *Good riddens*, his father would say, imitating the voice of the landlord, Mr. Dobson, who had taught him the expression. *Good riddens to high school.*

Yasha could blame his father's current despair on the institution of American schooling. And the Berlin Wall. He pictured Vassily scooping up a fresh mound of cream cheese with the edge of his bialy, and tearing a bite off with his small teeth.

This was the legend his father had told him: the Berlin wall had fallen, Russia's emigration laws had shifted, and Yasha's mother Olyana had said, "Let Yakov go to an American school." Olyana had grown up speaking French and English, with tutors. Vassily had grown up imitating the snorts of his family's pigs. Olyana had married Vassily, his father claimed, for a taste of the other side. The "simple," she had generously called it. Vassily could not imagine that the simple would hold her attention. Then the drama came. The drama appealed to her: the wall fell, the doors opened, and they left.

But they didn't all leave. Olyana had put on her best dress— brown with small green buttons at the back of the neck—and gone to her father's old accountants for the Moscow–Paris–New York plane tickets. Tickets were nearly impossible to come by. The men were good to her; she reminded them of her late father, their boss, a presiding member of the Duma, who had always paid them on time and celebrated every Christmas with gifts of herring. They gave her one first-class ticket, for herself. It was the only one they could spare. For her simple husband and her simple child, they gave a pair of standard seats, on a flight that would leave before hers. Three tickets of any kind was great luck, they said, considering the demand, may her father rest in peace.

Olyana came home to Vassily that night and allowed him to peel her brown dress from her body, beginning with the green buttons. Afterward, still undressed, she gave Vassily the two tickets. The tickets became fused in Vassily's mind with this moment of his wife's radiant nakedness, and he took them, and that evening he let Yasha, who was seven, hold them and measure their length with a ruler. Yasha couldn't remember the ruler.

He only remembered that the week after Olyana secured the tickets, he and his father entered New York City. Vassily's brother had been in touch with a friend of a second cousin. This friend lived in Brighton Beach. Yasha, not yet four feet tall, slept for three nights in the man's armchair, while Vassily slept on his couch. The apartment looked out over Oriental Boulevard, where prominent Cyrillic letters soothed Vassily's homesickness. One empty storefront flashed a sign: FOR RENT. CALL CHARLES DOBSON. On the phone, Mr. Dobson responded well to Vassily's accent, and assured him that Brighton Beach was where he belonged. The previous owner's ovens were still installed, Mr. Dobson said, and the upstairs space would accommodate the whole family. The Gregoriov Bakery opened its doors. In the attic apartment above the bakery, Vassily and Yasha made two beds—one single, one double. They waited for Olyana to join them. She did not.

. . .

Yasha chose *Out of bialys* from his original list and wrote a story in which his father had eaten the last one, and Mr. Dobson came by for a dozen for Mrs. Dobson's birthday, and Mr. Dobson was terribly disappointed and screamed, *Good riddance, Gregoriovs!* and kicked them out of their bakery forever, and the cat ran away out of shame. Yasha stood up and read it before the class, winning giggles from the two curliest-haired girls, Sidney and Alexa. They had loved him since tenth grade. Yasha figured that they mostly liked his hair, which was also curly. Sidney and Alexa were best friends, and admired and encouraged each other in loving Yasha as a team.

The girls, as well as most of his classmates, assumed that Yasha didn't like them. He did well on his tests and had a naturally sour twist on his lips and never stopped to talk in the halls. He was tall, and his shoulders were fully developed, making him look stronger than he was. The girls assumed that in Russia, Yasha had enjoyed a succession of fur-wearing, princess-like girlfriends. Of course, Yasha had been far too young in Russia for girls. And in America, throughout middle school, he had still been too Russian, and consequently, too shy. By high school, he had lost his accent and grown to a full six feet. He felt comfortable looking at the girls he liked. He could in most cases stare straight over their heads without ever making it known that he was paying attention to them—but he wasn't going to approach them. He'd had little practice talking to girls of any kind, and the American teenage girl was a particularly challenging place to start. In any case, Yasha didn't have time to try. He was due at the bakery immediately after school. His father relied on him to manage the afternoon rush.

The only girl he had ever managed to speak to, outside of class, before going home, was a redheaded flutist whom he'd seen perform in the symphonic band. He had complimented her fingering, a term he found in *A Flutist's Handbook*, and regretted it feverishly ever since. When he realized that this girl bore an uncanny resemblance to his mother, as he remembered her, he went off girls for a good year. He had never yet kissed.

. . .

"I have been given a few new piano students," Olyana had explained at first. "I need more time." She asked, "Is Yasha healthy? Is Yasha in school?"

"Yes," Vassily said. "Both. Please come."

"She is coming," Vassily told Yasha.

"I don't see her," Vassily's brother, Daniil, said when he called from Moscow. "I don't see her in your window."

"She is coming," Vassily told Yasha.

The Gregoriov Bakery's phone number was added to the public directory. Yasha's father was proud and flattered when she found it. Olyana called the store phone every couple of weeks.

"Is Yasha healthy? Is Yasha in school?"

"Yes," Vassily said. "Are you coming?"

"Our recital is in the spring," she said, or she said, "The Christmas Concert."

"I can't find her," Daniil told Vassily. "She doesn't live in your house anymore."

The phone rang, and Vassily took the phone into the bakery's bathroom.

"Is Yasha healthy? Is Yasha in school?"

"Yes," Vassily said. "Please come."

Yasha stopped asking about his mother after his third year in America, the year he turned ten.

Vassily did not visit a doctor during his first four years in New York. In April of the bakery's fifth year, Yasha saw his father faint while moving a twenty-pound bag of flour. Mr. Dobson scheduled and paid for a physical exam.

"They call it hypertrophic cardiomyopathy," Vassily told his son. "My heart muscle is extra thick," Vassily said, making himself laugh. His hair, waist, and legs had always been too thin. "They say many people live a normal life," he said.

When Vassily told his brother, Daniil replied with another piece of news. "I found her," Daniil said. "She has moved to her cousin's estate." Vassily wrote down her new phone number, and even the loops of the nines and sixes looked luxurious. He showed the number to Yasha, and said Olyana had finally found her way back to the grand from the "simple." "Damn the estate," Vassily said, in one of his life's few bouts of anger. The bakery was flourishing. Why give her family another reason to sneer at him, at his abnormal valve function, his latest inadequacy? Yasha was twelve years old. He had never seen his father so angry, nor felt less able, himself, amid his personal squirming, suddenly tall and usually silent, to confront his long-invisible mother. Father and son agreed to keep the news of Vassily's heart quiet, and Mr. Dobson scheduled a series of checkups with the cardiologist.

The slowness with which Vassily was forced to knead his dough, in order to avoid chest pain, made his bread fluffier and more elastic. The Gregoriov Bakery put the Arkady Bakery out of business.

Four more years passed before it was time to implant a defibrillator. This was the last resort, according to Vassily's medical pamphlets. This was what the doctors did when the heart was so unstable it needed to be monitored from the inside. Vassily retrieved the old slip of butcher paper from under the cash register, where he'd hidden his wife's number instead of throwing it out years earlier. Cornmeal had eroded the ballpoint ink, but each digit was still legible. He called, carefully entering the country code first. No rings, then a prerecorded message: Эта телефонная линия была отключена. This number has been disconnected.

Daniil had no new information. Vassily had no way of reaching her. The doctors allowed Vassily six months until the implantable cardioverter-defibrillator would have to be inserted over his right ventricle. In this six-month period, while he could still travel,

Vassily wanted to see Moscow one more time, face his wife's family, and demand her whereabouts. Yasha had finally stopped wondering where she could be.

. . .

Senior workshop ended for the day and Sidney and Alexa said, "Got bread?" to Yasha in unison. Yasha made it out of the room and down the stairs without having to look at the ceramic tea mugs they were working on together and had in Sidney's locker, if he wanted to see. Outside it was still dark, warm, and foggy. He descended calmly into the subway. When he got out onto the elevated platform at Brighton Beach, the air had grown even saltier, and the Friday-ness of the whole planet's atmosphere lifted him home, slowly, down Oriental Boulevard. Simon & Garfunkel's "Mrs. Robinson" poured out of the open door at Yefim's Barbershop. Yefim was singing along, and Yasha too continued the song's *da-doo*s as he walked past. When he finished singing "Mrs. Robinson," he began to sing "America." He had learned both off his father's copy of *Bookends*, the first album they'd bought in New York.

Yasha performed the opening hums of "America" with real zest, wildly off pitch, scaring a squirrel who had just found a piece of kebab meat. People liked him. Girls liked him. Girls wanted to show him their tea mugs. Yasha looked out toward the shore of Manhattan Beach and sang, "Let us be lovers, we'll marry our fortunes together." The waves were low and steady. Yasha felt a fortune coming to him. He intended to share it, whenever it came—whether it was wealth or a Ducati Streetfighter S—with his father. His father wouldn't be able to ride the Ducati. His father worried him. Certain mornings, his father stopped kneading, rested his floury hands on the counter, and breathed heavily for a few moments. When it passed, he began kneading again, with a little less force.

Yasha looked down at his own body as he walked. He wondered if he was still growing. He was tall enough, but he wanted his heart to grow stronger than his father's. He wanted to get from his heart its full worth: natural instructions for kissing, more courage at the right moments—the reckless blood-pumping that would make him a real American lover. It had been a decade since he'd arrived in Brooklyn, and now he was nearly a legal American adult, but today, for the first time—saluting a dog who'd just peed on a bag of garbage, smelling salt and exhaust on the breeze, scanning the straight course of the avenue beyond him—Yasha felt like a genuine New Yorker.

When he reached the bakery, his father was sitting just inside the window, chewing a toothpick, holding an envelope and a steel ruler.

"Just in time," Vassily said. He stood up, slid the envelope under a large knife, spat his toothpick out, and tucked his shirt into his pants. It was just before three o'clock, and the usual crowd would soon arrive—the delirious cookie children, a few nurses, Mr. Dobson, and the man they called "Dostoyevsky." Yasha put his books in the back and tied a black half-apron around his waist. His Garfunkely feeling of contentment had worn off a little. He cleaned his glasses and waited for the customers to come. The door opened.

Dostoyevsky arrived first. He had a beard and a straight nose and hair that looked meticulously combed. He'd come in the past couple Fridays, always wearing leather boots, his jeans rolled up as if to show them off, with a collection of child-sized instruments hanging off his shoulder. Tucked into the miniature guitar case he kept one or another paperback Dostoyevsky novel. He would place his order, and then read aloud while Yasha wrapped the bread. Yasha did nothing to encourage him. Still, the man came every week and read.

Today's quotation: "'He was seldom playful, seldom even merry, but anyone could see at once, at a glance, that this was not from any kind of sullenness . . .'" Dostoyevsky looked up at Yasha, and then back down. He went on, "'Maybe for that very reason he was never afraid of anyone . . .'" The man grinned and nodded broadly. Yasha handed him the sourdough.

"Thank you," Yasha said.

"Thank *you*," said the man, pushing his thick *Brothers Karamazov* back in with the miniature guitar. He met Yasha's blank expression with a face-stretching smile that lasted longer than Yasha could bear. At last, he turned to leave. Yasha watched him go. Hard to say whether the man just loved Russian literature or had lost his mind. Dostoyevsky walked cheerfully out to the street. His sourdough banged against his set of chimes as he walked. Vassily laughed and turned on the commercial-sized mixer.

"Just because I am Russian doesn't mean I am Alyosha, for fuck's sake," Yasha muttered.

Vassily laughed, then sneezed. "Yakov Vassiliovich," he said, attempting ceremoniousness.

"Hm?"

Vassily inched toward the knife that lay over the envelope.

"You see," Vassily began. Yasha turned to him brusquely, still irritated by Dostoyevsky's quote. The windows that spread out behind Yasha were full of a gray mist. Yasha's face was in shadow.

Vassily's shoulders sank, and he took a step back. "I am going to the bathroom," Vassily said.

"Okay." Yasha squinted and waited to hear the rest. "Is that all?"

Vassily didn't answer. He walked into the back office and closed the door. Yasha turned on the television that was hidden in the crevice behind the front door. Brazil was playing Portugal. From behind the counter, he watched the tiny running shoes racing after the ball. Beside him, the mixer folded the flour into the eggs, and the large bowl buzzed against the wall. Brazil scored a goal. Now there was the bowl buzzing, the eggs smacking, and the roar of the crowd. The screen switched to instant replay. Without his glasses, all Yasha could see was the same old homework geometry—the kicker's body was a vertical line, and his leg was horizontal, curving the trajectory of a small shooting sphere. Yasha followed the kicker's outward leg line, through the ball and the blurred mesh of the goal, just off the screen, through the window, and out onto Oriental Boulevard, where there was a woman beside the mailbox. It was his mother. There was a commercial break.

Yasha did not doubt his identification. Nicknames for "Mother" in Russian flooded him. Her chin, lips, and eyes matched both his memory and the only two photographs he'd seen of her in the last ten years. Her hair was still red. She had come. His mind emptied for a moment. Then he thought: Let her look for me, good. Yasha turned to see if his father had come back, if he too had seen her. The door was still closed. When Yasha looked out again his mother was running, clumsily, in heels, away from the mailbox and toward the elevated subway tracks.

· · ·

It was an ordinary Friday in Brighton Beach but now everyone was running. Even the man who was standing still on the curb seemed to be running backward at exactly Yasha's pace. When Yasha came to the end of the block he leapt down too forcefully and was shin-shocked, the sting rushing up to his knee. The discomfort as he ran made him feel old, older than his mother, who, from the back, could very well have been the flutist from symphonic band.

Yasha wanted to stop, or did not know why he had started. If she hadn't wanted to see him all these years, why had she come now? She kept on running, and he was close behind. She was thin and could twist between the street crowds. They were one window apart. Yasha saw his mother stop. They met in front of the chocolate store.

"Do not tell your father," she said, smiling horridly, resting her hands on her knees. Yasha forgot all his languages.

Being with her, face-to-face, Yasha felt like a child. The rumbling of train tracks above made it impossible to hear anything. His mother looked around at all the Russian shop fronts. She had painted a black line fanning out from the corner of each eye, and wore a necklace of small pink pearls. She looked so happy to see him, Yasha almost fell into her arms. To keep from hugging her, he crossed his arms behind his back and stood up straight.

In spite of his posture, he wanted his mother to touch him, to take his face into her hands. She only looked up at him. He wondered how he looked. He wondered if he looked seven years old to her, or like a "man," which was a stupid word that he hated having to think about. He hadn't yet cared if he was a man or not, he had been taking it all as it came—his height, his torso as it grew—but now she must have been evaluating him on the whole. Did he look right, or old, or even recognizable? She turned away from him and examined the candies in the window. His brain offered up one definite memory: that his mother was fond of milk chocolate, that they had, on some warm-weather day, shared a long bar of milk chocolate shaped like Saint Basil's Cathedral.

It started to rain. Everybody passing in the street seemed to be looking at her—she was wearing a bright blue knee-length short-sleeved dress that lifted in the wind. Her pearls were getting wet and extra shiny across her neck. She was smiling so ferociously, her arms were so thin, and her dress was so blue, that it was impossible not to look at her, to want to invite her inside.

His father must have been out of the bathroom by now. Yasha wondered if he was calling the neighbors, looking for him. Yasha had left the cash register and the door open. Why wasn't she saying anything? The only thing she had said, before she began her rapturous survey of the neighborhood, was, *Do not tell your father*. Yasha wondered if she was, at bottom, cruel. He wanted to get her inside. He wanted to touch her, if she wasn't going to touch him. It wasn't impossible. For the first time in ten years, touching her wasn't impossible. He placed his hand on her elbow and led her into the chocolate store.

His mother laughed.

"Sweets!" his mother said. The shopkeeper nodded her head and gave the blue dress a skeptical once-over.

"Don't you need a paper towel?" the shopkeeper said, in Russian. Olyana walked up to the cash register and responded in low, animated Russian—something about an umbrella whose handle had snapped off. Her Russian was strange. At home, she had spoken to Yasha almost exclusively in English—in her old-fashioned, tutor-taught British accent. She'd demanded that he speak English every day, "for his future." The kids at his Moscow primary school had nicknamed him Bill Clinton.

When she turned around from the counter she was already eating something—a single nonpareil.

"You live here," she said, part statement, part question, looking past him and out the window. She uncurled her fist, revealing two more nonpareils.

Yasha turned to the window, to see what she was watching. It wasn't pretty. Old men and women were buying tomatoes, and it was raining hard now, and the raised subway platform seemed to be dripping grit onto the street. Cars honked. Everything had gone gray with the clouds except two neon signs, one pink, one orange. They looked sickly and overcharged. His mother looked satisfied, and ran her now empty hand through her hair.

"You sent us here," Yasha said, and for a first thing to say, he thought that wasn't bad.

His mother's face lit up, as if it were exactly what she had wanted to hear. "Yes!" she said, and clasped her hands, "and look!" She looked at him from his toes to his hair. Yasha wished that he had showered. His hair was stuck to his head with sweat and rain, and he was still wearing, to his horror, an apron. "You look marvelous," she said, still not touching him. Perhaps, Yasha thought with some pleasure, she did not feel that she had permission to touch him, having so long ago given him up. Perhaps he wasn't really hers anymore. Perhaps that was fine. Perhaps it would be better, after all, to shake her hand, get a good look at her, and leave.

He glanced at the doorknob.

"Your father—" She caught herself and shook her head fondly. "How is he? And the bakery? Selling millions and millions?"

"It's our tenth anniversary." It wasn't really the right thing to say. He pictured the cruller twist and the everything bagel, hanging week after week in the window, barely recognizable as a "10." It hadn't, now that he thought of it, done much to increase their business.

"Yes, well, that is why I wanted to talk to you, absolutely now," his mother said. "I've been saying, *ten years*, good lord."

I've been saying, Yasha thought. Who had she been saying this to?

"Only let's take our time," she said, "yes," and turned completely around, flipping the bottom of her dress up into a high, floating ring. She tore a plastic bag from the dispenser and opened the bucket of gummy bears. She plunged the scoop as deep as it would go and came up with a heap of bears. After the gummy bears came the gummy worms, the sour cola bottles, the gummy raspberries and blackberries, the peanut toffees, the caramels, the Nerds, the Dots, and then one entire twelve-ounce brick of chocolate.

"It's Friday," his mother explained, in Russian, to the shopkeeper.

Their total was $35.50 and she paid with a fifty-dollar bill. She pulled it out of an orange leather wallet that was full of fifty-dollar bills. She carried no credit cards or identification. She put fifty cents in the tip jar.

Yasha's mother held the door open and motioned for Yasha to exit. He couldn't move. He was yearning himself desperately toward her and away from her simultaneously, making his stomach turn, and she was holding the door, and was he supposed to be holding the door?

Outside, the rain picked up right where it had left off, flattening his hair to his head. His mother didn't seem bothered by the weather in the least. She led him briskly down Brighton Beach Avenue, as if she had lived there all her life. As if she had lived there, with them, for ten years, at the Gregoriov Bakery, as she had once said that she would.

"What are you doing?" Yasha asked, after a block, stopping abruptly.

"Don't *stop*," she said, not stopping, "you'll get wetter. Let's go."

This made a certain, immediate sense. He walked, slightly behind her. The subway tracks above them veered north at Coney Island Avenue, revealing the sky again, such as it was, and Brighton Beach Avenue turned into Oriental Boulevard. They passed Joseph's and Jerry's, the twin pizza parlors—Yasha recalled his lunch, which he had eaten today, back when today had been the simplest possible Friday—and soon the chaos of the market dissipated, resolving into brick family houses, each with a healthy front yard.

"How sweet," she said, touching the red hat of a sopping wet gnome and flicking a pinwheel, which was spinning hysterically next to a birdhouse. She kept the candy bag closed with a clenched fist, giving the bag a kind of neck, one that she was strangling.

Upon first sight of the entrance to Pat Perlato Playground, Olyana hung a sharp right. She beckoned Yasha on with her free hand, stopped short at the gate, and looked out, admiring the shore. Manhattan Beach, a name that had long confused Yasha, made Brooklyn's thin barrier against the Atlantic Ocean.

"I've missed you," Yasha said to the back of her head, hoping that she wouldn't hear it through the wind.

"I've missed you *terribly*," she said, opening the low gate to the playground, "so terribly I thought I would burst."

She sat down, straddling a grasshopper that rocked back and forth on a giant spring. The only other place to sit near her was the adjacent dragonfly, which required a child to sit on top of the open wings, cross-legged.

Yasha was relieved that he did not have to say or think anything for the next forty seconds as he got himself onto the dragonfly. It was wet, and the wings were slippery. His legs were much too long, even when crossed. When he was finally seated, he looked like a mix of Aladdin on his carpet and Buddha on a windowsill.

"Did you ever play here?" his mother asked.

"It's for babies." Yasha looked out toward the shore. "Sometimes Papa and I used to build things down on the beach."

"The beach," she said, and offered him the bag. It was wide open, and she had rolled down the edges. The Nerds and Dots had blended and looked like confetti. He took a gummy worm.

"How extraordinary, to be on the water," she said. Yasha thought about Moscow. Locked into its own country.

"We like it here. Papa says, 'Brighton Beach, a Ton of Bright.'" His father had never said that. "Not that you picked such a good day—"

"Yes, I simply don't know what was I *thinking*, standing by your window like that. Vassily could have seen me. I mean, Vassily could have *seen* me," she said, biting into a caramel. "First you, Yakov. First you and me. Then, when we're ready, your father."

If he argued with her, Yasha feared she might disappear again. She was breaking the chocolate bar into chunks now, letting the pieces fall into the open bag. When it was all broken up, she handed the bag back to Yasha. The gesture reminded Yasha of kids at his high school, passing beers around the swing sets in Battery Park. She was so thin, and so strong, and so hungry; his father, in comparison, seemed barely alive.

"Papa's heart is too thick," Yasha said, hearing immediately how ridiculous he'd made the cardiomyopathy sound.

His mother, pouncing on his mistake, said, "You mean he doesn't miss me?"

"I mean the walls between his ventricles are stiff, and he has to sit down a lot."

She continued to pick through the candies. "He is older than I am."

"He's the one you should be seeing right now," Yasha said. "I'm younger than both of you. You can see me later."

"No, not right now, especially if he is ill. You know I am a great deal to handle," his mother said, biting into a toffee and smiling with her cheeks while she chewed, smiling so convincingly that Yasha smiled back on instinct. He corrected his face. "It wouldn't be wise to spring this whole thing on him just like that, dear," his mother said. Yasha wanted to know what "this whole thing" was. It didn't seem possible that anything could be larger or more terrible than the woman herself.

"Talk to Papa tomorrow, or I'll tell him you're here," Yasha said, and it felt like negotiating with a terrorist.

Yasha's mother slid off her grasshopper, shook the rain from her dress, and started walking toward the B train. Yasha followed.

"I'll come tomorrow," she said as she walked. Yasha had no means of guaranteeing the agreement. The only rules were her words, *I'll come*, and Yasha began to understand how easily the last ten years had happened the way they had. There was a veil over her, a touch of the preternatural—the air out of which she appeared, and into which she disappeared again, could have been outer space.

She climbed up the long, switchbacked stairway to the platform, two steps at a time. Yasha stood on the street with his arms by his sides, looking up. He could see her panties for a moment each time she took a double step. All the blood in his body seemed to pause in his heart and then rush out again to his limbs. When she reached the top, she pulled out a MetroCard and turned onto the Manhattan-bound track. So she was staying in Manhattan, Yasha thought, before realizing that there was nowhere to go in the other direction, and that she could have been riding the train to just about anywhere. Nothing, in essence, had changed.

. . .

He came back to the bakery soaking wet. His father hadn't called the neighbors, or the police, but looked bewildered. Yasha stood just inside the door. He looked at the space of the bakery. He wanted to thank his father for their house, their bakery, the food he had eaten for the past ten years, the Band-Aids and books, and for feeding the cat each time Yasha forgot. He looked at Vassily: middling height, gray hair, bulb nose, filthy pants. He wanted to say, You've done everything right. His father was about to become angry. Yasha said he'd forgotten his precalculus textbook at Joseph's Pizza and had gone to look for it but hadn't found it. He said he'd been all through the neighborhood. No one had seen it. He'd have to ask Mr. Usoroh for another one. Vassily shook his head and said there had been dozens of children while

Yasha was gone, all of them wanting black-and-white cookies. They closed up for the day. Both men were quiet and exhausted.

. . .

Saturday. Swarm of bagel customers, dearth of poppy seeds, Vassily's pants drenched in a bowlful of spilled eggs, Yasha's shoes untied, Yasha's shoelaces dragging through the egg yolks, the cat licking the floor all morning, Vassily many times kicking the cat, Vassily apologizing, talking to the cat, frightening the customers. The customers, usual. The Danishes, a little sour. No mother, no mother, no mother.

. . .

"When I die," Vassily said, sitting down after the rush, "put me with no people. Get me far away." He looked out the window and toward the beach. "Do you remember, Yakov Vassiliovich, about the reindeer hunters?"

Yes, he remembered about the reindeer hunters. It was his father's favorite story. He told it once a month.

"No," said Yasha. "What reindeer hunters?"

"The Sami," Vassily said. "They live at the top of the world." He blew his nose. "My father's hunting teacher was a Sami. Crossed the land bridge into Russia from Lapland. Not so many people there. Mostly ice." Vassily yawned and smiled at the same time, showing Yasha all his small teeth. "His name was Ommot and he used to teach me how to shoot. I think, growing up, I loved Ommot best of anybody."

"You know how to shoot?"

"I know how to shoot a reindeer."

"Have you ever shot a reindeer?"

49

"No," Vassily said cheerfully, "your father is a twiglet." A twiglet? Yasha imagined branches being shot to splinters by reindeer-hunting guns. "I wanted to live Ommot's life, the hunter's life," Vassily said, "but I didn't have it in me. I had bialys in me." Vassily's smile widened, making his teeth look even smaller. "I didn't live the life of peace. That was how Ommot lived, all those years, crossing Lapland, not so many people, mostly ice. He lived the life of peace. Peace." Vassily squinted. "Мир," he translated. "The word used to ring in my ears before I went to sleep. I was a boy. Well"—he straightened his back—"I can live the death of peace, at least. I can look out at that ice my whole death long."

Yasha pushed himself up onto the countertop and sat between the two registers.

"That's what I wish for myself—" Vassily said. "A death full of peace."

Yasha let his finger fall on the CASH button, made it ding, made the drawer shoot out, closed it, and did it again. He made it ding five times in a row. His mother, he realized, did not have much to do with peace.

A girl came into the shop. "Three Danishes, please," she said.

"They're a little sour today," said Yasha.

"But aren't you sweet," Vassily said, standing up from his chair with some difficulty. "If the Danishes are sour, one babka on me."

The girl smiled and ruffled her bangs. She had exceptionally thin eyebrows, big eyes, and not much nose, which made her look like a baby. Vassily gave her three cherry Danishes. She bit into one and declared it to be sweet. Vassily gave her a chocolate babka. "It's Saturday," Vassily said, and charged the girl for only the Danishes. Yasha's head chimed. $35.50. *It's Friday*. The fifty-dollar bills. Were they in on this together? Was it possible that his parents had, once upon a time, developed inside jokes? *It's Saturday*, his father had just said. Yasha imagined his mother's panties. He imagined his mother wearing different panties for every day of the week. *It's Friday. It's Saturday*. It seemed possible that his parents were, a decade later, in love. The girl left the bakery finishing the first Danish, leaving some flakes on the floor. Yasha ran to keep the cat from following her out.

"She was cute," Vassily said, "no?"

"Not for me."

"Women—" Vassily said, then stopped.

Yasha wanted to hear the rest of the sentence. Both men, at that moment, were thinking of Olyana. It was four o'clock, about the same time she had appeared the day before. Yasha looked out to the mailbox: no mother. He picked up the cat and held him. He wondered if the cat had some animal means of locating her. The cat bit into Yasha's chin.

"I loved your mother," Vassily said, sitting down again.

The cat bit a little harder, and Yasha dropped him. What could he say? Not I know, not Me too, not She's here, or could he?

"I loved your mother," Vassily said, more adamantly. "So. I was thinking—" He lifted the large knife that had been resting on the counter, but the envelope no longer lay beneath it. He looked up to the ceiling for moment, then at the large knife, then at Yasha, and then reached into the bialy bin. He stabbed a fresh bialy with the knife and cut it down the middle. He opened the refrigerator and took out the cream cheese. Yasha watched his father schmear his bialy professionally, the surface beginning to look like a circus tent: white and smooth, a few peaks. Just as Yasha was going to ask his father to finish his sentence, Mr. Dobson came in. Yasha had never been more unhappy to see the door open. His father was right about Lapland, Yasha thought. No people. Ice. Real peace.

. . .

Vassily and Yasha lived directly above the bakery. The apartment had the same shape as the store below it. Yasha slept near the window, and Vassily slept toward the back, over the ovens.

Yasha had just brushed his teeth and was doing push-ups at the side of his bed. His mother hadn't come all day. She had broken her promise, but so had he—he hadn't given his father a word of warning. It wasn't fair that he should have to do it. The news might make his father pass out or, worse, sound like a mean joke. Yasha's arms were burning, and he hoped it would show in the morning. If she came in the morning, he would look bigger. If she didn't come, he could punch something.

His father knocked on his door and whispered, "Yakov Vassiliovich?"

"Come in."

Vassily opened the door just wide enough to slip in and left it open. Yasha got up from the floor. His father had changed into his extraordinary pajamas. This was the first warning. His father's ordinary pajamas consisted of boxer shorts and a pink button-down shirt, once white, a casualty of an attempt three years earlier to sell pink cookies on Valentine's Day. He seldom wore his best: a gift from Mr. Dobson's wife, a matching set, consisting of a button-down top with a fish-mouth lapel and elastic-waisted bottoms, the whole set printed with small gray bagels. Vassily had rolled up the bottoms of his bagel pajama pants, as he had learned from Dostoyevsky. The envelope in his father's hand was the second warning. Septimos crept in the open door and sat beside Vassily's exposed ankles.

"What's in the envelope?" said Yasha.

"Tickets," said Vassily. "Happy birthday," he added hastily.

Yasha's birthday presents had generally come out of the oven, and were then treated with a double coat of frosting and sprinkled with M&M's to distinguish them from the everyday cakes. His father wasn't good at remembering dates, and the birthday cakes had often been a few days late. No gift had ever arrived early. Third warning.

"Are we going to a show?"

"You could put it that way," said Vassily.

Yasha took the envelope from his father's hands and studied the tickets. They were one-way flights, New York to Moscow, departing the following Thursday. There were only two.

"I have been thinking," Vassily said.

"Graduation," Yasha said, the first excuse that came to him. "On the twenty-ninth."

"It was a bad mistake," said Vassily, sitting on Yasha's bed. "I was thinking of the last day of school. I thought, Let's go fast. Wednesday school is out, Thursday we are out. What did I know about a graduation?" he said with some light in his eyes. "I never did one of those." He patted his thighs, and small clouds of flour erupted. "When school was out, I figured, it was out."

Yasha loved his father. When his father spoke, Yasha understood what he said. His father was sometimes eccentric, but never insane; not terribly attractive, but adorable, easy to adore. He smiled when he had amused himself and shouted when he was mad. His pants were yellow from dozens of broken eggs. His hair was gray and long around his ears. His core, Yasha suspected, was made of peace.

Out, I figured, was out, Yasha repeated to himself, hoping his mother would never show up again. "Let's go," Yasha said, "I don't need to go to graduation." If she did come again, they would be gone. Let her miss me, Yasha thought. "Saves a hundred dollars, no cap and gown," he said.

"So what, you can have ten caps," Vassily said, "with fur, even with earflaps." The wind made Yasha's blinds rattle against the window. Vassily said he would find Olyana, kiss her bare hands, show her his gray hair and their good-looking son. Vassily touched his own lips. He said he imagined his body growing thinner and his heart growing thicker until it all ended, at which point he wanted his wife at his side. He said they were low on juice and milk, and he would not go about replenishing. "Think of it as a vacation," Vassily said. "And when we come back," he said, grinning, "the doctors will cut my chest open."

. . .

At lunch hour on Monday, Olyana was standing at the school door. It was sunny, and she leaned against a pillar, fanning herself with one hand. Yasha had come outside for some air and a turkey sandwich. He was about to have a precalculus exam. He couldn't remember telling her where he went to school.

There were so many questions he would have to ask to begin understanding anything, questions of such different magnitudes: How did you know where I go to school? and Why didn't you want to raise me? and Do you know what we're about to do? She was wearing an orange dress today. When she saw him, she started waving jubilantly with her whole arm. He didn't want to go over there and be happy with her. He wanted a turkey sandwich, and to use the bathroom, and to study the law of cosines.

"Yakov!" she shouted, making a few kids on the street look at him.

He hurried over to keep her from shouting more. "Be quiet," he said.

"Heavens, why? Look, I've gotten us a few apples."

"I told you to come this weekend, and you didn't, but you're here forty minutes before my final exam, for lunch?"

His mother handed him a yellow apple. "Where can we find a good sandwich?" she asked.

Yasha closed his mouth and twisted it up. He felt tall again, and over-aware of his own arms, and hungry, and at war.

"You can find a good sandwich at the Gregoriov Bakery," Yasha said, "where your husband and son work." She was already eating her apple.

"Yakov," she said, "if I storm right in and talk to your father, with his sick little heart, after all these years, nothing will go right for any of us," she said, twirling her empty hand in the shape of an infinity sign, first out toward Yasha, then back to her.

"If you don't talk to my father before Thursday, you will have missed your chance."

"Thursday?" She laughed, and in doing so choked on a piece of apple. Her laughter flared up into coughing and then resolved into laughter again. "See what you've done? You've made me choke, with all your threatening. All right, little man, perhaps you can help me on Thursday. Perhaps Thursday will be fine."

Ten years ago, Yasha had needed his mother's "help" to pick out his school clothes, scramble his eggs, comb his hair. She denied him nothing in those days, no service, no affection, straight up until she decided to deny him a decade. Now he stood inches from her generous hands, feeling capable and cold.

"How could I possibly help you?" Yasha said.

"You and I will make a plan for your father tomorrow. You take your exam now like a good little man," she said, "and be sure to ravage it. *Ravage* it."

As Yasha marched up the stairs to Mr. Usoroh's classroom, her voice said, *little man, little man*, around his head in a loop. She cared less about everything than anyone he'd ever met. All the kids at his school, he himself, his father—they all seemed, in retrospect, to be bombarded by worries, to be hopelessly depressed, compared with his red-haired mother. She was one big victory. She made him feel so powerless, so without a body, he walked straight down the hall, looking for something to punch, turned into an alcove of senior lockers, pushed Alexa against her own locker, and kissed her.

They kept their mouths closed and touching for long enough to make Yasha feel certain it was a *kiss*, and then he stepped back and walked into the math room. From inside, he could hear ferocious squealing, not just from Alexa but from all the girls nearby. He looked back out the classroom door's window. Alexa was on the floor, trying to breathe through her giggling. The other girls had gathered around her, flipping their hair around and touching Alexa's knees. Yasha rubbed his lips together. The kiss had left no trace, hadn't even tasted like anything, and now it was over. Yasha still needed to use the bathroom. Mr. Usoroh was passing out the exam papers.

"Did you study?" a boy named Stephen whispered from his desk, next to Yasha's.

Mr. Usoroh asked the class to begin.

. . .

When Yasha came down to lunch on Tuesday, he needed his mother to be there. She wasn't. When he left school for the day two hours later, she was there, at the school entrance, wanting to go to Lincoln Center.

"Take me to the fountain," she said.

It was the second-to-last day of school, and it had been eventful—the school's heating system had malfunctioned and started pumping hot air into the classrooms, making everyone sweat and some freshmen cry; Alexa had followed him down every hallway, leaning against lockers, asking if he wanted to "do it again," and he did kind of want to do it again, but he walked right past her every time, leading her eventually to shout that she hoped he'd go back to Russia and stay there.

Was that what would happen? If they moved back to Russia, would his mother follow them back? Could they lure her there, trap her, and undo this enormous American detour? She was ahead of him now, skipping down a flight of stairs into the subway.

Yasha watched one serpentine trail of white bricks crawl across the tunnel wall as the train sped uptown. It was comforting to sit beside his mother, *any* mother, he thought, when the train rattled. The doors chimed, and opened, and closed. Everybody riding seemed half asleep. He closed his eyes and let the thick vibrations bounce him, babylike, on the lap of the seat.

They got off at 66th Street. The asphalt in the street was shining. On the east side of Broadway, a man was selling framed photograph prints. They were spread out on a folding table, the unframed prints collected in alphabetized bins. Olyana walked over and ran her finger across the surface of the table. She looked at a picture of the Brooklyn Bridge with a moon, then Marilyn Monroe, John Lennon. Behind those, in black-and-white, a little girl was kissing a little boy. Yasha looked at them—it only confirmed his feeling that he had come late to the whole kissing game. He could never have asked his father about such things, but his mother, who seemed be in a constant state of kissing— her whole body seemed to be tonguing the wind that blew around it—she had, without a doubt, much to say on the subject, and Yasha wanted, despite himself, to consult her.

Beside the kissing children lay a color photograph of Lincoln Center, the fountain centered and at full blast. The man selling the photographs smiled at Olyana—Russian nose, yellow dress. After looking at her, he looked up above her head at the scrolling text of the AMC Loews movie theater. She took the five-by-seven print of Lincoln Center and dropped it into her large shoulder bag. By the time the man looked back down at his table, she had closed the gap, rearranging the rectangles into an evenly spaced grid. She picked up the photograph of John Lennon and looked at it intently.

Yasha's hands started sweating. He looked at the man behind the table, half hoping for confirmation that he hadn't seen, half hoping for him to call the police. If they took her away now, he would have some time to think. They'd have her cornered, he and Papa, if she were in jail.

"Poor man," she said. "Simply too tragic." She put the Lennon portrait back on the table and thanked the seller.

Yasha thanked him profusely and wished him a great summer. The man told him to take care of his lovely mother.

"Take a walk through Central Park!" the man shouted after them.

"Yes, how would you like to spend a little time in the park," his mother said, "not just today, I mean every day, if you liked?"

"You just stole a—" They were still within earshot of the man. "There is something in your bag," Yasha said. He didn't know how to make his face look appalled enough.

"There are many things in my bag, Yakov," Olyana said. "What about yours?" she asked. "Where are your books? Have you left them at school? At the bakery? Tell me," she said, turning east onto 67th Street, the trees of the park coming into view, "how do you like working in the bakery? Truly, how do you like it? Are you tired of all the bread?"

To Yasha, bread was clean and homogeneous. Bread had no veins and no gristly parts. It broke down into sugars, and filled one's stomach. It soaked up everything else. It won.

"Tired of Brooklyn, maybe?" his mother continued. "Perhaps you would like to live in Manhattan? You could live with me, in Manhattan."

The traffic light changed, and they crossed Central Park West. Eastward-driving cars came rushing up from behind them and drove straight into the park, each car making its own whoosh.

"You live in Manhattan?" Yasha said.

"I have been here for three months. At Ian's apartment in Tribeca. I will need your help to stay longer." She looked at Yasha intently.

Yasha didn't want to look at his mother. Hearing her was enough. A man was riding a unicycle up the park's western bike path, and Yasha watched the rider's knees moving in nearly hypnotic circles.

"Who is Ian?"

"We are going to be married," his mother said.

At that moment, as if to distract Yasha from his rage, the unicyclist lifted his cap to Yasha and rode faster to pass a horse carriage. They all seemed to be circus attractions, hired by his mother, the ringleader.

"You are married," Yasha said. "To Papa."

"If I ever bring myself to see your father," she said, "I will ask him to be free."

To be free, Yasha thought. To be free to be free to be free.

Who had been free, all these years? Yasha watched four more cars whoosh under the footbridge. Hadn't everybody? She had stayed in Russia, to be free. They had come to Brooklyn, to be free. They had opened a business, made some money, been free. She had met another man, in her freedom—"Who is he?" Yasha asked.

"An American, Yakov, just like you. Good lord, I could call you Jacob!" She laughed, and he could see her ribs stretch out her dress. "He has an awful lot of money and could have done whatever he wanted, and what he wanted, bless him, was Russia!" The yellow material of her dress was elastic and became paler when it stretched. "He came to me asking for lessons. What could I teach him? He plays like a dream, my student."

"Papa was your student," Yasha said. This fact had always started the story, the story of how his mother and father met, which Yasha had sometimes asked his father to tell him at bedtime, before he stopped asking about his mother altogether.

"Teachers, and students—" she said, resting her hand across her collarbone.

Yasha took a step into the park, turned around, and looked back at her, carrying her large bag, carrying the hideous photograph, which lay illuminated in Yasha's vision as if by an X-ray. He looked at her hands, the nails cut short, the fingers long, and could not remember how her skin felt—could not remember if she had often held him. He could only recall her hands touching her piano; her playing on certain weekends four-hand duets with his father, who had never been a fine pianist. His father, her first student, replaced by a second student, a finer pianist, a wealthier man, no doubt a childless man, no doubt a man who asked nothing of her, no doubt a man who bought her all these colorful dresses, no doubt a paradise.

"When we're married we'll live here in New York, with you, I hope."

"We are leaving New York," Yasha told his mother as simply and loudly as he could. "To look for you, in fact." The perversity of his family's many overlapping errors, and his singular power to make things right, or more wrong, made Yasha giddy. "Papa bought tickets to Moscow. He thinks he's going to find you there. He wants—"

"How absurd," his mother said. "Listen. You must tell your father, tell him, Mama is here, she is terribly happy, she has made a new life for herself, and the best thing to do—the only civilized thing—is to let the woman go. Just like that. Then you give him these." She retrieved a manila folder of papers from her bag. "And see that he signs. He will sign if you ask him, Yasha."

"He will die if I ask him," Yasha said. "But you're right, he would die faster and harder if the news came directly from you." His mother stood clutching the thin stack of divorce papers, a stack no thicker than a bialy. "We are leaving on Thursday," Yasha said. "We are going to *conquer Moscow*, Papa keeps saying, and have a great time while we do it. Papa hasn't gotten out of the bakery since . . . well, actually since we moved in, but we're going all-out this time. He calls it *Gregoriov's Last Great Adventure*. If you want to break his heart, you can wait until we're back and they've implanted his defibrillator. Maybe with that thing in his chest you won't ruin him completely."

"By that time the police will be after me." Yasha could think of a million reasons to arrest her, but she provided one that hadn't occurred to him. "They'll kick me out of this country," she said. "You must understand—no divorce, no marriage, no residence permit, for an alien like me," she said.

"They won't find you so fast," Yasha said. "You're very hard to find." Yasha thought of his father in the bathroom, talking into the telephone, asking her to come. He thought of a faceless man who must have been in the room with her during those calls, kissing her neck while she said, *Soon, soon, soon.* "Your bogus wedding can wait a little while, can't it?" Yasha said. "We won't be gone for ten years. I promise. Tell your fucking boyfriend—"

"Ian," his mother said.

"Tell Ian he can hold his horses."

A speckled, sad-looking carriage horse clopped just then over the footbridge. Yasha had taken over as ringleader; the actors and animals were taking his cues now. Following the horse he had conjured, Yasha turned and walked out of the park, two blocks west to Broadway, down from 67th to 59th, picking up into a run that led him into the waiting mouth of the B train.

At the bakery, he found his father singing the Simon part and Mr. Dobson singing the Garfunkel part of "Homeward Bound." Mr. Dobson was slapping a loaf of rye against the counter, keeping time, which helped, as neither man was singing in tune. His father was throwing out all the bread in the store. He walked around with a big black garbage bag, emptying all the baskets.

Home! (He dumped the challahs.)

Where my thought's escaping!

Home! (He dumped the babkas.)

Where my music's playing!

Home! (He dumped the egg, everything, and onion bagels.)

Where my love lies waiting silently for me. (He dumped, finally, the bialys, tied the bag up, and threw it to the floor beside the cat bowl.)

"Silently for me," Vassily whined, solo.

"Dum, dum dum dum, dum dum," crooned Mr. Dobson.

"Yakov Vassiliovich!" said Vassily, looking up.

"Jesus Christ," said Yasha.

"It's only Mr. Dobson!" said Vassily. "He's our final customer."

"The Gregoriovs visit the homeland!" Mr. Dobson sang out.

Vassily started shimmying his shoulders—a dance Yasha would never have expected to see his father's body perform—and waving his hands in the air. The fourth finger of his left hand still bore a gold ring.

"Papa," said Yasha.

"Yasha!" said Vassily. "I have some shirts to show you."

"When do you leave?" asked Mr. Dobson.

"Thursday," Vassily said. "Back before winter, but who knows when?"

"Come here, Sam," Yasha called. The cat looked up at him. Yasha lifted him under his front legs and held him up, while his father hoisted the bag of bread over his shoulder, knocking the cat bowl to the wall. Vassily opened the door.

Yasha looked out the door in the direction of the ocean. Rows of clouds pushed inland. His father had written *BACK INDEFINITELY* onto a piece of butcher paper and hung the sign on the front door. Yasha inhaled, and the bakery smelled empty.

"Well, my dear Gregoriovs . . ." said Mr. Dobson.

"*Good riddens*," said all three men, each at his own pitch, and it sounded more like harmony than any of their singing.

. . .

After school on Wednesday, Yasha said goodbye to Stephen, did not say goodbye to Alexa, and ran directly to the subway. Now that he'd asked his mother to stay away, it seemed only more likely that she'd appear. She hadn't been at the school door, and Yasha feared that he would find her at home with Papa, getting her papers signed if it cost her Papa's life. Yasha rode the empty subway home standing up, in preparation.

When Yasha got to the Gregoriov Bakery, it was closed. The lights were off, and the shelves empty. The door to the basement was propped open, and from the sidewalk he could see a single lit bulb dangling from a cord. He ran down. Vassily was there, alone, his jeans rolled above his knees, frantically swatting at a foot of water with a garbage bag.

"Flood," said Vassily, his forehead covered in sweat. "The whole boulevard. The pipes are telling us, Get out of here!" He laughed and dragged his wet hand across his forehead, making water run down his face. He was smiling, but the drops resembled tears, and Yasha was paralyzed. "Help me clear this out, Yakov Vassiliovich," Vassily said, "so we can go upstairs and pack."

"Has anyone come to see you today?" Yasha asked in a quiet voice, knowing that the answer was no, knowing that his father would hardly have been in flood-fighting condition had the news been broken, but needing to check, all the same.

"Only Dostoyevsky," his father said. "Mr. Dobson is too soft to handle a second goodbye. I told Dostoyevsky to get his sourdough at Ilya's this summer. He looked very upset. I told him that

64

I would read to you while we're away. I told him not to bother reading to old Ilya."

Yasha laughed, not at old Ilya, their fat, friendly competitor of seven years, but at his mother. She was incapable of doing anything, Yasha thought, feeling some relief, and some pity. She was incapable of showing up, even when she needed to for her own sake, even to make her own gross wishes come true.

"Put that flour in the garbage," Vassily said. "I'll get the pump."

Vassily and Yasha worked together for an hour. Vassily, sweating, chattered on the subjects of suitcase name tags, a brown dress Yasha's mother had once worn, airplane drink menus, walking shoes, and a haircut he would get from a man in Kitai-Gorod. Yasha filled three garbage bags with pounds of wet white bread flour. Vassily finished pumping the basement and ushered his son upstairs, with modest shoulder dances and some clapping, for one last Brooklyn night. Yasha, seventeen, wanting to get his mother back but refusing to take her back, wanting distance, wanting the place he was from, wanting a little time, wanting his father to breathe air that had been blown through the sky and not baked, said nothing to stop their journey.

• • •

The next day, Yasha carried Septimos to the fence of Mr. Dobson's yard, kissed his head, and lowered him into the garden. Around the cat's neck, a red string was tied with a note that read *Call me Sam.*

• • •

Olyana Gregoriov placed an international call from Ian's apartment at 480 Leonard Street. When Daniil picked up, she spoke clearly: "Vassily will soon be in Moscow. When he asks for me, tell him I am in New York, in love. My cousin is on his way to your house with some papers. My youngest cousin. You needn't spend any time with him. See that Vassily signs immediately. Once he has signed, call this number, and calm him down. I've heard he isn't well."

. . .

That evening, a new upright piano was delivered to Ian's apartment. Yasha's mother christened it with Scriabin. Daniil had fallen asleep reading through the divorce papers that Evgeny had delivered, and the pages fell to the floor as he rolled in bed, dreaming about his brother and a pack of hounds. At the back of a Delta Airbus, Vassily stretched his legs into the aisle, while Yasha looked out the window. Alexa looked for Yasha on the Sunset Terrace at Chelsea Piers. It was prom night.

PART THREE

· · ·

The Yellow Room

To get to the Leknes Artist Colony, I had taken one train from Oslo to Trondheim, another from Trondheim to Bodø, and completed the journey by boat. The boat's name was Hurtigruten, and it had been commercially crossing fjords since 1893. A man named With had captained its maiden voyage. A man named Nils would fetch me (they used the word *fetch* a lot, the Norwegians, and never in a canine context) from the Hurtigruten's landing dock in Stamsund.

In Stamsund, in a loading area surrounded by small red houses, a man stood beside a brown car, holding a green can of beer and a kitchen rag. Seeing me, he waved his rag in the air, not smiling. I smiled furiously. I was sweating from working my suitcase down the Hurtigruten's loading ramp. I wheeled it to him over loud pebbles. He popped open the trunk and said, "Nils."

I was delighted. Here was a man so blank, so short, so clearly unflustered by these raging mountains, so disinclined to make a new friend—he couldn't have had less to do with pregnancy, or divorce, or New Jersey. Here was mankind in his original state, I thought, in all his innocence.

He finished his beer while he drove. The mountains we drove through were horrifying—many-peaked and oversized—a species of mountain far wilder than the snowcapped triangles of picture books. The fjordwater that cut between the mountains was bright turquoise. Nils and I made our way up the E10 road across Vestvågøy, the fifth of six islands in an archipelago called Lofoten. It was two latitudinal degrees north of the Arctic Circle, separated from mainland Norway by the Vestfjord and mercifully warmed by the Gulf Stream. Tall flowers grew along the side of the road. Behind the flowers rose sheer gray rock. We drove until we reached a clearing, in the middle of which stood a long house with a curved roof that ended in dragon gargoyles. A stake with a blue sign read BORG. A shorter stake with a white sign read VIKINGMUSEET.

In the museum's lobby, I signed the receptionist's log. Nils led me out a side door, across a field, and into an empty barn. Light poured in through attic windows and shone on Nils's brown sweater, brown shoes.

"You are to be my apprentice," Nils said, and I felt I was being both knighted and warned.

"Yes," I said. I'd seen pictures of this barn in the fellowship brochures, but its setting hadn't been mentioned. I asked, "Is the Yellow Room part of the Viking Museum?"

"The Yellow Room stands alone," Nils said. Then, flinging out his arm, he added, "These are my walls." I looked around and found three of the barn walls painted over in a patchwork yellow mural. This was no simple monochrome; he had harnessed the difference between mustard and saffron to create the subtle outlines of fish, hexagons, extraordinary asymmetries. Nils pointed to the fourth wall and said, "Yours." Three virgin brushes, an emptied bucket of Troms frozen prawns, and an assortment of acrylic tubes lay heaped at the base of my wall.

"The minister comes in one month," Nils said. "The Yellow Room will be inspected by KORO officers, and if they like it, they will put me on the map." I was surprised that Nils would use this colloquial expression, and then he pulled out an actual map. Small orange *K*'s marked hundreds of spots across the Norwegian mainland. A thin line connected each *K* to a thumbnail image: massive sculptures, neon light displays, geometric domes. Nils dragged his finger up the country, then across the Vestfjord to the amoeba shapes that represented the Lofoten Islands. "The government wants more art up here in the northern districts," he said. "They pay for it. They give it to the people. And the people actually come to look." Nils looked around the barn, giving each wall its turn.

"Use these walls as an example," Nils said. "The fourth must be painted immediately, to be dry when the officers come. You will have time and silence, to concentrate. You will be alone in here. I will be painting the exterior." I didn't say anything, and Nils consoled me with "Music will play," pointing toward a miniature battery-powered boom box I hadn't seen in the corner. "Schubert," Nils said, squatting and turning the volume up on a melody that had been playing all along. He said, "'The Trout.'"

I listened, and the yellow walls pulsed when I blinked.

"Come," Nils said, after a few measures. "The chief wants to meet the New Yorker."

We walked toward lush black smoke and entered the museum's smithy. The blacksmith welcomed me and suggested that I forge myself a nail. The chief was on his way. I sat beside a freestanding anvil, and the blacksmith presented me with a tiny hunk of iron. I only managed to strike the thing once, and weakly, each time the iron was hot. I struck four times. Then the blacksmith stuck the mangled nail back into the coals. Nils excused himself for a moment and vanished.

"I am Sigbjørn," the blacksmith said, and with his free hand he shook mine.

"Frances," I said.

He nodded. Sigbjørn had the build of a soccer player. He was thin and of medium height, but his frame suggested agility and power. Sandy hair had begun to recede from his temples, and he hadn't shaved in a few days.

In a long, continuous gesture, Sigbjørn removed his tongs from the coal pile. The nail's shaft was square from my four petty blows. Its tip was not sharp enough, and its head was not flat. He cooled the metal in a bucket of water. When its color had returned from orange to black, he placed the nail in my palm.

"You know about the sun?" Sigbjørn asked, plunging a new piece of iron into the coals. I told him I did not. "It never goes down," he said, smiling. I was looking at the black stripe of iron in my hand, the darkest thing I would see for several months, when the chief entered and told me to call him Haldor. He was bald, had a red beard, and wore a red felt tunic. A leather belt cut into his significant belly, and a royal blue satchel hung over his left hip. The whole outfit was trimmed with what looked like teeth. He walked straight past me to the fire the blacksmith was goading and reached from his hip to the smoking coals. He stood a moment warming the one hand. Nils reappeared.

"New York," Haldor said to Nils.

Sigbjørn rolled his sleeves all the way up to his shoulders, revealing his grotesquely wide forearms.

"We don't know why she wanted to come here," Sigbjørn said, "to Borg!"

"Have you done some shooting? Have you mounted the boat?" asked Haldor.

Sigbjørn said, "She hit the nail."

"The boat goes at two." Haldor pulled a wristwatch from his satchel. "Good time," he said, replacing it.

"Take her to the boat. She cannot be only painting all the time, as you are," Sigbjørn said to Nils.

I watched Nils consider this—he looked first embarrassed, then puzzled. He shifted his kitchen rag from one pocket to another.

"She has come here to paint all the time," Nils said.

"She lives at the asylum?" Haldor asked.

"Where?" I asked.

"*Ja,*" Nils said. "We have not gone home yet. She has only just come from Bodø."

"Straight to work," Haldor said. "Nils. Take her home. Be civilized."

Sigbjørn wiped coal onto his bruised leather apron. His movement made the teeth on Haldor's tunic shake and clatter. Nils, the only modern man in the smithy, coughed from the fire's smoke.

"How long will you stay?" Sigbjørn asked me. "*If* she stays," he said to Nils.

"Until the wedding. My sister is getting married," I said to everyone in the hut.

"Fine!" Haldor said.

"In California," I added, and turned my head to the left, as if it were the West.

"Fine!" Haldor said again.

Sigbjørn pulled a glowing orange lump from the coals. He began to whack it mercilessly.

Over the steady noise, Haldor said, "You will not leave us before the KORO inspection, I hope." He looked to Nils and added, "The government is hard to please."

"It is true that Nils is needing help," Sigbjørn said. He kicked open a small door and emptied one bucket after another of ash, water, and scrap iron into the back field. The wind mixed the lighter pieces into a black vapor and spread the rest across the grass.

Right then Nils hurried out of the smithy, and I followed. The chief and the blacksmith remained, speaking all at once their own language. Nils was walking very fast in the direction of the docks, where I could make out a few figures and the approaching prow of a boat. We walked away from the sparse trees that surrounded the smithy. They added a bark smell to the hut's smoke, and a few clouds rolled in from the water we were now running toward, making it all smell of camp, campfire.

"Why are you running?" I shouted ahead.

"Bad time," Nils cried without turning his head back to me.

"I thought the chief said good time!"

"You see the boat?" Nils flung out a finger and shook it.

I caught up with him, and we ran the last stretch of the road side by side. Nils's legs were short, like mine, and we pumped our arms. We were kicking dirt from the road onto the many roadside flowers—these were not house orchids, my mother had never told me their names—and into shrubs hung with dark berries. We both began to sweat. When it seemed we would have to stop to catch our breath or wipe our foreheads, we stopped. The path had ended.

In the water, a twenty-foot Viking ship was being roped and stocked by the deckhands I'd seen from the hut. They were sweating too. The clouds that had passed over the smithy were gone again, revealing a very high sun.

"You will paint all of the time," Nils said, his tone both commanding and beseeching. "Today," he said, "okay, the boat. I will fetch you after the ride. So, home for the evening." He told me that we would be working long days. We would begin tomorrow, formally. For tonight, he suggested that I try painting the ox that roamed around the asylum, for my leisure, for an exercise. Then dinner, he said. He had a fish in the freezer. I didn't tell him I didn't eat fish. I figured it would count as blasphemy in this country, though I hardly knew where I would find other food.

The Viking ship's deckhands waved their blond arms at us. The boat was long and thin, vegetable-like; it had the shape of snow pea and the color of a turnip. Nils led me down the hill to the dock and exchanged a few words with a deckhand. Dozens of passengers had taken their seats, and the crew had untied the boat. I climbed aboard. Nils started back up the hill.

A girl with muscular arms said, "Welcome." She wore an upturned sack with holes cut out for her head and arms and had a rope tied around her waist. *"Velkommen,"* she said to us.

• • •

Fifty strangers and I rowed the ninth-century ship out to sea. The strangers were mostly small families—one child with two parents, or two children with their dad. The families, clumped, sat at the center of the deck. A few individuals had taken the single seats around the edge of the boat, where they could look out at the water. As we rowed, the girl captain hollered again and again, "Haroo!"

Over the course of our rowing, the roles shifted. I saw the younger children squint their eyes and become older, concentrated. The fathers, in their shorts, reverted to little boys, looking up at the girl captain, then down at their own legs. The single adults around the perimeter rowed without thinking, lost in separate dreams of the same sea. I was a poor rower. I did not manage to tilt the oar correctly, and I was distracted by my own separate dream:

My sister, wearing a Viking sack, stood at the mast. I looked down at the water in panic. Its color was changing, darkening. We were far out at sea for such an old boat. Sarah was far out at sea for such a young girl. I had to believe she was ready, because she had looked me in the face and told me so. None of us, I saw on the faces of the boys and girls on the center benches, were ready to be where we were—ever farther out in the water, closer and closer to Greenland. The captain was constant, shouting "Haroo!" every other minute.

I looked at the captain's blond hair and knew my black-haired sister was at that moment sharing our childhood bunk bed with her fiancé. Scott was visiting my parents for the first time since the announcement, spending the weekend at our old apartment, which was slowly being dismantled—my mother taking her things down from the walls, my father folding and refolding his two pairs of pants.

The water grew brighter, shallower. The captain shouted what turned out to be her final "Haroo!" We had rowed in a tidy loop. I saw Nils standing by the dock. We tied the prow's dragon head to the dock posts. I thanked the captain, complimented her on her sack, and ran up the hill from the water.

"Not enough hours in the day for boat rides," Nils said when I reached him. We started for the parking lot. I looked up at the incredible, never-setting sun. There would be countless hours in the day.

. . .

Toward the end of our fifteen-minute drive to the artist colony, Nils admitted that the main building had previously been a mental asylum, but he assured me that he had repainted the outer walls blue. Upon arriving, I discovered he'd not just painted them blue, but seven shades of blue, in a wave pattern. The asylum building was three stories high, and ours was the only car in the lot.

"How many artists live here?" I asked.

"You and me."

While Nils dug around in the trunk, I stayed in the passenger seat and tried to calm myself by watching the wind bend the parking lot weeds. They were the same tall, voluptuous flowers that grew alongside all the roads, and the light in their petals was whiter and cleaner than any I'd seen before. Nils came around the passenger side and knocked on my window. If there was anything worse than being an artist colony's only artist, I thought, it was being the second. Still, I got out of the car and followed Nils through the asylum's unlocked front door. He walked straight down the ground-floor hallway. I followed him with my suitcase. We passed a large bathroom and stopped at the second door on the left.

It was the room he had chosen for me. I didn't know which room was his, even which floor. Nils carried my suitcase up in his arms over the threshold of the room. I knew I was marrying myself to something right then, stranded and strangely overjoyed, on this nontropical island in the middle of the Norwegian Sea.

There was a bell ringing, and out the window of my room it proved to be the collar bell of a sheep. Four sheep had entered the parking lot.

I advanced to the windowsill and Nils retreated, leaving me to my new quarters. I stared at the animals, the only other living creatures in sight, and it was so easy to cast them as my family: I, the littlest with the clanging bell; my sister, the gangly-legged female closer to the road; my father, the curly one who hadn't been sheared; my mother, the lean, round-eyed matriarch. It was good to see us again. It was good that we'd transformed and were adapting to new environments, growing steadier hooves.

I turned away from the mirage in the window and made my bed with white sheets and a striped blanket that Nils had left for me. The hallway bathroom didn't have any toilet paper. I wondered again about Nils. It was easy to imagine that Nils never pooped. I didn't know where he'd gone. I walked as quietly as possible and peeked inside the first floor's kitchen, but he wasn't there. I stood in the center of the hall and stared to the hall's end in both directions; it was long and full of terrible little doors. One could go insane from the floor plan, if one wasn't already.

"Nils!" I shouted.

From the parking lot, echoing down the corridor, a long, low, "*Ja?*" It could have been either man or animal answering me. No lights had been turned on in the asylum. I ran toward the smell of sheep dung that wafted in from the open entry. Nils stood centered in the parking lot, his trunk open, the sheep shy and keeping to the lot's distant corner. I approached Nils, and the sheep drew farther away, out toward the open back fields.

"Where are you going?" I said.

"Town," he said. "Where are you going?"

"Town," I said, thrilled that there was such a place.

. . .

We drove down the hill and the town came into sight immediately—it wasn't far, and it wasn't large. I had never lived in a town. When I thought about it, I had never visited a grocery store by car. The Gristedes where we shopped in New York had been on the ground floor of our apartment building. My bedroom's fire escape hung six stories above its front door. I had occasionally walked down to it barefoot. And when I thought about it, I didn't know what I needed from this town. Some milk. A couple pounds of pasta would last me a long time, if Nils wasn't driving down again soon.

Halfway between the asylum and the town, Nils pulled over and turned off the car. "It's blue," he exclaimed, pointing down to a rocky lake beside the road, and also up to the sky. "Blue and orange. Are complementary colors," Nils said urgently. "If you look at something orange, a paper, for fifteen seconds, and then you look at a white paper, your eye makes blue. The same with yellow and violet. I use yellow and red, and the eye wants violet, so it is living."

"It is living," I affirmed, and Nils restarted the car, looking relieved.

It ran for only two minutes before we entered the REMA 1000 parking lot. We pulled in behind a departing station wagon and joined the shoppers. While I hadn't caught the population number for Leknes, it seemed the entire town was in this grocery store. A long line formed behind each of the six checkout counters. It wasn't surprising, somehow, that we all needed milk.

The terrain of these northern islands could only be tempered by protein, by sips, by cups, the smallest things under our control.

I marveled at the firm red peppers that had made it up here. This was a very unusual dot of land, stationed in arctic waters. An older woman went ahead and put two of the peppers into her basket. I switched into gear.

"Milk," I said aloud, and looked to my side for Nils. He had wandered out toward the bananas. Nils's expertise was so convincing, in his painting (I wanted to learn) and his driving (I would never learn) and his never worrying (you're either born this way or not); in my helplessness, I wanted to enter into complete symbiosis with him: eating whatever he ate, paying squarely for my half, following him here when he came and home when he went. Home to an asylum, I thought. I pushed myself toward the refrigerators.

The milk was sold only in paper quarts. It came in seven colors. A man reached in front of me and selected a green quart. So did I. (It turned out to be kefir, a sour milk delicacy that is as thick as yogurt.) I imagined putting the kefir in my tea and cereal, so I found those things in their aisles too. I selected a hunk of cheese from a massive array of cheese hunks, all inscrutably brown. I found Nils.

His basket was full of fish and beer. He looked into my basket and nodded at the kefir, impressed.

I didn't feel comfortable asking Nils about toilet paper, so I asked him where I could find spaghetti. We walked together past the ice cream section, past all the tomato-stewed-mackerel pastes for bread, past the frozen pizza section, past the wall of bread loaves—unsliced and sorted by coarseness—into the very back of the store, where we found the pastas and sauces. In an adjacent housecleaning aisle, I found all the toilet paper I could ever need, sorted according to indecipherable descriptions of softness. Nils joined the checkout line. I caught up with him and placed my items on the belt behind his.

The cashier looked at me, turned to Nils, and said, *"Pussy?"*

Nils said, *"Ja."*

I said, *"What?"*

The cashier bagged Nils's beers and advanced my pasta to the bar-code scanner.

"Pussy?" she asked me.

I didn't respond.

"A bag, a bag," Nils chimed. "Do you want a bag?"

I said, "Please. Thank you."

The cashier bagged my items, double-bagging the quart of kefir.

We drove home to the asylum.

. . .

Nils and I each had our own floor, and each floor had its own industrial kitchen. I could hear Nils's footsteps in the kitchen directly above mine, shuffling between the sink and the freezer. I put my purchases in their right places, doing little to fill the vast emptiness of the cupboards.

Out the kitchen window, fields extended back toward the horizon, which I had always known to be a line, but in this case was a mountain wall. Farmhouses dotted the fields, each with a truck at its door. Nils had stopped moving above me. The colony fell silent. For the first time I was afraid of its size, its noiselessness, its solitude. My parents wanted to know that I'd arrived, and I wanted to hear their voices. I retrieved my laptop from my quiet new room, carried it back to the kitchen, and centered it on the table, watching trees shaking in the window behind the screen.

My mother was also shaking. Behind her, bowls lined across the counter were filled with raspberries. I looked into the tiny camera and told them I had arrived safely and had been warmly welcomed. I told them I was comfortable. I didn't tell them about the three-story building where I lived with one middle-aged man.

"You're way up there," my mother said.

"And they're here," my father said.

"We put them in your room," my mother told me. "Scott took your bottom bunk." I pictured Scott climbing up the bunk bed's ladder at night, my sister a brunette Rapunzel.

"The schmo waltzed in here asking me how the *scribbles* are coming along."

"He doesn't have a good heart," said my mother.

"I'm losing my stomach." My father showed me how white his tongue had turned. "I have to keep myself from retching."

"I have to start melting the ice cream." My mother turned her back to the camera and shrank on my screen as she walked back into the kitchen. I saw her bend down to the freezer, the rear pockets of her jeans suddenly visible, and set two pints of Häagen-Dazs on the counter.

"I was hoping," I told my father, "that we could take this as a new era. And buck up."

I thought it was a new era. One in which the constant fret over why Sarah was still *dating* this person would be relieved by the sheer elevation of her *marrying* him. And that my family could, consequentially, buck up.

"I can't stand to be in a room with him," my father said. He pinched the bridge of his nose.

My mother ran back to the screen from the kitchen, wiping freezer frost onto her apron, shouting toward the computer, "I am frightened for her!"

"Why couldn't she marry somebody more like me?" my father asked.

Outrage blacked out my thoughts for a moment, and when they came back, I found myself thinking about the Viking ship. How the families and the strangers had resembled one another. How each husband had been born and raised a stranger to his eventual wife, and their eventual children had each arrived as a stranger to both parents. I couldn't really say what a stranger was anymore, having encountered Nils—who was both stranger and sole companion to me, for the time being—and these islands in general, whose mountains were transforming in my perception from dinosaur spines into my most reliable friends. My sister's fiancé was hardly, after three years, a stranger to us. All the same, my parents did not seem interested in expanding our family.

"That's a ludicrous thing to say," I told my father.

"No." He leaned close to the webcam, such that his hair filled the whole of my screen.

Sarah had taken a stand, he went on to say, against the values with which they had raised her. Against the artistic, which this guy wasn't, against the Jewish, which this guy certainly wasn't, against the delicate and the disciplined, both of which my father had counted out from Scott's first mention of Xbox, against the essential fineness my family valued and could not find in the Glennys of San Francisco. He took it as a personal rejection.

When I didn't answer, my father resumed the conversation with a story of the dinner they'd all shared the night before. They had been sitting at the table, Scott speaking about how excited he and Sarah felt, and my mother had gone into her bedroom and begun to cry.

"It's not right," my father said.

My mother left the screen again, and I saw her by the fridge, blueberry cartons stacked from her hands to her chin. She had served vanilla ice cream with mixed berries every summer that I could remember. The same white porcelain bowls. It was sooth-ing to see the tradition return, though I wondered whether any of them could stomach ice cream at that moment, and the kitchen was being packed away, each appliance into its original box, the boxes split between my parents according to who used which more.

"They'll be coming out of the room soon," my mother said, "for ice cream."

"I wish they'd stay in there," growled my father.

My mother asked him to set the juices out on the table. I told them to enjoy the visit and celebrate Sarah. My mother spilled half a carton of blueberries onto the floor and dove down to clean them up. My father signed off.

I looked up from my screen and out the kitchen window. In the fields, the trees were still shaking. I saw the asylum's pet ox wandering between them and testing his horns against the trunks. I wanted, as many often want, to talk with the animal. The only way was to keep perfectly silent. The ox lifted his head, walked a little way into the open, and stood nobly by a patch of low-growing crops, waiting for his portrait to be painted.

· · ·

Nils started the car just before midnight, when it was still very bright, and we drove northwest from Leknes. It was the clearest night he'd seen on the islands.

We listened to Radio Norge, the national station, whose most frequently played song was Dolly Parton's "Jolene." Nils announced he would speak only in Norwegian for the rest of the night. When he flattened his Lofoten map over the dashboard, allowing me to pick a direction, I pointed at the word EGGUM. It was a place near Borg, up the road from the museum, on the northern shore. His reply was, *"Det kan vi."* That can we.

Along the way, vocabulary basics. One sheep on the roadside: *Sau*. A horse: *En hest*. The horse: *Hesten*. Nils pointed a finger to his chest, said, *Jeg*, pointed at me, said, *Du. Jeg*, I said. *Du*, he said. We were getting somewhere.

We hunted the midnight sun, and found it behind each mountain, over every pond and fjord, doubling itself on the smooth surfaces of those waters, and in the windows of Nils's car, and on the lenses of his glasses. We wanted to get somehow closer to it, as close as possible. That's how Eggum helped us. As shown on Nils's map, it was the northward-facing, beachy top of our island. Between Eggum and the North Pole lay one final landmass, a polar-bear-inhabited block called Svalbard. But Eggum was inhabited by people, if sparsely, and was even marked with a sculpture of a human head.

When we sat on the beach there, between the sculpture and a damaged World War II radar fort, our eyes met the sun's stare. Nils filled two tin mugs with instant coffee and balanced them on a flat-topped rock. We sat on a boulder that faced due north, and in the glare of that final waterfront I couldn't say how much of the night we would spend there, or what kind of togetherness ours was.

I wanted to keep the conversation simple, to avoid a host of complications. Waves made the rocks look like dolphins jumping, I told Nils, or a whale's tail flipping up. "*Ja*, but it is rocks," Nils said. He looked at his watch and said, "*Klar?*"

One o'clock, two o'clock—these were the hours in Lofoten when the sun came down to the sea, colored the water and mountains, and sat on the brink of the horizon before starting back up again. It never left our sight, or the sight of the world, whose ponds and grasses seemed to be watching the sun along with us, mimicking it and lighting up for all the night travelers to see.

Nils said, "*Bra,*" with great sincerity in his voice, meaning, "Good."

These hours were characterized by a wildness of colors, the combined power of a sunset and sunrise. It was easy to watch the horizon for hours straight, the sun in perpetual motion, the sky turning orange and cranberry until at three it returned to blue, and I felt ready for bed. Nils rose from his rock and said we would begin Yellow Room work in four hours. He called himself *kjempetrøtt*, "super-tired," to teach me *kjempe*, the prefix that super-sized anything. Best to sleep now, he said, if we were to sleep any.

Radio Norge filled the slow ride back with Journey, A-ha, Dolly Parton, and a metal band called the Sins of Thy Beloved.

The light behind the mountain at Utakleiv Beach was gold; it looked like a biblical place. The foothills were patchy, balding. Tall plants formed patches for the road's elbows. In every meadow grew white and yellow grasses. Waterfall veins streaked the mountains, and a little rain in the air prepared the sky for rainbows. We drove through a passing wink of colors, a natural hologram.

It had been a very long day, and this had been our day off. I pictured the barn's thousand wooden surfaces that needed sanding, priming, painting. I didn't know whether Nils would become my friend or my uncle, whether he had a wife, whether, in the absence of all other society, our ages separated us as much as they otherwise would. The space we shared was immense, and we were both petite people who barely filled our own rooms. I took off the clothes I had worn since boarding the Hurtigruten, twenty-four hours and many fjords earlier. I stood by the window and nobody could see me—even the sheep had gone.

Nighttime, though it was completely indistinguishable from the day, was a relative of other darknesses in other parts of the world, I remembered, where men lost their minds. It may have been merely the hallway I feared. I had nothing to fear from Nils. Had he wanted anything from me, he could have taken it easily in the kitchen, or the car, or the empty places along the northern shore where we'd pulled over. He hadn't made any such move. The parking lot lay illuminated in the perpetual morning out my window. I drew the curtains and locked my door, foolishly, against the empty asylum, or against my only companion, or against anything that woke in the weird bright night.

. . .

The next day lasted three weeks. The sun stayed above us, as if it had nowhere else to be. Nils and I spent mornings in the barn and nights in the car. We slept at miscellaneous times—drawing the asylum's curtains, we could choose when night was. The barn grew richer and wilder. It was the only marker of time passing. As Nils made his way around the exterior walls, covering the brown wood with his signature marigold, a square sun seemed to rise from the hilltop. From down the road, there it was: a small, brilliant box. Up close, it was strange and enormous. Its lemon color loomed over the lime-green grass. Nils considered trimming the windows and doors in white, to add a little mildness, to serve as cream. He expected the KORO officers would be mild-mannered men.

Haldor and Sigbjørn taunted us eagerly. When Sigbjørn came out from the smithy at museum closing, covered in smoke and iron residue, he looked at us, covered in yellow paint, and called us sticks of butter. Haldor liked to remind me that there were no barns in Manhattan. He asked me if I was homesick, and I told him about my parents moving out of our home. He asked me if I was lonely, and introduced me to Frida, the museum's Icelandic sous-chef, and Kurt, the museum's German chef. Kurt's girlfriend, Agnes, had come with him for the summer, and had been hired to tend the museum's stables. Haldor didn't introduce me to Agnes, because she terrified him.

Agnes had the body of a fourteen-year-old, the face of a forty-year-old, and the ferocity of a wolverine—if I rode in the truck with her, on a lunch break or in the evening, she screamed for me to unbuckle my seat belt. Why a seat belt, she screamed, was I scared? She was under five feet tall. She was the only person at the Viking Museum who could tame an enraged Icelandic pony. I could see her some days driving between the museum and the stables in her little gray Volkswagen, hollering along to death metal with her windows down, her pearl earrings slamming one at a time into her neck.

Every morning Kurt prepared breakfast for the staff and for visitors. Afterward, he prepared one individual meal, on the museum's only pink plate—a gift from the Princess Mette-Marit upon her visit five years earlier—and carried it to Agnes. He lived for her, and I rooted for him. If Agnes was near him, he was picking the pony hairs out of her sweaters. If she was off working, he was writing messages to her over the tops of sausages, in thin lines of mustard. He'd bring them to her, one in each hand— *liebe* in the left, *dich* in the right—for their lunch.

Nils and I slept less and less, and started painting the inaccessible places. I climbed tall ladders to yellow the rafters; Nils lay with his ear in mud to yellow the foundation.

The world was perpetually visible, so I looked at it. Conditioned by hours in the Yellow Room, I saw the landscape in colorblock. The midnight sun came in shades of pink. The fjords rushed up onto white-sand beaches, and the sand made the water Bermuda-green. The houses were always red. They appeared in clusters, villages, wherever there lay flat land. Mountains rose steeply behind each village—menaces and guardians. Each red house was a lighthouse, marking the boundary between one terrain and another, preventing crashes, somehow, providing solace. Nils told me, "There are no dangerous animals here, *bare flott*," which meant either "only nice ones" or "only ticks."

The sky often split into two opposing weathers: blue over the mountains, where the many peaks had ripped the clouds open, and white over the water, where the clouds collected again, blanketing the fjord. At night, out the colony windows, silent machines passed through crops, and in the morning, great white plastic-wrapped bundles appeared, preserving I didn't know what until I didn't know when.

Even at midsummer, snow remained on the highest peaks. The mountains were writing something with those high ridges; there was surely calligraphy there. Where the mountains ended, a line of cursive ran across the otherwise blank sky, four thousand meters up, where it could be read by everyone. People who'd lived in Lofoten all their lives had surely translated those scripts, I imagined, at crucial moments, when they needed to be told.

One triumphant evening, Nils and I bought tickets to a screening of Harry Potter at the Leknes movie house. Nils didn't know anything about Harry Potter. When I tried to give him a basic introduction, he didn't understand the word *wizard*, but after he looked it up in the dictionary and found that it meant "trollman," he was excited.

Dead fish hung by their tails from wooden racks, mouths open, all along the side of the road. Nils said they were dried cod, for the stockfish export—Lofoten's once-great industry. The fishermen were late in collecting them this year. As the weeks passed, the fish dwindled in number, until only the bare racks remained. Nils was pleased that there would be no dangling heads when the inspectors came—with all those sharp teeth taken out of the sky, he said, the barn would have less visual competition.

The lights stayed off in the colony, and when the sun rose or fell to tree-level, perching briefly in the branches, it looked like a bird's nest in flames.

I set up an easel near the window where the ox most often appeared. Painting the animal at night, from a distance, was a relief after days spent with my nose against splintering walls. When it rained, the sky reflected itself in the ox's wet horns, and the horns turned cloud-gray, aging the beast considerably.

Nils finished the barn's exterior walls. Our sun on the hill stood irrefutable, and we began to apply details to the surfaces—thin shapes drawn in white-pink, barely visible, but making the mono-chrome shimmer into motion.

At the end of each day's work, Nils wanted to drink box wine. The government controlled all alcohol sales in the country, and he bought the boxes in bulk from a state-owned outlet in Stamsund. At the upstairs kitchen table, he handed me full glasses, and I shared my brown cheese with him. We read *Lofotposten*, a thin local newspaper that included photographs of every child whose birthday it was that day. He'd take out a pen and circle grammatical forms for me, using the simplest articles as examples.

RAMBO, KITTEN, RESCUES OTHER KITTEN, ON A
FARM NEAR TANGSTAD

A kitten / the kitten / this kitten / that kitten
En kattunge / kattungen / denne kattungen / den kattungen

I learned a great deal of Norwegian this way. When the sky darkened slightly, we got in the car to chase the midnight sun. The roads were visited nightly by arctic foxes, little things, and lined by construction machines. We'd stop to examine abandoned backhoes whose digging claws rested on the ground, mouths open. I crawled inside each claw and sat bunched up in the corner, while Nils took notes on the machine's industrial yellow.

My work on the fourth interior wall progressed until it was nearly indistinguishable from Nils's original three. We would soon be ready for inspection, and indeed the men were due in less than a week. Haldor and Sigbjørn became nervous, and kinder. An approved KORO installation would mean much-desired traffic for the museum. And they knew what it would mean to Nils—at least, they could imagine what rejection would mean to Nils.

It was the Thursday before the government's Sunday visit, and Nils and I were driving from Leknes up to the barn. There had been a storm overnight—we had woken to find the radish fields beside the colony flooded, and the ox gone. Now the sun had recovered and spread through the washed air, glinting off the road and the roofs of passing cars, making us squint. I'd never seen such strong light. Nils was terrified, imagining the exterior wall damage. I was dazed, watching bluebells shoot past in the side shrubs, when a black line bisected the pale world.

A boy was walking up the road's shoulder. His back was to us, and he wore black clothes from neck to toe. He had the darkest hair I'd seen on these blond islands. He walked slowly, and quickly fell away behind our car. I rolled down my window, stuck my head out, and looked back at him. His head was down, and curly hair fell over his face. He looked no older than eighteen.

I shouted, "Need a ride?"

He looked up for a second, but I couldn't hear if he spoke.

Nils grunted for me to sit up straight. He rolled up my window from the control panel on his door. We didn't have time for rides, he said. The barn had come into view, and immediately we saw what had happened: the top coat of paint, which hadn't been completely dry before the start of the downpour, now formed a bleary film over the surface of the wood, threatening to drip uncontrollably.

We spent the day holding paper towels up to the barn walls. Nils suggested we slam the towel once, as if crushing a bug, and then not move until the paper had saturated. The goal was to absorb the excess moisture without smudging the wet paint. Sigbjørn helped us. Haldor's hands were enormous, and Nils worried they'd make more mess. By early evening we'd soaked up all the dripping but stripped a good deal of the color. A new coat wouldn't dry by Sunday. As it stood now, the barn looked decades old and severely faded. Nils went into the smithy to dry his hands by the coals and think. I sat in the barn, listening to his Schubert. When he returned, we began to add thin layers to tiny areas, blowing on what we'd painted. We added only some patchy brightness over the course of the next ten hours.

Leaving the museum for the night, I saw a light shining in one of the guest rooms. The head I saw in shadow, racing around the room, was too high to be Agnes's, and too slight to be Haldor's. June had ended, and I felt a change coming—the KORO officers were on their way, maybe this was the first of them.

• • •

In the morning, I was hungry and the sun was back to the top of the sky. Nils had left a note under my door that said he was doing some detailed repairs he'd rather do alone, and that I should get a pancake. I had been hearing about a pancake stand. It was straight up the mountain from the artist colony, the REMA 1000 cashiers had told me. I put on a dress and started walking.

After nearly a mile of climbing with nothing in sight, I began to suspect that there never had been any pancake stand. I kept on, despite feeling hopelessly duped by the whole pancake story. My beacon came in the form of a shabby roadside sign that read PANNEKAKE and listed hours of operation. I turned off the road and walked down a short driveway toward a gigantic house.

Following the signs inside, I entered a room full of tables. It was the largest restaurant I had ever seen. The dining room was a square expanse with windows on every side, framing the ubiquitous mountains and fjords and *geitrams*. Nobody was there, nobody at all. I went up to the counter, read the laminated menu, and waited awhile before a woman appeared. She flicked the lights on over the dining tables. I asked for a pancake with blueberries, bananas, and chocolate sauce. She took my kroner and said, "Next."

The boy in black stood behind me. He stepped up to the counter and ordered a pancake. The woman asked if he wanted any toppings. There was a long pause. Then he said no.

I stared at him, trying to take in the details I'd missed from the car. I couldn't believe I'd gotten a second chance: here he was, not lost to the road, no windows to roll up between us. As he paid, I studied the way his glasses (black, like his clothes) rested on his nose, partially obstructed by his unstoppable hair. The register's cash drawer slammed shut and the boy turned away. I watched him as he walked toward the far window. He stood up tall and straight, and rested one hand on the back of a chair. He seemed to fill the room.

The way he looked at the fjords out the window reminded me of the way I did—it was a foreigner's awe. Even his *no* to the cashier had betrayed an accent of some kind, and my basic loneliness, though I had come to accept and even enjoy it, reached out toward his.

The waitress disappeared into the kitchen.

I didn't dare walk any closer to him, so I found myself shouting from a distance again: "Are you from around here?"

He continued to look out the window.

Given that there were only two of us, I couldn't have been speaking to anyone else, but I took a step in his direction and tried again.

"Er du Norsk?" I said.

When he finally turned my way, revealing an expression of intense weariness and irritation, he mustered the word "What?" and sat down in a chair, his back to me. No, he wasn't Norsk.

My pancake arrived. I took it from the waitress's hands and found a fork and a place to sit—I chose the table farthest from the boy, and sat with my back to his back. I saw the waitress bring out his plate. Looking down, to keep from looking at him, I poked at the pancake with my fork. It was thin, dense, and elastic. It lay like a bedsheet under the chocolate sauce. When I heard the boy begin to eat, I ate. Each bite was sweet, slippery. We chewed in the silence of the great room, making just a little noise between the two of us, until we'd both finished and the deeper silence resumed. Perhaps the boy hadn't liked being identified as an outsider. I felt I could amend things by sympathizing.

The waitress circled around us, gathering first my empty plate and then his. I rehearsed a line: I'm not from here either. Nice to see another stranger in town.

When I stood up to walk to his table, he'd gone.

· · ·

Just as well, because it took ages to find a bus stop, and ages until a bus came, and by the time I entered the Yellow Room, Nils was beside himself. I found him sitting on the floor of the barn, clutching the boom box to his stomach. Haldor was standing over him. I suspected something terrible had happened—Haldor never entered the Yellow Room.

"There you are," Haldor said to me. "If I could trouble both of you a minute." Nils popped open the CD deck, placed one finger on his Schubert CD, and closed the lid on his finger, again and again.

"Going to need a favor," Haldor said.

"Inspection in two days," Nils said from the floor. "No favors."

"Inspection in two days, fine, but, funeral tomorrow," Haldor said.

Nils stood up.

"Who's dead?" he asked, so mercilessly direct and Nils-like that I nearly laughed.

"I do not know the man, and I very much do not know how to bury him. But the museum has agreed to do it. It will only take a few hours. I must ask you both to join me at Eggum, at midnight, Saturday. I have promised a proper ceremony."

"Eggum?" I asked. I imagined hot colors and holograms.

"According to the family's request," Haldor said. "The man has asked to be buried *at the top of the world*."

"Eggum is not the top of the world," Nils said. "There's Svalbard."

"Can't dig through the ice on Svalbard. This is the closest they will get, and they know it."

The two men switched to Norwegian, for more efficient arguing. I recognized the words for "no," "sleep," and "absurd."

Haldor ended the escalating dispute by pointing at me, shouting, "Then she will!" and leaving the barn. In the moment the doors were open, I saw, walking between the museum's archery targets, the boy. I followed Haldor out of the barn.

The boy walked aimlessly over the museum grounds, and when he reached a nearby hall, I saw him open a door I'd never opened. His appearances no longer charmed me. For somebody so good at keeping his business to himself, I thought, he had little business in there—I ran to catch the door as it closed behind him.

Inside, axes everywhere. Axes with decorative holes in their middles and with gold inlay. Axes with smooth-edged blades, others eroded, toothy. One ruby-encrusted axe, resting on blood-colored satin. He stood in the shadow of a royal axe display case, leaning against its pedestal.

"Are you lost?" I said. "Are your parents here with you?"

I'd later learn it was the worst thing I could say. At the time, he merely looked at me, said, "They are not," and tilted his chin up.

"What are you doing here?"

"What are *you* doing here?"

"I am painting a barn," I said flatly. "It's an art project."

Then, as thoughtlessly as he'd entered, he exited the Axe Hall and looked up the hill toward the barn. Nils had resumed his work on the exterior, reaching a paintbrush far above his head. He looked small against the high wall.

"People waste their lives in so many ways," the boy said.

Before I could find an equally insulting retort, Haldor appeared, exclaiming, "I see you two have met!"

Now the boy looked me in the eye, and he looked alarmed. "What have you told her?" the boy asked, his voice suddenly childish.

"We will need her help with the ceremony," Haldor said.

I stared into the boy's black shirt, comprehending it. I was prepared to start over, to console him in any possible way, when the boy said, "I don't need help."

He looked at me the same way he had on the road—with the hollowed-out face of an empty person. I could see that he meant what he said.

Robert Mason hummed his curse in my ear: I didn't—I couldn't—help anyone.

"If he doesn't need help," I said to Haldor, "the Yellow Room does, and I'd prefer to—"

"Let me have a word with him," Haldor said, and pulled the boy away. They walked past the barn to the lobby. Nils stopped painting, threw his brush down into the grass, and lit a cigarette. He walked toward the parking lot and took a seat on the hood of his car. He didn't see me where I stood near the Axe Hall. I turned and walked down to the fjord.

. . .

It was high tide, and the water was clear and turquoise. A little way beyond the museum's marked territory, I passed a woman who was swimming in her underwear. We nodded shyly at each other, and I walked on. When I got to a place where no one could see, I took my clothes off and swam naked in the fjordwater, which was warm after many days and nights of sun.

I could see through the clear water to the bottom. I found a large shell, but there was a creature alive inside, so I did not take it. Two long shells lay open, their mussel plucked out. I lifted these from the sand. Inside, celestial blues turned white at the bright point where the shells linked.

Spider threads stretched over my socks and underwear when I found them again on the rocks. I wrung the water from my hair and tried to find the spider. It had moved on to a nearby beer bottle. Earlier bathers had left some junk in the sand, but wonderfully, the paperback they'd discarded was in English. I found a concave boulder and crawled down into the hard dent to read.

Pan's back cover suggested that Edvarda would meet a tragic end. I turned to the last page, hoping for instructions on how bodies are buried in the Far North. I could not imagine Eggum accommodating the ceremony I understood a funeral to be—rectangular plot, bordered by other plots, rain the worst possible weather, the gatherers in dress shoes and black umbrellas. On Eggum the beach boulders would be larger than any casket and furthermore threaten to crush the dead. The wind could blow hard enough to remove the mourners' tears from their cheeks. And there was no place for the dead on that shore. Everything that wasn't rock had been taken or canceled by the sea.

I knew only one funeral by heart. My grandmother had died on Yom Kippur, the most sacred day of the year, in September 2001. We buried her in a Jewish cemetery, and given the burning towers I had just seen out my high school's windows, I wasn't sure the world would be around much longer, and I was afraid and missed her terribly.

In *Pan*, Hamsun's Edvarda was carried to her funeral in a white boat.

I lay my bright body over the rock. I took care not to crush the twinned blue mussel shells. Sometimes the waves made a sound on the rocks like footsteps, and I would lift up and look over my shoulder to see who was coming. There was never anyone coming.

PART FOUR

The Top of the World

The flight to Russia had taken ten hours. When Vassily and Yasha landed at Domodedovo, they found Daniil waiting in short-term parking lot A. Yasha hadn't seen his uncle in ten years and was pleased to discover he hadn't much aged, only widened, the way a tree grows.

Daniil drove them through the suburbs of Vidnoye, Tsaritsyno, Danilovskiy—his namesake—and the Tagansky District, and finally entered central Moscow, where the first Gregoriov Bakery maintained moderate business on Arbat Street.

The bakery's cashier welcomed the family with warm blini. Exhausted from travel, Vassily ate a pancake and walked around the corner to Daniil's house, where he took a nap. In the evening, the men played cards and taught Yasha how to swallow vodka without clenching his throat. Vassily refused to drink and told Daniil about the defibrillator they'd soon insert. Yasha told Daniil how much stronger Papa would soon be. Daniil said the surgery was overdue. After Vassily won his third consecutive round, they cleared the tables and slept well.

On the morning of their second day, Vassily felt it was time to focus. While Yasha was in the kitchen, curing an unprecedented hangover with buttered bread, Vassily brought Daniil upstairs to have a talk about "the woman." They sat in Daniil's small account-ing office, which had once been Vassily and Olyana's bedroom.

Vassily asked his brother whether he'd heard anything from Olyana. Daniil had been dreading the conversation, but took the question as a sign that Vassily was prepared. In one flustered monologue, Daniil relieved himself of the facts: Olyana was in New York, she lived with a musician, and here were the papers she'd sent along in the mail. He handed the paper-clipped stack to Vassily. Vassily stared at the cover page of the divorce agree-ment for a long time before he began to read.

Daniil excused himself and returned to the bakery. Vassily took a walk around the house. Her belongings were gone from their old bedroom's closets, except for a black-lacquer jewelry box that contained a few bracelets and her wedding band. Vassily returned to the office, sat, and signed on the numerous lines. Gone was gone; he felt no need to refuse the bureaucracy. The difference between losing her and freeing her was not so great.

Vassily and Yasha went for a walk that afternoon, and though Vassily intended to tell Yasha, he found he couldn't bring himself to say it out loud. The weather was mild for midsummer, and they walked without talking much at all, sharing the peace that was most familiar to them.

When they returned to Daniil's house, Vassily climbed the stairs, entered the kitchen, and suffered a cardiac failure. Yasha wailed for help, and Daniil ran in, only to witness Vassily's collapse, which would prove irreversible.

After the ambulance, after the hospital, after the long ride home and the unsleepable night, after the dawn that had no right to break, after the inedible breakfast, after his body had begun to reject its own agony and the convulsions stilled, Yasha remembered his father's instructions. On the back of a bakery receipt, he wrote:

Ommot's route
Lapland
Top of the world
Real peace

Yasha gave the short list to his uncle, and Daniil recognized Vassily's fantasies instantly. The imagery stemmed from their childhood, their long-dead hunting teacher. Daniil told Yasha these ideas were whims, but Yasha was inconsolably serious, and began researching funeral homes in the Far North. Yasha said that his father had spoken this wish back at home, and on the plane to Moscow, and in the airport, and before bed his final night. He refused to ignore what he'd been so plainly told. He had, on the other hand, been willing to ignore his mother's wishes, and common sense, in making this pointless trip. Yasha admitted that his mother lived in New York. Daniil admitted that he knew. Yasha said his mother had wanted a divorce. Daniil said he'd given Vassily her divorce papers.

Having confused each other with their overlapping revelations, neither man knew whom to blame for what. They followed Vassily's wishes. Daniil called Olyana at the number she'd provided. A man picked up. Daniil could not find a way to address him, and instead said only, "Olyana Gregoriov," which succeeded in bringing her to the phone. By that time, Yasha had contacted the Viking Museum of Borg, Norway, and reached an agreement with its chief. Daniil gave Olyana directions from New York via

Oslo to Bodø, saying he'd meet her there with the body. Olyana called the sons of the men who'd once helped her leave Russia, now asking for their help in the cross-border transportation of human remains.

Yasha traveled ahead, alone, to coordinate the ceremony. He took two planes, a boat, and a bus. The museum gave him a room, and a revised quote for the funeral expenses. It fell just within Daniil's stipulated limit. The island where his father would be buried had one main highway, and Yasha walked it aimlessly, stunned by the sparse population, the perpetual light, the one enormous restaurant where he ate all his meals, and the staggering mountains around it.

Vassily's embalmed body was flown out of Russia and over Lapland.

. . .

Olyana arrived in a long black dress, her hands in calfskin gloves, her feet in platform boots. For luggage she carried only a shoulder bag, which the receptionist carried into Room 20. While a bed was made up for her, she stood in the middle of the museum lobby's pentagonal floor, arms straight and neck long, as if to invite predators. It was Saturday afternoon. The Viking Museum was open and full of visitors. Nobody came near her for ten minutes, until Yasha entered the room.

"I begged you," he said. He stood opposite her, recovering from a long sleep and a longer anger.

"*Yakov*," she said, sounding relieved to find him alive.

"I begged you to leave him alone," Yasha said.

"I begged you to tell him yourself."

"I told you he couldn't bear it."

His mother removed one glove, then the other. "The news would have hit him more gently," she said, "coming from his son."

"His son refused," Yasha said.

The men's bathroom door opened, and Daniil appeared.

"So you tried his brother." Yasha turned to his uncle. "And you did it," he said to Daniil, having failed to say it in Moscow. "You did exactly what she asked. She told you to make Papa sign, and you made him. You didn't even hesitate, did you?"

Daniil paused. "I *did* hesitate."

"He could have lived a little longer," Yasha said. He looked at his mother, whose short red hair was pulled back in purple barrettes. "Married to you on paper," he said, "what would it have hurt you?"

"I did it," Daniil said. He held his black cap in his hands, the way Yasha's mother held her gloves, and they both appeared to be holding dead dolls. "You are right, Yakov," his uncle said, "I gave him the papers. I did."

"It was the best thing to do," Olyana said.

"Explain to me how killing him was the best thing to do!" Yasha shouted.

The girl and the barn-painter entered the lobby, raised their eyebrows at Yasha's shouting, turned left, and walked down the hall toward the guest rooms. They carried a couple of bags into Room 18 and closed the door.

"What a funny little house," Olyana said.

"It's a museum," Yasha said. "And what do you care? It was Papa's idea."

"Darling, I had no idea what you were saying when your uncle called about your father. I could hear you in the background. You were simply incomprehensible. *Ommot's route, Ommot's route*, and then gibberish."

"I had to find a place near *the top of the world*," Yasha said, as simply and slowly as he could, given the pace his pulse had assumed since the sight of her monstrous boots, "the way Papa wanted it, that we could get to by following Ommot's hunting route, the way Papa wanted it, that would agree to host a funeral. You can imagine there weren't too many options. This was the best I could find."

"And it's marvelous!" His mother swept her arm from the floor to the ceiling. "Isn't it?"

Yasha didn't know whether or not he'd gotten it right. He needed to ask his father. Daniil was now the closest to his father he could come.

"Where is he?" Yasha asked his uncle.

"In the parking lot." Daniil opened the lobby door and ushered first Yasha then Olyana outside.

The casket was narrow and unpainted. Yasha wondered whether Daniil hadn't hammered the wood together himself. It looked measured to his father's shoulders, which had never been broad. It was tapered at the feet, not very deep, and looked like it would weigh nothing, like nobody was in there at all.

Haldor came marching toward them from the water. When he reached the mourners, he bent himself over, completely, at the hips, bowing to Olyana, who returned his bow with an aristocratic inclination of her head. She touched her hand to her heart.

Daniil reached his arm out toward the casket and declared, "Vassily Gregoriov."

Yasha looked at the casket again, and his eyes teared up.

Haldor spun around and marched back to the museum. He came out again with a dolly that rolled unevenly over the gravel.

The wood of the dolly was darker and thicker than the casket's. There was no equipment in the world, Yasha thought, that could have been built for this purpose, for the death of his particular Papa. Haldor freed a gravel pebble from the bearings of one of the wheels. Yasha thought: Nothing could make this easier.

Daniil and Haldor lifted the casket off the truck and placed it on the platform of the dolly.

"My brother wished to be buried at the top of the world," Daniil said. Yasha heard his father's accent in his uncle's voice—two smart brothers, who knew English well, but rarely spoke it aloud. "There was a Laplander we knew as children," Daniil said. "Our father's hunting teacher. Came from these parts. One of the Sami. Let us shoot with his bows. He put an idea in Vassily's head."

"It is an idea I understand," Haldor said. "The north is very attractive. It should have been a pleasure to meet Vassily Gregoriov."

Olyana shivered in her black dress and ran her hands through her hair. She said, "His heart went out." She made a vague hand gesture that looked to Yasha like a butterfly shooting out of her chest.

Haldor gave a brief account of his aunt Hilde, who'd had heart trouble as well, and who'd lived to the age of ninety-four, though not without several trips to the hospital at Bodø, to which they'd often had to take a night boat, and one time a twelve-person plane.

When Haldor finished they were quiet again.

"She was trying to divorce him when he died," Yasha said to Haldor. Yasha's eyes were blurred with crying, and he wanted to keep things straight. "I don't even know whether he signed the papers," Yasha said. "I was too *distracted* at the time." He turned to Daniil. "Did he sign? Did he manage to sign before—"

"Yes," Daniil said.

"So he's a free man," Yasha said, looking down at the wood. "There lies a free, dead man."

"Please," Haldor said. "We will take very good care of your father. Come inside. Eat. Rest. We have several hours until midnight."

"Have your men done this before?" asked Olyana.

Yasha looked around for Haldor's men. He didn't see any.

"And why midnight?" she continued.

"It is our best hour," Haldor said. He turned out toward the shore.

Yasha followed the chief's stare. The surface of the fjord looked like a sheet of metal marking the planet's edge.

Haldor led Olyana inside, telling her about the midnight sun. Daniil followed behind them, listening. Yasha approached the casket. It was low and steady. The wood had hardly been sanded, but it was even and flat. Yasha lay himself down over the top of it. He was taller than his father, and longer than his father's casket. His dark brown dress shoes hung off the end, toes pointing to the ground. His head was turned to the right, cheek to the wood. He let his arms fall freely down along the casket's sides and onto the ground, where his fingers could lodge in the gravel.

From a distance, a set of hips came toward him, filling his hip-level vision. He stayed still. In comparison to the rough wood under his cheek, and the horror below the wood, the moving figure that now approached him seemed an emblem of the living world, sent to reclaim him. She stopped directly before him, the fly of her jeans parallel to his mouth. He felt his arm reach up, without consciously moving it. He felt her hand accept his. She lifted him with one hand held and the other guiding his back, turning him toward the lobby. On their way inside they passed the painter, who was walking to the barn. He looked unstrung, as though he'd either just rolled out of bed or hadn't slept for days.

"Be right there," she said.

"*Please*," the painter said.

She led Yasha to the row of guest rooms, and Yasha pointed to Room 16. They stood outside the door for a moment.

"What's his name?" Yasha asked, nodding up toward the barn.

"Nils," she said. She grimaced. He recognized her expression from the last time they'd spoken. The receptionist walked past them now; the girl's arm was still around Yasha's back, and Yasha wasn't embarrassed. He wanted the girl to look at him kindly again.

"What's your name?" Yasha asked.

"Frances," she said.

She didn't seem to have any interest in him—she didn't crowd him the way Alexa had, nor was she running away, his mother's signature trick. He had nothing in particular to say to her, but he wanted to keep her attention—her level, undemanding attention. He wanted to simply say *Please*, as Nils had.

"I have to go," Frances said. She went.

Yasha found her stunningly reliable.

. . .

It was dark inside Room 16. Yasha considered what might have happened had Frances stepped inside with him. When he parted the thick, sun-blocking curtains, every corner was blasted with a brightness he hadn't anticipated. The walls were orange, the floor red, the ceiling blue. It felt like being inside the guts of an animal.

The room had two twin-sized beds against opposite walls. One bed frame was made of metal, the other of wood. Yasha sat on the wooden bed, still unmade from the night before. His hands looked freakishly white against his jeans, and the light in his eyes made the room fade, and his cheeks sweat, and his mouth dry. He yawned, swallowing and loosening his jaw.

As the light settled in his room, the colors mellowed slightly. Yasha focused on what lay outside. From his bed it seemed nothing but water, but standing up at the window he could see the shore that came first. Flat white sand. The water looked tropical and freezing. It was cleaner than Manhattan Beach—no cigarettes, no tubby Russians, no babies, no person of any kind, and no trash. A wild boar ate in its pen, on a small patch of grass between the beach and the museum.

Yasha yanked open the room's rickety window. The air that came in felt like it had never touched anything before touching him right now, like it came directly from the place where air is made. He was glad to be up here. He wasn't exactly glad to be at the Viking Museum. Vikings would always mean death to him now, just as they had to lots of people, he supposed. But he understood why his father had wanted to come up here. It was good here: far, high. He wondered why his father had never come up here while he was alive.

Things his father had done in his life: collected frogs, repaired radios, learned English, learned French, learned how to make bread, learned how to play the piano, married his piano teacher, moved to Brooklyn, opened the Gregoriov Bakery, painted the name Gregoriov over their awning in big blue letters.

Things his father had loved: the awning, a bialy in autumn, roller skates, his wife, the baby his wife gave him, the patronymic system that injected his own name into his son's name, binding them forever, the Atlantic Ocean, fishes, the place he came from, the place he moved to, the whole planet, flour, yeast, salt, the subway named B.

Yasha wanted to schmear cream cheese on a bialy for his father. He wanted to serve it to him. The loss was spread unevenly over the day: he had been able to wake up this morning, and he was up on his feet, at least, thanks to Frances. Now that he was alone, the absence drew its invisible weapons. His gut-colored room was full of violence. He lay down, his head hanging off the side of the bed. All he could see was the red floor. The window, still open, let in a breeze that smelled of horse and pasture and lulled Yasha with its oxygen. The red of the floor disappeared and returned. It alternated with brown. When the light moved across the floor, his eyelids changed in color.

The sun was high. It could have been ten in the morning, or noon, or eight at night. It could have been midnight. No, it wasn't midnight yet. Frances would be with him again at midnight. He would be with Papa again at midnight. Yasha pulled his head back onto the bed and pressed his face into the mattress.

. . .

Yasha slept for several hours, then woke up with a start, stood up, and left his room. He followed the smell of bread down the

hallway, past a large metal sculpture of a tree, past the receptionist in the lobby, and straight ahead through the open double doors
of the Ceremonial Hall. It was seven in the evening. Soon they
would need to gather the necessary tools and drive the casket to
Eggum, but the museum staff was dispersed—the Ceremonial
Hall was empty. Then came the sound of boots stomping down
the hallway.

"You haven't eaten, my darling," his mother said. "You're
starving."

"I ate," Yasha said. He hadn't, and he was starving.

"What did you eat? This?" She surveyed the buffet platters:
the bread was unsliced, the tea was red, the eggs were runny,
and everything was pickled. She reached out and touched a
piece of fish. It shook under her touch, and she drew her hand
away.

"Herring," she said. "My father's favorite. I always hated the
way it wiggles."

Yasha couldn't remember Russian herring. He could barely
remember Brooklyn bagels. He saw a block of brown matter on a
silver platter, and a cheese slicer with a handle in the shape of a
bearded man. He gripped the man's face and shaved off the top
of the block. It tasted like nuts, caramel, and potatoes. It looked
like solid peanut butter. A note lying before it on the table, in
angular, rune-like handwriting, read, BROWN CHEESE.

"My darling," his mother said while he was looking down at
the cheese. "Here we are, aren't we? Here we are." She flapped
her hands in the air, indicating the general space of the hall.

He did have a kind of urge toward her—to hold those hands,
or let them hold him, for once, because it was Saturday, and they
both knew what that meant. But he didn't reach out to her, and

his mother put her breakfast together. She sawed two slices of bread from the loaf. On the side of her plate she added a packet of mayonnaise she mistook for butter. Yasha stuffed a thin, heart-shaped waffle into his mouth.

Haldor had changed into a white tunic. He entered the hall now, looking clean and capable; his beard looked extra red. He bowed with his whole body again, deeply, to Yasha's mother.

"It is a dark day," he said.

Olyana nodded. Yasha looked out the Ceremonial Hall's windows. The sun was as bright as it had been for the past thirty-six hours. The fjord was calm. The wild boar was sleeping.

"The darkest days are made of a weather we cannot help but admire," Olyana said. She set her full plate down on the buffet table and picked up one of her slices of bread.

"Your English is very fine, Mrs. Gregoriov," said Haldor.

"Chief Haldor"—Olyana curtsied—"my father was a wealthy man. If you can consider any Russian rich." Nobody laughed, so she went on. "We had—we had so many pleasures. I grew up with tutors, you can imagine, and extra rooms, and herring in the morning. It wasn't for me, such luxuries," she said. "I married a baker."

She held the bread up as evidence. She chewed. Haldor spoke about the darkness of Russian bread compared to the darkness of Norwegian bread. The Norwegian bread, even at its darkest, was lighter than Russia's black bread. Yasha didn't know what they were talking about, or why they were talking. He asked to go back to his room. As he walked away, he heard Haldor begin to speak about sunberries.

. . .

There was no such thing as sunberries. There was no such thing as chitchatting about imaginary fruit on the day of your husband's funeral. Yasha grabbed the doorknob to his room. Through the door of the room next to his, he heard Frances speaking. The museum had given her Room 18 for the night, to spare her the trip back to Leknes. All this meant to Yasha was that Frances would be separated from her teacher and their strange yellow barn. She would be sleeping one wall away from him. Somebody answered her—a few people, but none of them sounded like Nils. He stepped over to her door and listened.

Frances was saying, "Their children will not be assholes."

"How do you know?" a man shouted.

"Like father, like son!" a woman shouted.

There was a silence. Yasha knocked on her door.

"One second!" he heard, and shuffling. *"Ett øyeblikk!"*

When she opened the door, she was wearing yellow short-shorts. He couldn't look at them, but he couldn't look too hard at her shirt either. He was pretty sure it had flowers on it. He looked down. Her legs were tan and smooth.

"Sorry," Frances said, "I didn't think I was needed until ten."

"You aren't needed," Yasha said. He regretted saying that. "I wanted to thank you for before," he said. "I'm interrupting."

"Ongoing family crisis," she said. "Is there anything you—" she hurried to tighten the drawstring of her shorts. "Anything you need?"

Behind her, Yasha could see her laptop open on a little desk by the window and a tiny man and woman on the computer screen. The woman waved slightly. He waved back. The woman waved more vigorously.

"Who's your friend?" came from the laptop's speakers.

"This is Yasha," Frances said, turning away from Yasha, leaving the door open and walking back to the desk by the window.

"Yasha, Yasha, Yasha," said the man.

"Are you the dad?" Yasha said.

"I'm the dad."

Yasha nodded. "My dad just died."

The man and the woman stopped bobbing around.

"I'm sorry," said the woman. "We've just been hearing about the funeral your family has planned. How extraordinary it will be."

"I only told them about his wish," Frances said, "the top-of-the-world one."

"He makes dying sound good," the dad said.

"*Saul*," said the mom.

Yasha took in Frances's room. Like his own, hers had two separate twin beds. The bed she slept on was made, the other had paintbrushes and necklaces scattered across it. One change of black clothes lay neatly folded in her open closet, and the window curtains were drawn to the side, revealing her head-on view of the wild boar's pen. Her toenails were painted orange.

"My parents needed to talk to me before the ceremony begins," she said.

"Where do your parents live?" Yasha asked. He didn't know why he'd entered her room, but having been admitted, he wanted to stay.

"New York," her parents answered in unison.

Yasha sat in Frances's desk chair. "I used to live there."

"In the city?" the dad said.

"In Brooklyn," Yasha said. "The Gregoriov Bakery."

"Your family?"

"My father and I," Yasha said. He looked at Frances. "I didn't know you were from New York."

"Born and raised," said the dad. "Now, you, I think you were born somewhere else."

"*Saul.*"

"I mean, just maybe! Were you born somewhere else?"

"Please don't interrogate him, Dad," said Frances.

"Russia," said Yasha.

"See!" cried the dad.

"I'm sorry," said Frances.

"It's no problem," Yasha said. "I didn't need anything." Squatting to speak into the microphone, he said, "It was nice to meet you both." Frances looked embarrassed. He liked having embarrassed her; he hadn't thought he was capable. He left.

Her dad's voice, audible from within the room, restarted the conversation with, "Well, he . . ."

Yasha walked back down the hall, toward the door that led out to the parking lot, to see if the casket was still there.

"Who lives in that room?" Yasha's mother called to him. She was standing in the lobby, looking at the Yggdrasil tree sculpture.

"No one," Yasha said. "A girl—"

"Yakov," his mother said, "you didn't tell me you'd taken a lover."

"Jesus Christ," Yasha said.

"We don't use that expression. Look at this," she said, forgetting his lover. "It says it's a tree of life!"

Yasha approached her with caution.

"And there's a goat!" she said.

He looked up at the enormous metal sculpture. There wasn't any goat. There was, as far as he could see, one bronze tree trunk, anchored in three places to the floor of the lobby, with many branches extending up toward the lobby's low, domed ceiling. He noticed, for the first time, four wooden dwarves, which had been glued to the ceiling, evenly spaced around the tree. Each dwarf wore a shirt with a different letter: N, S, V, and Ø.

Still, he couldn't see any goat.

"Where?" Yasha said.

"'The goat stands on the roof of Valhalla and eats its leaves,'" Olyana read from a plaque, bending down to the height of the pedestal. She looked very funny to Yasha, so short. Her whole body was collected, a clump, under her long black dress. When she stood to full height again, he could see that she had always been taller than his father. She was almost as tall as Yasha. On the plaque, where she pointed, a diagram showed the complete system of Yggdrasil.

The sculpture replica was incomplete. There was no miniature Valhalla under the tree, only a metal floor molded to look like grass. Yasha put both his hands on the trunk.

"Don't touch," Olyana said. "It says don't touch. Don't touch the tree of life. Well, can you imagine!" she said, smiling. "Four dwarves are responsible for holding up the sky."

"Where do you think Papa is?" Yasha asked, not smiling, still touching the tree. "With the dwarves in the sky or down with the goat? I think he's under the goat. In the big hall."

"Yasha. You think your father is in Valhalla?"

"I do."

"Well." She ran her hands through her hair. The corners of her mouth, which were giddy by nature, fell.

"'Valhalla,'" she read from the plaque. "'The hall of the slain. At Valhalla, dead warriors drink mead from the udders of the goat called Heiðrún. But there is never so big a crowd in Valhalla that they don't get enough pork from the boar called Sæhrímnir. He is boiled every day, and comes alive every evening.' Well. Your father was no warrior, Yasha," she said.

"And he didn't like to eat red meat. But where do you think *you'll* go?" Yasha said. He pointed to the diagram, tapping at three different places. "Asgard? Valhalla? Niflheim?"

"Stop that, dear." Olyana said.

"No, really. Where do you think?" Yasha bent down the way she had. He sensed that somehow he was gaining on her. "See, if you go up with the dwarves, you have to deal with the wolves who are chasing the sun, and if you go down under the tree's roots"—he kicked the trunk and lost his balance, then got it back—"there's a crazy hedgehog down there, chewing at the roots, pretty rough, and below the hedgehog there's a serpent, and you—"

Olyana read aloud over Yasha's talking. She bent down next to him, at the level of the plaque, their shoulders touching. "'THIS COSMIC PILLAR,'" she read, "'at the centre of the world is described as a giant ash tree'"—she swept one arm in a rainbow motion—"'binding together the disparate parts of the universe.'"

Yasha went quiet and let her big voice bounce off the lobby walls. He looked at the tree. Here it was, binding together the disparate parts of the universe.

"Don't worry," Yasha said, standing up. "Papa isn't with the goat. I don't know where he is, you don't know where he is. That's okay. It's good where he is. He has lots of flour and ovens there, and when *you* die, you won't have anything because you don't love anything."

Olyana was still crouching when she looked up at her son. She was red now, not only in her hair, but in her cheeks and neck. As she blushed, her eyes darkened.

Yasha turned away from his mother and found Haldor's great belly waiting directly behind him. They were standing nose to nose.

"We are prepared," Haldor said to Yasha, "and at your service," he continued, bowing to Olyana. Yasha wondered how Haldor could have arrived so soundlessly.

"Yes, my son was just telling me something terribly interesting," Olyana said, running her hand through her hair and then reaching it out to Haldor, who held it. "About Valhalla."

"Valhalla!" Haldor said, helping her up. "I didn't know it was familiar to you."

The three of them turned back to the tree. Its bulging roots sank into the lobby floor, as if continuing into the underworld.

"You would have made a fine Valkyrie, Mrs. Gregoriov," Haldor said. "They were tall women, like you, with wings."

"I would have made a fine goat," Yasha said.

"No, no," Haldor said, shaking a finger, "at Valhalla it is a very special goat. Very special goat, Heiðrún. Mead comes out of her . . . her . . ."

"Nipples?" Olyana said.

"*Ja,*" said Haldor.

Nobody spoke.

"We go the way to Eggum," Haldor said.

. . .

It was undeniably Saturday, and closer by the minute to midnight. Yasha couldn't stop the time, now that it had come. They were all doing what they were supposed to be doing. Everybody was doing so much that Yasha had nothing to do. Frances was filling the bed of a pickup truck with blankets. Nils had excused himself from the funeral. The inspection of his life's work, he'd apologized, would begin first thing in the morning. He needed to prepare, and to sleep. Frances, he'd said, would unfortunately have to go directly from the midnight funeral to the early inspection.

Yasha helped her with the last blanket. Next were the sheepskins; they piled those on together. Frances filled a crate with thermos bottles, and Yasha packed the collapsible plastic tables. The deck was almost full. Haldor threw a great mass of rope on top of the sheepskins. Yasha loaded one red-handled and one yellow-handled shovel onto the pickup.

A young man pulled a utility trailer into the parking lot. He smiled at Frances, and then stopped smiling when he saw Yasha.

"Your father will ride here," he said.

"Who are you?" Yasha asked.

"Sigbjørn. The blacksmith."

Yasha examined the trailer. It was silver, and it hadn't been cleaned.

"Yakov Vassiliovich Gregoriov." Yasha shook Sigbjørn's hand. He took off his thin green sweater and wiped down the surface where the casket would rest. He clumped the sweater into a ball and rubbed out the dirty corners.

"Superfine," said the blacksmith.

When the trailer was clean enough, Yasha tossed the sweater aside. Frances and Sigbjørn hitched the trailer to the back of the pickup truck. Haldor wheeled the casket out on its dolly, from a back door marked PRIVAT.

"Come now," Haldor said to the men.

Uncle Daniil, Chief Haldor, Sigbjørn the blacksmith, and Yasha gathered around the casket. The sun was still high but falling slightly behind Daniil, casting Daniil's hat-wearing shadow onto the wood. The shadow fell upside down over the casket—Daniil's head at Vassily's feet. Yasha studied his uncle's face. His uncle looked down at the casket, unaware of being watched. Yasha examined him: there was Vassily's nose (bulbous), Vassily's hairline (surprisingly unreceded), Vassily's ears (small). Daniil did not have Vassily's eyes. Yasha's eyes had never resembled his father's either. His father's eyes had been water-colored.

Yasha wanted to open the casket. Fast, once.

"Daniil—" he said.

"Yes?"

"Can we open it?"

"Open it?"

"Open it."

"No, I don't think we can open it."

"No?"

"You see," Daniil said, "well, it is not hard to pick the nails, I only hammered them. But Yasha," he said, "Yasha. You want to do it? He is resting. He looks sick inside."

Everyone looked at the casket.

"I haven't seen him in six days," Yasha said.

"I haven't seen him in ten years," said Olyana.

"My father died in 1999," Haldor said.

Daniil rubbed his face, took off his cap. "He is resting."

Yasha looked at the casket again: still sunlit. He thought about the sunlight passing through the wood, through his father's eyelids and into the green of each eye. They would become brilliant, some days, when the ocean light came in through the bakery windows and slapped his father straight in the face. Those were moments when his father's face was so bright, Yasha could see every nose hair in perfect clarity, and the lake-like green of his eyes. The bakery, which was otherwise a dimly lit place, darkened their color into something more leaf-like on cloudier days.

Everyone was waiting for Yasha to respond. Yasha turned to his mother, who was checking that her earring was still in place. Ten feet behind her, sitting on the back bumper of the truck, Frances was staring at Yasha almost tearfully, making Yasha feel suddenly proud. This was his father, his father's funeral they were all attending.

"Don't open it," Yasha said. "He's resting."

"Then we heave it up," said Sigbjørn.

"Yes," said Daniil.

All four men bent their knees and extended their arms. The casket sat between them, shivering on the dolly.

Frances made runway hand signals, guiding the men backward and the casket onto the trailer. When it was in place, Haldor picked up the coil of rope and wound it around the casket four times, securing it to the trailer. Yasha and Frances climbed onto the bed of the pickup. They sat side by side on the sheepskin stack.

Daniil and Sigbjørn sat in the backseat while Haldor drove and Olyana sat passenger. The truck drove slowly, ceremoniously.

• • •

Vikingveien, the portion of the highway that ran past the museum, soon forked west into Eggumveien, which passed the fifty-odd houses that made up Eggum village and terminated in a sheep field. A narrow dirt road continued past the sheep, between six red fishing cabins, and out toward the northernmost tip of the peninsula, where a government-sponsored sculpture installation—a human head that seemed to turn upside down as one walked around it—stood mounted on a thin pedestal. Eggum Beach sprawled on, boulder by boulder, seemingly without end, to both the east and the west. North of Eggum lay the Norwegian Sea. At the far side of the Norwegian Sea lay the North Pole, and then the world started again on the other side.

Yasha and Frances sat on a wooden bench beside Eggum's ruined German radar station. Yasha stared at a gyrating sixteen-legged spider, which split into two spiders who ran away from each other and met again on the underside of the bench.

"Ugh," said Frances.

"Do they bite?"

"Don't all bugs bite?"

Yasha smiled—they were both New Yorkers.

"Here, we have the cheeses!" Haldor shouted from the base of the radar station. "And buns, and butter, and coffee. So many cups as you like!" He had set up a plastic table, and Sigbjørn had covered it with a sheepskin. The skin was thick, with uneven clumps of wool, making the coffee cups wobble. The hairs below the thermos were already stained brown.

Daniil ate three buns. He looked starved, as if he had carried his ruined brother here on his shoulders. The Gregoriov family had never believed in reunions. Now they were all here. Here, in a way. Yasha imagined the brothers as boys. Daniil would have been taller. Vassily would have been faster. When he thought of his father, Yasha thought of a living, breathing, sneezing, baking man. They hadn't yet brought the casket down from the silver trailer. Yasha imagined his father sneezing inside his coffin.

There would be nowhere for the snot to go. It would gather on the inside of the wood. Yasha imagined Vassily sneezing, underground, forever.

"What time is it?" Yasha asked.

"Now it is nearly fifteen over twenty-three—"

"He means eleven fifteen," said Sigbjørn.

"I apologize," said Haldor. "The point is, forty-five minutes remain."

It could not have possibly been eleven fifteen, Yasha thought. He looked up. Bright blue. He looked out. Never-ending sea. He looked right and left. Rocks.

"Is it going to get dark at some point?" Yasha asked.

"No," said Haldor. "Did it get dark last night? No. Not all the way dark. Only a little bit pink. It will not get all the way dark tonight either, which is good, I think, for your father."

"Dancing—" Olyana said, with a look of inspiration on her face. "There should be dancing, in the light," she said.

She might have been fun to be married to, Yasha thought at the same time as he considered tackling her. Here she was, talking about dancing "in the light." She really was detestable. She might at least have made Papa laugh. Or dance. Papa did dance occasionally. He had danced, if just with his shoulders, the night they closed the bakery.

Frances kept to herself, staring at the sand, but she was laughing quietly.

"If you danced, Mrs. Gregoriov," Haldor said, "none of us would refuse to join you."

Frances laughed harder.

"It can be that you are laughing too much tonight," Sigbjørn said to her.

"It cannot be," Yasha said.

"I'm so sorry, Yasha," said Frances. "I'm not laughing. I'm doing the thing when your body gets confused about grief and just shakes a lot. You know? I'm not laughing. I'm shaking."

Yasha wondered what other things her body did; he thought about gripping her small shoulders and moving her nearer to him.

"Shall we dig?" Haldor asked Sigbjørn. "Better to have the hole cleared, such that we fill it at midnight."

Yasha looked up and saw tears falling down his mother's face. There, Yasha thought. There, it's occurred to her.

"Mrs. Gregoriov," said Haldor, "I have upset you, and I will never forgive myself for it."

"You have not upset me, dear chief," she said. "The hole upset me. Digging the hole. That we dig for Vassily."

Yasha was upset about the hole as well. He was also upset about the rocks, and how they might roll over in a storm and damage the casket, even once it was underground, and about all the waves, and the tide, and about the last time he'd stood in the basement with his father, the night it had flooded, and his father had rolled his pants up, and Yasha hadn't even touched his father's calves, even though they were right there and covered in hair, hadn't celebrated them at all. He mourned that he hadn't sat down in the floodwater and hugged himself around his father's leg while it was a leg, while his father stood on it, and now Papa was lying down, and would be lying down forever, and he had lain down over his father's casket. He wondered whether Frances had thought him pathetic for doing so, and whether fruits grew faster on trees when she laughed, and whether she liked him, because he actually liked her so much, and because he was ashamed to like anyone when today was Saturday, and the one person who had loved him all his life was, in the end, no bigger than a hole.

"He was my brother," Daniil said.

Yasha wondered whether his mother would have the courage to say, "He was my husband." If she said that, she would also have to say, "And my new boyfriend's name is Ian."

Olyana said nothing. She was smoothing her black dress down against her stomach over and over, with alternating hands. She was thin, almost concave. Her arms were covered in prominent goose bumps.

Haldor and Sigbjørn started to dig. Before sitting down, Yasha checked under the bench for spiders but didn't find any. The wind picked up, blowing the hairs of the sheepskin into the cheese on the platter. When Haldor shoveled sand over his shoulder, it spread through the air. Some of the sand landed on Yasha's raisin bun. He ate it, and then ground the grains between his teeth until they disappeared.

· · ·

At ten minutes to midnight, Haldor shouted, *"Klar!"*

"It means 'ready'!" Sigbjørn shouted, somewhat frantic.

"Ready," repeated Frances, hopping up and clearing the coffee cups.

"What are we to do?" his mother asked.

"It is a question many have wondered," Haldor said, "since the beginning, and so they wrote the sagas, to give some answers. Because none of us know."

Yasha did not find this helpful.

"Who will lift the casket off the trailer?" Yasha asked.

"This funeral may feel to you like Ragnarök, the End of the World," Haldor said, "but I can assure you, Mrs. Gregoriov—"

"My name is Olyana."

"Olyana!" Haldor's face seemed to expand for a moment, and then contract again: "I can assure you that the world begins again after the End of the World. Two people survive, and their children fill the new world. So says the great saga, the Edda, in its very first section, called *Gylfaginning*, which means, 'The Fooling of Gylfi.' If you have read the fifty-second chapter of *Gylfaginning*, the chapter called, 'After Ragnarök,' you see there, it is not the end. We bury your husband tonight under the midnight sun to show it is not the end—to show there is light, even in a time of darkness."

This was better, Yasha thought. This was something. Some way to make sense of the sunlight. It was five to midnight. The sky was the same pale blue as Frances's coffee cup. Yasha craved some sense.

His mother surprised him with her practicality just then, asking, "But what are we to do, now, with the casket?"

Sigbjørn stepped forward, out from behind Haldor, who had concealed him completely, and said, "The casket is light. I can move it."

"I can help," said Daniil.

"Superfine," Sigbjørn said.

"What will I do?" Yasha asked. He straightened his back to its full height, dropped his shoulders, leaned his chest forward, pulled his arms back, tilted his chin slightly up and to the side, and placed one hand in his pocket.

Frances started to laugh again.

Yasha took her hand, silently congratulated himself, and walked her to the hole. They had cleared quite a bit of sand, and the hole was far deeper than the casket was tall, offering some protection from the boulders and the wind. It looked comfortable. As if in response to Yasha's thought, Sigbjørn began to line the inside of the hole with sheepskins. The grave was built into an inverse animal, all the wool facing in. The space was insulated from the damp sand, and from the North Pole, which was perpetually ending the earth out there in the water. Everything our skin keeps out must stay out, Yasha thought, far from Papa, who will lose his skin, over time. The image of his father's skeleton blinded Yasha with its clarity and whiteness. Sigbjørn and Daniil went off to retrieve the casket.

They buried him under devastating sunshine. Brilliant light gleaming off the shovels and the casket's brass nails. Brilliant light on the hair of the mourners and the pistils of the wreath flowers and the spotted backs of the things living in the nearest woods. Birds in the sky were black, in silhouette, before the sun. Light covered the water, making the water a sky, making the sky a body of water.

They lowered the casket on two ropes. One band of pink light lined the horizon. The blond wood caught the pink in its grains and released, from Papa, Yasha thought, a blush.

"We gather at the top of the world," Haldor began, "to bury Vassily Gregoriov."

"Vassily Andreovich Gregoriov," said Daniil, "may it please our resting father."

Haldor was not a priest. He was, by trade, a tour guide. The rocks rising from the shallowest water had grown as black as the birds, backlit, and were predators to Haldor's improvised ceremony. Farther up, where the shore ended, the wartime radar station blinked its old red bulb. The shoreline was cluttered with mountains, each mountain transforming, where it met the sea, from rock into water. Waves rushed up toward the mourners but did not reach them. They stopped some way down the shore, split into foam by the boulders.

Haldor pulled a small book from inside his tunic, opened it, and said to Daniil, "Your brother," and said to Olyana, "your husband," and said to Yasha, "your father, Vassily Andreovich Gregoriov, asked to be given, after death, to the top of the world. Why did he do this?" Yasha saw Haldor's eyes move to a slip of paper taped to his book's inside cover. He had prepared a speech. "It is, it must be, for the same reasons that the All-Father, Odin, journeyed north in the time of the gods. It was to greet the powers that dwell here, the guards who look after the edge of the earth." Haldor faced the mourners. "Fortunately," he said, "the world begins again, on the other side, for example, with Canada."

Frances laughed, then Sigbjørn laughed, then Yasha laughed, then Olyana laughed.

"What, Canada?" Haldor asked meekly.

"Go on, Haldor," Yasha said.

"I did not mean it to be a joke," Haldor said. "I was only thinking about the land on the other side of the pole, those countries. I thought of Canada first, though, to myself, I wonder why Canada is not spelled with a K. The meaning was to say that the top of the world and the end of the world are not the same"—he drew a breath—"and that Vassily's ending is another one of these endings that can mean beginnings after." He was sweating under his eyes.

"Bravo," Olyana whispered with aggressive sincerity.

"We read from the fifty-third chapter of *Gylfaginning*," Haldor said, gathering confidence. "It is called, 'The High One Describes the Rebirth of the World.' It is my favorite chapter."

Sigbjørn bowed his head. Yasha noticed the military shortness of the blacksmith's hair and the perfect sphere of his head, hovering moonlike over the hole. Haldor's little book looked tiny in his large hands. In his "chief" posture, he stood with his feet apart and his chest high. Haldor was no priest, but he was righteous. He had the once-removed righteousness of an actor playing the President.

"'There will arise out of the sea,'" Haldor read, "'another earth most lovely and verdant, with pleasant fields where the grain shall grow unsown. Vidar and Vali shall survive; neither the flood nor Surtur's fire shall harm them. They shall dwell on the plain of Ida, where Asgard formerly stood.'"

In Yasha's imagination, the plain of Ida looked like the museum's lobby: a place with a great tree at its center. He didn't mind much, one way or another, how these worlds looked; it was soothing to hear all the vowels in their names, pronounced slowly and openly by Haldor's big mouth, in a foreign accent, each word washed by the wind. Ida might look a lot like Eggum, Yasha thought, turning briefly back toward the sculpture of the human head, the signature of this strangest possible place. He wanted to ask: Isn't this strange? Papa, isn't this strange?

"'. . . Thither shall come the sons of Thor, Modi, and Magni,'" Haldor was saying, "'bringing with them their father's mallet Mjölnir. They will all sit down together and converse, talking about things that happened in the past, about the Midgard Serpent and the wolf Fenrir. Their food will be the morning dews, and from these men will come so great a stock that the whole world will be peopled.'"

Olyana looked up—she had been staring down at her own breasts, touching her fingertips together. She turned out now over the water, toward the sun perched on the horizon line, soon to start rising again.

"'The sun will have borne a daughter no less lovely than herself,'" Haldor read, "'and she will follow the paths of her mother, as it says here . . .'"

And Haldor read to the end of the fifty-third chapter, and Yasha wondered whether Haldor had seen his mother look out over the water, and whether the ceremony was for his father or for her. Sigbjørn's head was still bowed in grace, and Frances had clasped her hands behind her back, a tiny soldier, contributing her best seriousness and her best sympathy. Yasha had no requests to make, no changes to make to this ceremony. Whether his mother was mourning, or hopeful, or bored, or empty-headed did not matter to Yasha, because it hadn't mattered for the last ten years, not as much as the bakery or feeding Septimos had mattered. Yasha had let Septimos go; his mother had long ago let her family go; and Yasha himself, he felt with dread excitement, had been let go, now that Papa had gone.

Then came the sound of sand hitting the casket—Sigbjørn had gotten hold of the red-handled shovel and had begun to fill in the hole. Yasha forgot all his peace at the sound of the sand and his mother's voice.

"What are we doing?" she asked, which seemed to be the only question she had asked all night.

"It is only the first bit of sand," Haldor said, closing his book. "We must begin to fill in the grave, such that your husband is buried by dawn."

"He's not her husband," Yasha said.

"What?" said his mother.

"No?" asked Haldor.

"He's not your husband!" Yasha shouted. "You're somebody's girlfriend." He turned to Haldor and said, "She lives with a man, in Tribeca." He looked at his uncle, and then back at his mother, and then down into the hole. "I am his son," Yasha said. "And that's all."

"You are also *her* son," said Sigbjørn, pointing the shovel at Olyana.

"You *are* his mother, aren't you?" said Haldor.

Olyana ran her hands through her hair and said, "I am Yakov's mother. Vassily was my husband. The rest is only about cats and apartments." She made a flicking gesture with one hand. "Let me bury him."

Haldor whispered, "Dear Olyana," but she snatched the shovel from Sigbjørn's hand. Haldor, now defenseless, touched at his beard absentmindedly. Sigbjørn dropped to the ground and sat, holding his knees to his chest. Nobody knew what was wrong with him. He was not, in any case, attempting to retrieve the shovel from Yasha's mother. Olyana stood with all her limbs spread apart, the red handle clutched in one fist. Frances kept her own hands behind her back, her hair covering her face. It did not seem possible to Yasha that they could both be called women.

Things had been moving very, very fast, Yasha thought, while everybody remained silent. It had begun the day his mother appeared on Oriental Boulevard. He'd chased her, they'd run a good distance toward Brighton Beach, and it seemed they hadn't stopped running. Yasha had run off with his father to Russia, his father's heart had run out, and they had all run up here to the damn North Pole, where he'd found the first girl he really—

"What's wrong, Mrs. Gregoriov?" Frances asked.

That is what happened, Yasha thought, as her voice confirmed it.

Olyana lowered her shovel, but not completely to the ground. "I cannot remember the blessing," she said, and then lowered the shovel completely.

The word *blessing* startled Haldor. He flipped furiously through his tiny book.

"There is a prayer we should say. I learned it for my father's funeral and I do not remember how to say it. I do not remember how to say it!"

Haldor left his position at the head of the grave and walked around to Olyana. He gently freed the red handle from her fist. Frances came over and stood between them. Everybody was on one side of the grave now, except Yasha, who stood directly opposite, looking very tall and gangly against the open beach.

Olyana turned to Frances and said, "You're Jewish."

"What?" said everyone.

"I am Jewish," said Frances simply.

"Of course she is," Olyana said to the group. "New York, brown hair, I mean, look at her!"

"*Mom,*" said Yasha, who realized he'd never called her "Mom" before, only "Mama," and not often that. "Mom" was what the kids at his high school said into their phones, after school, when they were begging for something.

"I only want to know if she knows the blessing," Olyana said.

"What blessing?" said Frances.

"The one I said for my father."

"*Mom,*" said Yasha.

"I am certain you know it. Of course, I should know it, only we were hardly Jewish at all. We pretended not to be. It was easier that way." She turned to Haldor with an expression that begged his pardon. "And of course my father died, so I learned the Jewish words, all nine of them or whatever it was. It was the only way we could bless him, I mean your grandfather, Yakov."

It was impressive, Yasha thought, the way she played to her audience, getting everyone involved. She was putting on a show, and she looked frighteningly radiant, like a star.

"I know the Mourner's Kaddish," Frances said. "That's all. I think you say that later. I don't think it's for right now."

"How does that go?" said Olyana.

Frances said, "*Yitgadal v'yitkadash.*"

"It's not that one," said Olyana.

Yasha said, "Let her finish."

"No, no, it's not that one," his mother said, lifting one hand to block out the sun, which was getting higher and into her eyes. She squinted, and paced up and down the length of the grave. "Not that many *y*'s. It's a short one." She turned to Sigbjørn, who had no idea, and looked insulted by the words *short one*.

"I thought Papa wasn't Jewish," Yasha said. "Only you are, sort of."

"I am," she said, "which means you are, Yasha, dear, and we are the ones who are mourning."

"The only Jewish thing Papa knew how to say was *mazel tov,*" Yasha said.

"He learned it at our wedding," said his mother.

Haldor opened his book. "Perhaps—"

"The blessing is not in your book, my dear chief," she said. "Lord," she said, "I miss my father. I miss that man, herring and all. I miss this man." She used her sun-blocking hand to point down at the casket. Her face was lit again, and shone as if the light came from under her skin. "I miss my son," she said. "Look how tall he is. I can hardly believe it. Of course I am a long-legged woman, but Vassily was so short."

Sigbjørn looked down at the casket.

"Heaven pity me," Olyana continued. "I lose everything."

"I don't pity you," Yasha said to his mother, across the grave.

Olyana was in her stride. What had happened by the Yggdrasil tree—when she had been crouched, and shocked, and nearly defeated—would not happen again. There were too many people watching this time, and her dress was thin, and she was cold, and strengthened by the cold. Yasha saw this, and braced himself.

"When I ask heaven to pity me," his mother said, "I ask heaven, not you, Yasha, dear. Then, of course, heaven will need to pity you too, for sending your poor father off to Russia, looking for me, when you knew very well I was not there. We'll see if heaven forgives you for that."

Frances turned, confused, to Yasha. Yasha's fingers cramped.

"When I call to heaven," Haldor said, passionately raising one arm, "I am asking Baldur, and Frey, and Skirnir, Frey's man-servant—"

"I sent *myself* off to Russia," Yasha said, "to get *away* from you." He glared at his mother, but her expression did not change. He turned to Haldor. "We are not Vikings, Haldor," Yasha said. "Frances, please, say the blessing you know. Stand where Haldor stands."

Nobody argued. Frances pulled her hair off her face and gathered it at the nape of her neck in a twist that immediately came undone. The group stood evenly spaced around the hole. The circus, Yasha thought, was over, and the band of pink light that had lined the horizon was sinking, gradually, into the sea.

Frances said, *"Yitgadal v'yitkadash sh'mei raba."*

There was a pause. She whispered to Yasha, "Say *amen*."

"Amen," said Yasha, with all his might.

"B'alma di v'ra chirutei v'yamlich malchutei b'chayeichon uv'yomeichon uv'chayei d'chol beit Yisrael, baagala uviz'man kariv. V'imru—"

She looked at Yasha. Yasha said, *"Amen."*

"Y'hei sh'mei raba m'varach l'alam ul'almei almaya. Yitbarach v'yishtabach v'yitpaar v'yitromam v'yitnasei, v'yit'hadar v'yitaleh v'yit'halal sh'mei d'Kud'sha—"

Olyana shouted, *"B'rich Hu!"* She beamed.

Frances went on. *"L'eila min kol birchata v'shirata, tushb'chata v'nechemata, daamiran b'alma. V'imru . . ."*

At the sound of the pause, Yasha said, *"Amen."*

"Y'hei sh'lama raba min sh'maya," Frances said, *"v'chayim aleinu v'al kol Yisrael. V'imru—"*

"Amen," Yasha said.

"Oseh shalom bimromav, Hu yaaseh shalom aleinu, v'al kol Yisrael. V'imru," Frances said, followed by a final *"Amen,"* which Yasha missed.

Olyana was delighted. "I simply don't know how I remembered it," she said, in the silence after the prayer. "Of course, my mother would have known it, maybe taught it to me. I haven't forgotten it all, bless me."

Yasha looked to Frances, attempting to communicate a gratitude he'd never felt before. Frances looked back with a sleepy, glad face.

Olyana walked around to the other side of the grave. "Your girlfriend has been a wonderful help, Yakov," she said. "Thank you," she said to Frances.

"Oh, no—" Frances said.

"You *have* been wonderful," Yasha said, hoping that Frances might let the "girlfriend" part slide, or even roll with it.

"Is anybody in need of refreshments, coffee?" Haldor asked. "Cheese?"

"We are not finished with the burying," Sigbjørn said.

Haldor opened his tiny book, and then closed it and put it away somewhere under his tunic. "Forgive me, forgive me, forgive me," he said. "Let us dig."

With the prayer said, and the sun rising, and the wind slowing down, it was—everyone seemed to agree—time to dig, time to bury the casket and the skins. It was cold, and the sand would undoubtedly make Papa warmer, in one way or another, whatever warmth could mean to him now. Frances left her spot at the head of the grave and motioned for Yasha to step forward.

I am still alive, Yasha thought. He picked up the yellow-handled shovel and joined Sigbjørn in shoveling sand. When the casket was no longer visible, he gave the shovel to his mother, an action that made him feel profoundly merciful. He watched her heap a few rounds and was moved, despite himself, because burying was the worst sport, and his mother performed it gracefully. Toward the end, Sigbjørn handed the shovel to Haldor. To prevent Haldor and his mother from finishing the digging together, Yasha asked Haldor for the red-handled shovel, and heaped, with his mother, the last of it.

. . .

They sat on the beach with the grave filled in behind them. Rocks the size of station wagons filled the shore; there weren't many good places to sit. A few rocks had smooth tops, with lichen for padding. They all sat facing the sea. Yasha had his own boulder, and his mother had her own—a larger one way down by the water, with a slight incline, like a pool chair. Daniil got up and washed his face with a little seawater.

Yasha turned back to the now barely discernible grave. Haldor, and the blacksmith, and now Papa—they belonged here, Yasha thought. This was their place. Daniil would go back to Russia, which had always been his place. Yasha, and his mother, and Frances—they did not seem tied to the idea of *place* altogether, as far as he could tell. They were the anywhere sort, just like his cat had been.

His mother leaned back with her eyes closed, sunbathing. There was nothing left of the sunset-sunrise that had stretched out around midnight. The sky was simpler now, less theatrical, and it was strangely unsurprising to see her there, taking in the early light, saying nothing. It was as if they were all waking up, waking up their bodies, each still grappling with a question from a dream. His mother, reclining on her rock, with her body unfurled, looked unquestionably like a woman. Yasha had in some sense never understood her this way—he didn't know if she shaved her armpits or legs, what creams she kept by the mirror, whether she slept naked or in yellow shorts, like Frances. No—his mother would not sleep in shorts. Yasha wondered if it had been a pleasure for his father to sleep beside her. He could hardly count the pleasures now divided from his father by sheepskins, wood, and his uncle's flimsy brass nails.

Under an ordinary sky, blue and recognizable as morning, they started to pack the truck. They had forgotten to use the blankets, though the blankets would have made the rocks more comfortable, and the pile lay folded on the bed of the truck. The only sheepskin that remained above ground was the coffee-stained one from under the refreshments; the thermoses were mostly empty now and the plastic tables cleared, ready to be collapsed. They had less to bring back, Yasha knew, than they'd carried out to the beach. The trailer lay empty, still hitched to the pickup truck.

Haldor again took the driver's seat, Olyana the passenger's. Daniil sat alone in the backseat. Yasha and Frances sat out on the bed of the pickup, with only the one stained sheepskin beneath them. The two shovels rattled across the floor as the truck moved, slamming into their feet. Sigbjørn sat on the empty utility trailer, facing Frances and Yasha. It was perverse, Yasha thought, for Sigbjørn to sit in the casket's place. Besides, he didn't know what sort of hand-holding he would have dared had Sigbjørn not been there, but he couldn't do any of it now.

"My grandmother," Sigbjørn said, apropos of nothing, "is waiting at home for me. I wonder if she soon will die."

It hadn't occurred to Yasha that Sigbjørn had a home outside the Viking Museum, much less a grandmother.

"How old is she?" asked Frances.

"Eighty-seven."

"How old are you?" asked Yasha.

"Thirty-one," said Sigbjørn. "And you?"

"Twenty-one," Frances said.

"Seventeen," Yasha said, simultaneously. Hearing Frances's answer, he added, "I'm turning eighteen in August."

"I'm turning twenty-two in August."

They drove very slowly up the hill and out of the parking lot, the German radar station blinking apathetically behind them. Yasha turned back one more time toward the beach. It looked like a beach. It did not look like a cemetery. It was what Papa wanted, Yasha told himself, and not not beautiful—

"How old is your mother?" Sigbjørn asked.

"I have no idea," Yasha said, dazed. "Fifty?"

Sigbjørn went quiet.

"What did your mother mean when she talked about going off to Russia?" Frances asked Yasha.

"I don't want to talk about it," Yasha said.

"All right," Frances said. Yasha recognized the flash of disappointment in her face and didn't know how to fix it. "In other news," she said, "I guess we might share the same birthday?"

"We might," Yasha said.

They passed the head sculpture, the fishing cabins, and the sheep. The dirt road gave way to Eggumveien, and the truck picked up speed. Haldor was speaking to Olyana as he drove, but Yasha couldn't hear what he said. They would soon be back at the museum, and then what? Would they leave in the morning? It hadn't been possible to think of anything after Saturday, and now it was Sunday. The party would be dispersed. The world seemed open to them, and Yasha wanted to stay put.

"Well, what's yours?" Frances said.

"We could just find out," Yasha said, trying to buy time. "Every day in August, it will either be both of our birthdays or not."

"It's only July."

"Your barn gets inspected in a few hours. Then where will you go? I'm not going anywhere," Yasha said, with so much conviction he surprised himself.

Frances was surprised too; she leaned back slightly and rested her head on the back of the truck's cabin. Yasha didn't dare face her. He waited.

"I don't know," she said eventually. "I have to be at a wedding in September."

"I'm going to work for the Viking Museum," Yasha went on, too anxious to ask whose wedding she meant. "They must have something for me to do here, and who knows where my mother is going?"

Frances did not seem prepared to engage in the details. She was still leaning back, out of Yasha's peripheral vision. She did not reply.

Yasha said, "I'm done with high school." He didn't know if that had been a smart thing to say to a girl who was almost twenty-two. "I'd rather stay here than go back to my father's bakery without my father." Frances said nothing.

Sigbjørn said, "If my grandmother died, I would not want to dig for her. That would hurt all of me. Arms and heart. Better to burn her. Or ask someone else to dig. *Ja,* ask someone else to dig."

Yasha stood up and stumbled across the moving bed of the truck. He stepped over the shovels, pushed both his hands down on one of the side walls, and jumped out of the truck, onto the road. His legs were long and shortened the fall. He only had to shake his ankles out for a moment before starting to walk. Then he followed the truck at its donkey pace, head down and hands in his pockets.

Sigbjørn turned around in the trailer to face him. Frances leaned against the side where he'd jumped.

Yasha slowed his pace to create more distance between himself and the truck. There was only a short way left to drive, and he was inexpressibly thankful to be walking it alone, without Frances's silence or Sigbjørn's mumbo jumbo. The night had been impossibly long.

. . .

Nils stood in the parking lot. Beside him stood a short blond woman. Haldor parked the truck and opened the passenger-side door for Olyana. He and Nils patted each other's backs. The woman shook hands with Olyana, who, to Yasha's relief, hadn't noticed his jump. His mother was shivering. Yasha had almost caught up with the group when Frances bounded past him and threw her arms around Nils.

Yasha ran after her, but could not join the embrace. When they finally separated, Nils began a hurried, whispered account of his trouble sleeping and his decision to check the barn once more. Yasha stood slightly too close to the two of them, trying to catch Frances's eye.

"I am Yasha's mother," Olyana told the blond woman.

"Frida," the woman replied. "The sous chef."

"Our head chef, Kurt, is already preparing breakfast," Haldor said. "Frida prepared the refreshments for tonight's funeral."

Everyone remembered that there had been a funeral. Olyana's shivers were intensifying. Haldor lifted Yasha's discarded sweater from the gravel, shook out the trailer's dust, and wrapped it around Olyana's shoulders.

"Let me take you inside, Olyana," Haldor said, and led her toward the museum.

"Let me clear out those trays," said Frida, and she rushed over to the truck. Daniil followed her, offering to carry the thermoses.

"You ought to get some rest," Frances told Nils.

"That's right," Yasha said, too eagerly. Nils turned to Yasha, arched his eyebrows, then turned back to Frances and said she was probably right.

"I can take Frances back to the asylum now," Nils told Haldor, who had just reached the lobby door. "Thank you anyway for giving her a room."

"Only a pleasure," Haldor said. He opened the door and Olyana strode through it.

Nils walked slowly toward his car. Frances stood frozen in place. Yasha stood behind her. He couldn't shout, Don't go. He dragged his foot through the gravel, disrupting hundreds of tiny pebbles and hoping their noise reached Frances's ears.

"My things are unpacked here," Frances told Haldor.

Yasha had seen her room—how little she'd unpacked. A toothbrush. A few paintbrushes scattered over her second bed. The change of black clothes she currently wore. She had no reason to stay at the museum, unless he had become a reason.

Nils stopped walking.

"Go on without me," she told him. "I'm here, and I'm half asleep already."

"You have everything you need?" Nils asked.

"We will make her comfortable," Haldor declared. He walked into the lobby and straight toward a supply closet.

Nils gave one glance to Yasha, and Yasha hid from it, turning his eyes down to see the line his foot had drawn in the dirt. Again, now, he heard Nils's slow steps, this time moving farther off.

Sigbjørn detached the trailer from the truck and wheeled it back toward the shed. Passing Yasha, he stopped. He rested the trailer hitch in the gravel and placed both of his hands on Yasha's shoulders.

"You were superfine tonight," Sigbjørn said. "We will be seeing each other."

"I don't think we would have made it through the night without you," Yasha told him.

"Only a pleasure," Sigbjørn said. "Of course, very sad." He bade them a hasty and serious goodnight, then wheeled the empty trailer away. Yasha tried to picture Sigbjørn's grandmother, eighty-seven years old, likely named Gerta, or Blorg.

Nils's car coughed and started.

"Hey, Frances," Yasha said. "You want to get out of here or what?" He felt he was catching a ball that had been thrown to someone else, and now he had to run with it.

"Out of here where?" she said.

"The lobby," Yasha said. "Yggdrasil."

They linked arms, spontaneously and a little childishly, Yasha thought, and walked up toward the lobby. When they got to the door, Yasha unlinked his arm and held the door open for her. He extended his other arm fully out to the side, like a butler, and made a small bow. Frances giggled, and Yasha grew pale.

The tree of life stood there, bronze and reaching up all its branches. The four dwarves, each in his little shirt, were still glued to the ceiling. Yasha remembered what his mother had said about the dwarves holding up the sky—his mother, where was she? His head filled with a number of answers, most of which involved Haldor.

"What did you want to do here?" Frances said.

"Check out the dwarves," Yasha said, which sounded like something only a moron would say, and which made Frances nod blankly. She turned away and looked through the window that showed the barn. The inspection would begin in a few hours. The flat, open calm her face had shown after the funeral had been replaced by strain and worry. This wasn't his moment.

"I have to say goodnight to my mother," he said.

"I understand," said Frances, with a little disappointment in her voice, Yasha hoped.

They walked down the corridor. Yasha walked straight to the door of Room 20, not in fact knowing whether his mother would be inside, and Frances stopped in front of Room 18. The doors were several feet apart from each other, making it impossible even to hug.

"Goodnight," Frances said. "Sleep well." She opened her door and disappeared.

Yasha knocked on his mother's door.

"Come in," Olyana answered.

Yasha had not yet been inside his mother's room. When he opened the door, he found her lying in a large bed. He walked closer and saw that she had pushed her twin beds together, one wire and one wood, of even heights, making a functional queen size. She lay covered by two overlapping blankets, each wide enough for only one half of the bed. She wore a nightgown, an elegant one, high-necked, cream-colored, and patterned with vines of small flowers. The gown was more dignified than Yasha considered his mother to be, though it was no more dignified than she considered herself to be, and he realized this as he came to the side of her bed.

"I miss Papa," Yasha said, before he could stop himself.

"I do too."

"You didn't miss him for ten years."

"I did," she said, "but I went about my business." To Yasha, the word *business* meant either bread or sex. "You will be fine without your father," his mother said. She removed the barrettes from her hair and set them down on her table, alongside her watch and bracelet. "You were fine"—she smiled—"without me."

"How could you possibly know that?"

"Now as to whether you'll be fine without your girlfriend," she went on, "harder to say. What will you do, my darling? Bring her home to Brooklyn? Where does she live?"

"She isn't my girlfriend."

"Heaven knows she won't want to live over that bakery," his mother said, fluffing the hair that had been flattened by her barrettes. "But for love, perhaps, as I did—imagine two generations of women, moving into bakeries for love!"

"She is not my girlfriend!"

His mother settled fully into the bed, pulling a duvet over her breasts. She looked regal, and powerless. "Very well," she said, "she isn't."

It was an argument Yasha hadn't really wanted to win.

"I don't know why she isn't," he said.

"You're a bit moth-eaten."

"I'm what?"

"A bit of a shabby flop," his mother said.

Yasha looked at the lacy collar that frothed around her long, thin neck and said, "You're a bitch."

His mother felt her forehead with the heel of her palm, as if taking her own temperature. "I heard you at the funeral, little man. You do not pity me. You needn't use uglier words." She turned away from him. "I must sleep. Chief Haldor was kind enough to come by and give me this tea." She pointed to a mug that was still completely full. "He has things to say to us in the morning. Let us meet for breakfast at nine."

It was probably three o'clock in the morning. The grass was full of sunshine. Yasha felt he'd been useless all night. He didn't know how to make anyone tea. Tea tasted like soap. He hated tea, and he hated himself for hating tea. He had no idea what he would do come morning, unlike that miserable painter and his pretty apprentice, who had something big to do. He had led Frances back to the lobby and paid more attention to the ceiling than to her. On his mother's bedside table, under the barrettes, the watch, and the bracelet, a form titled PETITION FOR DISSOLUTION OF MARRIAGE lay flat, bearing his father's signature.

"I can't wait until you're gone again," Yasha said.

"I think I'll stay a little while," she said, "before we go back to logistics . . ." She waved a hand over the papers. "Take in the fjord country. What about your girlfriend, Yakov, is she taking off? Cut your hair," she said. "It will give you a better chance with her."

Yasha left the room. In the hallway, he could hear Kurt in kitchen, chopping, and Frida talking about a vacuum.

He walked a few steps down the hall and stopped at the door to Frances's room. Frida's vacuum started up in the kitchen. It made a howling sound that Yasha couldn't bear. He had become terribly, terribly tired. He was a *shabby flop*. He pressed one palm against Frances's door, then the other, then his forehead, making three dull thuds. A latch moved, and suddenly the door opened. Yasha fell forward into the room. He stood just over the threshold as Frances cleared her second bed of a dozen multicolored gel pens, a necklace bearing a figurine of a ballerina, a bundle of paintbrushes, and her socks, which had been set out to dry. Yasha saw the open expanse of the cleared bed, removed his shoes, and lay down.

. . .

The wild boar was awake and rubbing itself vigorously against one side of its pen. A new load of apples had been thrown in, reddening and brightening the ground. Yasha had one eye open. The other had not yet given up on sleep. A blanket covered his body, though he could see his feet sticking out at the far side. No shoes. It was true, then, the final image his consciousness was now offering up—that he had knocked, or in a way, fallen, on Frances's door, and that he had taken his shoes off by the door, with a kind of diligence he could not this morning fathom, and gone to sleep on her second, bare bed. He rolled his one open eye, as slowly as possible, to the left.

Frances was there, in her bed. She too was covered entirely by a blanket, except for her shoulders, each marked by a thin gray strap. Yasha was perfectly awake now. So was Frances. She lay on her side, facing Yasha, her hair tied up in a bun. The room was about twelve feet wide.

To speak would require a significant movement of the lungs, parts of his body buried deep under the covers and practically nonexistent; the realm of what existed had drastically contracted, in the last forty seconds, to Frances's face and shoulders, his own feet, and the wild boar. He had no idea what Frances was thinking. The width of the room felt engineered for the special purpose of reminding Yasha that he would never, in all his life, touch the gray-strapped shoulders of the girl across from him. He imagined his married life taking place in the black-and-white bedroom set of *I Love Lucy*, the beds always separated, her hair always in a bun.

Yasha wanted to cross the room and join her in her faraway bed, something he should have tried last night, with the pretense of being too tired to think, if only it had been a pretense and he had been able to think at all. He'd chosen the wrong bed. The right room, at least, he told himself, and wanted so badly to stand up just then, but couldn't, because of his pants. That would pass soon. As he was checking the contour of the sheets over his crotch, Frances pushed back her covers, shattering the room's stillness. It hadn't been a bra. She was wearing a gray tank top, and the yellow short-shorts. "Morning, Yasha," she said, as she walked to the small sink at the foot of her bed.

Yasha imagined a HELLO! MY NAME IS name tag that read MOURNING YASHA and knew he would be wearing it for a long time.

She ran her toothbrush under the faucet. "You were really tired," she said. "Sleep well?"

There she was, brushing her teeth in front of him, an intimacy that flattered him tremendously. He turned away from her shorts, in the hopes of eventually standing up. The blinking clock radio on her night table read 9:09.

"We have to go to breakfast," Yasha said.

"Weckfeth?" She spat her toothpaste into the sink. "News to me. What have I missed?"

Yasha wanted to answer that question at length, starting with his mother's breakfast plans and progressing in time through his crusty childhood and his interest in building origami cubes out of MetroCards, but it was 9:10 now, and she was in pajamas, and he was still wearing his funeral clothes.

"I'm going to change," he said, and stood up. It wasn't too bad down there. He didn't need to tuck it under his belt. Even better, she hadn't seen him check. She was still bent down over the sink, rinsing her mouth out with cupped handfuls. She looked like a rabbit. He didn't want to leave.

"I'll be back in a minute, in a different shirt," he said. "I'll pick you up," he was pleased to say. "We'll go together. Breakfast in the Ceremonial Hall, with my mother and Haldor. *He has many things to say to us.*"

"If I'm not in the barn in about five minutes, Nils will weep," Frances said. She wiped her mouth with a towel and buttoned a collared shirt over her tank top, hiding the straps Yasha loved. "The officers arrived an hour ago."

"I forgot about the inspection."

"Turn around, would you?"

Yasha obeyed and presently heard the unmistakable sound of her shorts falling to the floor. A moment later, when he was permitted to turn, he found her fully dressed.

"Let's go," she said, leading him to the door.

Yasha wanted to go with her. To go anywhere, shamelessly. Instead, he stood still as she walked off toward the exit, toward the barn, where Nils stood waiting.

"We should stay," Yasha called.

"Why not?" Frances answered over her shoulder. "We've got nowhere to go." She tucked her shirt into her pants and rebundled her hair at the top of her head. Yasha wished her luck, then wished himself the same.

· · ·

Haldor wore his Sunday clothes at the breakfast table: a black tunic with white accents that made him look vaguely like a minister. Olyana wore a silk blouse with enormous sleeves. She and Haldor sat across from each other at a table neatly set for three.

"You may stay until and no later than the first of September," Haldor said, as soon as Yasha sat down. Haldor held his knife in one hand and his fork in the other, sharp ends up.

"How did you know I wanted to stay?" Yasha said, hearing his own voice sound miserably young.

"Why only the first of September?" his mother added right away.

"Yakov," Haldor said, "your mother and I have spoken."

Your mother and I! Papa himself had never used the phrase. Papa himself—it had only been nine hours since they'd buried him. Papa's *self* could not have decomposed yet, not entirely. Yasha took up Haldor's position: fork in one hand, knife in one hand, sharp ends up.

"Frances also wants to stay," Yasha told Haldor. "I can only stay if she stays with me." Olyana smacked the back of Yasha's hand approvingly. His knife jiggled. He wanted to tell her that she had nothing to do with it, but he wasn't sure that was true.

"Everyone can stay," Haldor said, "until I leave for a twelve-night cruise of the Baltic capitals," he said. "The ship departs from the Oslofjord on the first of September, which is also the day we close the Viking Museum for the autumn. Of course," he said, "this is not a co-in . . ." He turned to Olyana. "Co-in . . ."

"Coincidence," said Olyana.

Haldor smiled and waved his fork in the air, saying, "Olyana and her English." He started over. "This is not a coincidence, as it is I who plans the calendars."

Kurt appeared beside their table, bearing a tray full of meat.

"Certainly you are ready for your breakfast, Yakov, after last night's labors. Kurt!" Haldor said. "Deal out the sausages."

Kurt served Haldor first, filling his plate with four sausages that were four different shades of brown. He served three to Olyana, and two to Yasha.

Yasha was about to demand that Kurt fill his plate properly, when Haldor said, "Your mother will be joining the museum staff, in the position of Acting Valkyrie." Olyana's eyes flashed with pride. "We need her for battlefield reenactments. Yakov, you can choose jobs one by one. The same for Frances. I will pay you both by the day. We will need help with the Icelandic horses— they are very short and hungry—and the kitchen, and the cleaning, and sometimes the boat."

"We aren't quite ready to leave this marvelous place, are we, little man?" Olyana asked.

Yasha chewed slowly and absently. Behind Haldor, out the window, at the top of the hill, a line of four inspectors filed into the barn. He couldn't see Frances or Nils. He imagined them welcoming the officers, both terrified. Nils no longer seemed puny to Yasha, nor did the barn seem inconsequential. Nils had something to show for himself, and he had Frances at his side.

"I didn't think you all would want to stay here," Haldor said.

Yasha and his mother said simultaneously, "I do."

Kurt, who was still standing beside the table, said, "Orange juice?" To which Haldor bellowed, *"Ja!"*

There were questions, accusations, building up in Yasha's mind, and he was thinking of when to spring them. Questions about Manhattan, and Brooklyn, and the fall. Questions about who would visit Eggum regularly, after September, to check that the grave was intact, if they could find it out on the beach.

Questions about Icelandic horses. Questions about Frances and Nils.

Haldor seemed content. He was done with his meat, and his belly brushed the edge of the table. He stretched his arms out at his sides, as if to hold both Yasha's and Olyana's hands. Yasha's fingers reflexively bunched into a fist. But Haldor only let his arms drop and said, after a yawn, "I am so glad you both can stay."

Olyana said, "I am sure Vassily is happy to have us here a little longer."

"Excuse me," Yasha said. He stood up, pushed his chair in under the table, folded his napkin neatly in half, and slammed it onto the table. He walked out of the Ceremonial Hall, through the lobby, past Yggdrasil, and out the museum's back door.

. . .

Yasha had not yet explored the full grounds of the museum. The hours preceding the funeral had been filled with sleep and food. A complete Norse arena lay just outside his room. Families had come out for the museum's activities. He walked down the beach toward giant archery targets. A ten-year-old girl was aiming a child-sized bow and pulling back, with all her strength, a magnificent arrow.

Yasha stopped a good distance away, so as not to distract from her shot. She let the arrow go—it flew up for a moment before plunging into the dirt, well short of the target. A slightly older boy came trotting up behind her, teasing her from atop a shaggy pony. A woman arrived at the far side of the shooting fields to greet her children. She was standing at the foot of a trail that stretched behind her, and as she rushed to the now crying girl, Yasha ran past them to the opening where the woman had stood. He lacked a sense of direction, a map. He wanted to know where everything was. He followed the trail along its short curve to a hut. The hut had no front door, its whole front gaped open, and smoke bloomed from it in spurts.

"Superfine, Yasha," Sigbjørn said. "Good morning."

Mourning Yasha, Yasha named himself again, though he was relieved to see Sigbjørn's familiar biceps, and shook his sooty hand.

"We're staying," Yasha said, wiping the soot down the front of his pants.

"Who is staying?"

"I am, and Frances, and my mother," Yasha said. "My mother is the new Valkyrie."

Sigbjørn pushed a narrow piece of iron into a pile of burning coal. "Frances is not staying," he said. "Her sister shall marry. In California."

"She has a sister?" Yasha said. Sigbjørn nodded. California, at that moment, was the farthest, largest, warmest place Yasha could imagine.

"The wedding isn't until September, that much I know," Yasha said. He hadn't asked her the right questions in the back of the pickup truck. "What else has she told you?"

"Nothing. New York, her sister, California."

"Have you spent much time together?" Yasha wondered whether Frances had ever seen Sigbjørn's home, had ever met his grandma Gertblorg or Ingavildabrun or whatever.

"I helped her make a nail. Her first day. Then she ran away with the short man, Nils, to the boats. You have a special interest in the girl? Some choice she has," Sigbjørn said. "A man twice her age, or half!"

"I am not half her age," Yasha insisted, "I am exactly four years younger."

"*Ja vel,*" said Sigbjørn, pumping hard on a lavishly ornamented pair of bellows.

Yasha could see Sigbjørn's point. Perhaps Nils was not his rival—perhaps neither of them stood a chance. Yasha needed to talk to her. He needed to see her thin gray straps, which had become in his mind the pillars of an ancient temple, in whose inner chamber she slept.

"Your uncle is leaving," Sigbjørn said, when he stood from the bellows.

"When?" said Yasha.

"Do you not hear the taxi?"

Yasha ducked out of the smithy and saw Daniil in the parking lot, stuffing his bags into the trunk of a car. He sprinted back through the archery field.

"I came to say goodbye at breakfast, but your chair was empty," Daniil said.

"Don't go yet," Yasha said.

Daniil closed the trunk.

"I have left the shop to the mouses," Daniil said. "The customers will think I am also dead." There was still one Gregoriov Bakery open in the world, the original, where his father had started his business, wooed his mother, perfected the egg glazing on challah braids. "Come to Moscow sometime," Daniil said. "It will never be so sad again."

Yasha agreed. The only promise anybody could make him now was this: he would never lose his father again. It was a vaguely hopeful thought, but the immediate effect was devastating. "Eventually," Yasha said.

Daniil pressed his large, open palm over the top of Yasha's head, and then pulled Yasha into him, his arms closing easily around the boy's back. Yasha pressed his face into his uncle's chest, craving contact with the only other living Gregoriov. Daniil released him and got in the cab. The driver pulled out of the lot, leaving Yasha with a view of the barn, outside which Nils, Frances, and the four inspection officers stood talking.

Yasha walked into the lobby so he would be there when she returned. He leaned an elbow against the trunk of the tree sculpture and turned toward the open hall. Beside the buffet table, his mother stood on a three-foot raised platform, surrounded by women wearing upturned sacks. They were pinning wings onto her back. One woman measured the length of her shoulder blades, another straightened her feathers. His mother's head reached almost to the hall's molded ceiling. Her back was turned to him, casting a shadow that spilled out of the hall and nearly up to his feet. She was colossal.

The lobby window revealed the figure of Frances, running in from the barn. An attendant pierced the skin of Olyana's neck with a pin. Yasha turned at the sound of his mother's shriek, and Frances rushed into her room. In the quiet after the shriek, Frances's door slammed. Yasha followed her down the corridor and knocked. No answer. She was inside. He could hear her. She was crying. He knocked harder. She wouldn't answer. She was crying hard. "Frances," Yasha said into the keyhole. She only cried. He stood with his hand on the knob. There was a flurry of sound in the hall and Olyana, her wings in place, stepped down, to the cheers of the women, and began to move in his direction.

PART FIVE

. . .

The Other Season

On Sunday, July 8, the Yellow Room passed its inspection, and my parents RSVP'd "No" to my sister's wedding. It was a last stand, they wrote, in an email I received after the KORO officers had gone. They couldn't prevent the marriage, but they could refuse to participate. If Sarah wanted to ruin her youth by getting married too soon, to an idiot, and not even a Jewish idiot, then let her, they said. The word *youth* dizzied me. Little did they know, I thought, about the seventeen-year-old boy who had spent the night in my room. He was about to turn eighteen, I assured myself. I tried calling Sarah. She wouldn't pick up, and her voicemail was full. Yasha knocked on my door while I dialed her number, both of us relentless. Eventually a text message arrived: I'll call you back when I stop crying.

So I cried along with her. The KORO approval had put Nils in high demand: a welcoming panel waited for him in Bodø, and he intended to spend the rest of the summer at his home studio, assembling a full exhibit of paintings for the Tromsø hospital. In rooting for the Yellow Room, I hadn't anticipated the consequences of victory. Nils planned to abandon our asylum in a matter of days. It was no place to live alone. Yasha intended to stay out the summer, and he stood at my door, wanting to know what was wrong, wanting to know what I'd decided. I wanted to stay with him, that much I'd known since the moment after the Mourner's Kaddish, but I no longer knew how, my apprenticeship abruptly over. After a while he gave up knocking, and when I came out, he'd gone to feed the ponies. I didn't see him for a week. Nils and I had packing to do in Leknes.

On Nils's last night at the asylum, his room was fully packed. I'd never seen his bedroom door open before. I'd had a feeling it was messy inside. It was open now, and the room bare, the hallway full of boxes. Across the hall from his room was the bathroom he used, full of toilet paper. Nils pooped after all. Out the window of his bathroom, I could hear the sheep poking around for weeds in the parking lot, the bells on their collars jingling.

He was going back home, to the even farther north. His house lay in the northernmost part of the Norwegian mainland, not far from the Finnish area known as Lapland. Nils had been secretive about his relation to the Sami, Norway's indigenous reindeer herders. He was either of Sami origin himself or had a special interest in them—he'd started to study the Sami language some years ago—but he'd never made it clear. I wished he could have spoken to Yasha about them; for all I knew, Nils had known Ommot. In either case, where Nils lived, at the real top of everything, not far from the North Cape, the Gulf Stream that surrounded the Lofoten Islands was too far off to warm his town, and it was dark in the winter, and cold, and he'd lived there a long time.

In the kitchen, his boxes lay surrounded by stacks of old *Lofotposten* and the last of his red wine. Wanting to hold on to something, I grabbed the refrigerator's handle. I pulled the door open: Nils had removed his fish mustards. I had plenty of brown cheese left.

The midnight sun's purest season was ending, on its way toward the equal Polar night. The sun would now dip under the horizon for an hour, during which the sky would turn impossibly brighter than it was before, and then rise again slightly east of where we had seen it last. We knew it couldn't have fallen far, and the sea suggested from its depths a hidden basket, sun-sized, from which the sunrise would soon begin. The world felt smaller, the star larger. The sky felt less and less like a sky, more like the inside of a brilliant hot air balloon.

I joined him at the kitchen table, bringing the brown cheese and a slicer. Nils opened the CD deck of his baby-blue boom box. From his backpack, slung on the floor between a box and a bubble-wrapped painting, he pulled out the 1995 audiobook recording of Hamsun's *Victoria*, read aloud in English by Knut Norgaard. This was the hour the sun failed. The field outside the window was dusky enough, for the first time, to see the reflection of both our heads in the glass.

"'Victoria,'" Knut wailed, "'Victoria!'"

Our wine shook in our glasses.

"'If she knew that he was hers utterly, every second of his life! He would be her servant and slave and sweep a path before her with his shoulders. And he would kiss her delicate shoes and pull her carriage and stock her stove with firewood on cold days, stock her stove with firewood tipped with gold, ah Victoria!'"

When I looked to Nils, wanting to tell him that I loved this, I was astonished to find him crying. Was he crying? Nils cried, and the whole planet grew quietly darker. Knut's wailing kept coming out of the boom box. Where had the sun gone? Its colors still lined the horizon. I knew Nils was capable of leaving behind colors. I pictured streaks of acrylic paint.

I didn't know if somebody would be there waiting when Nils got home. He'd mentioned his old mother and father, a sister who had children, and his house near Lapland where the pipes often troubled him with their freezing. He wore no ring, and mentioned no wife, and I couldn't bring myself to ask. We'd eaten dinners together, just the two of us at a small table, and perhaps he hadn't lived that way with a woman, I thought, or not for a long time. We'd spent ages in his little brown car, the Norwegian radio hosts making him laugh, the wild animals by the roadside delighting me as I looked out, understanding nothing. It had been an idyll, and he was upset either by the memory of it, or in anticipation of his faraway winter.

Knut went on. Victoria and Johannes had their unfulfilled romance. Nils and I had our fulfilled unromance. I saw my profile in the window reflection; it was the same as my sister's. I pictured her standing in Mrs. Glenny's garden, holding her new husband's hand. My father was standing behind them, shouting something unintelligible. My sister's face wore a stern, stubborn, unrevealing expression. What kind of fulfillment, what kind of romance, was hers?

Victoria proved to be a short novel, but by the time Knut was done reading, the sun was moving up from the horizon again and Nils was calm. I was not; I sat ripping up the cardboard of the empty box of wine.

We began making promises to each other—small, obvious things to say: I will write you; I will come back here one day when you come back; maybe it will be summer again, we'll go driving; in the meantime I will visit the Hirschsprungske in Copenhagen, the Frick in New York, and send a postcard, your favorite Turner, your favorite Krøyer, the one with the man and his wife and their dog in moonlight on the beach. Other artists, he said, had noticed great light before us.

It was nearly two in the morning and the parking lot was full of newly risen sun. Nils told me he would take care of himself. He would be driving for thirteen hours. I told him I wanted to stay in Norway a little longer, see if I could help Yasha recover from the funeral, until the sun went down, really down, and stopped coming up again. Then I'd go looking for it way out West at the wedding, in California, which was one answer for where the sun went. I promised him a postcard from San Francisco that he didn't seem to want. He wanted to get going. He made a padded nest for his paintings in the backseat of his car and took one more look at the colony's blue facade. I said goodbye. My arms were at my sides and he hugged me over them, such that I couldn't hug him back. It was good enough, I guess, because he left.

. . .

Yasha had learned that the gas pedal was the smaller one, which was strange. He had learned which position the seat should click into in order for his legs to fit. He resented having to keep his foot on the gas pedal the whole time. It should have been pump on, pump off. And nobody needed this many mirrors. There were never any cars to his right or left, never any cars behind him. He hadn't lied—Haldor had said: *Can you take these wooden poles to the beach?* Not: *Yasha, do you know how to drive?*

So what if his father had never owned a car? So what if he had always relied on the B train? The Viking Museum relied on its trucks, its tractors. Haldor could drive them, Sigbjørn could drive them, and Yasha was doing his best. This glimmering Mazda was the largest vehicle the Viking road could support, and as he drove, Yasha feared the whole thing might topple into the fjordwater, poles and all. So far, all right.

The road began at the museum's parking lot and ran up along the water toward the stables, past the *lavvo*s where they stood on the beach, each lavvo a twenty-foot teepee. Yasha stocked the lavvos with firewood and pig meat, with sheepskins to cover the benches in preparation for a feast—"Odin's Victory Feast," if the guests paid one thousand kroner; "An Evening with Baldur," for five hundred; "Frigg's Potato Patties" for children's birthday parties. On off days, he took the sheepskins away, cleared the burned-up coals, swept the bread crumbs out from under the feast tables.

This work somehow resembled the work he'd always known. As before, he looked out on a beach as he worked, which made the air salty and the light unpredictable. As before, there were chunks of crust to be cleaned from the floors. But no cat. Yasha wanted his cat; he felt certain the cat would be valuable to him up here, biting Haldor when he came too close to his mother, luring Frances with its pointy ears, sleeping on his chest at night. He wondered whether Mr. Dobson had taken Sam in, whether he'd given him a new name. Yasha had some business to do with Mr. Dobson. An obituary for his father. A report on his cat. An expiration date for the Gregoriov Bakery's lease.

It had been a week since he'd seen Frances. He'd missed his chance to kiss her after the funeral. Now his father's voice filled his head each night, through his sleep, for the past few nights, asking: Why not? Why not? Why not?

Yasha began unloading the poles. They were three times Yasha's height and thick as lampposts, and each lavvo required nine of them to stand. They filled the bed of the pickup and stuck out the back as he drove. It did not make the driving easier. When unloaded, they revealed the spot where he and Frances had sat on the sheepskins the night of the funeral. The museum would have to build three more lavvos for the first of August, for the whale meat festival, more special and more expensive than even a Victory Feast. There would be a fire, and the meat, and dancing and horn-blowing on the beach. Sigbjørn and Haldor had promised to help him build the extra lavvos later. It was hardly a job for one man.

One man, Yasha thought. The word *man* now always made him think of his mother. She said it so often, *little man, little man*, and she was the only person who said it to him. She had herself escaped human gender altogether, evolving so quickly and so successfully into a Valkyrie. She wandered the museum lobby in costume, looming behind visitors and reciting her lines: "'I am sent by Odin to this battle, and I choose which man gains victory, and lo, which man will die!'" He'd seen her frighten adult men. Yasha still had no use for the word *man*, which he couldn't apply to himself (a few days short of his eighteenth birthday) or to his father (was a dead man still a man?), nor had he any use for the word *woman*, which he could only think of applying to Frances, but which seemed to call attention to her age, and his age, and her maturity, and his immaturity, and her body, and his hands.

His uncle, whose hands were far larger and more capable, was long since back in Moscow. The image of Daniil with his bags in the parking lot stuck with Yasha—it was as if Daniil had come and gone with no change in baggage, as if he weren't forgetting anything, as if he hadn't left anyone behind in the sand. Yasha couldn't comprehend going back to Russia. Russia had come to mean only great separation: the country that kept his mother, the country that killed his father. To go back there now did not reverse enough, did not return what it had taken.

The poles, now off the truck, looked like pick-up sticks in the sand. He had dropped them at the wrong angle, perpendicular to the water, and waves wet their tops. Yasha took off his shoes and socks. He gripped his toes into the sand—it wasn't hot, the sun up here was cold—and dragged each pole around until it lay parallel to the shore and the horizon. They made the beach look like his mother's music paper. Seabirds would land on the lines and make notes. The pale wood caught the sunlight and Yasha wondered whether it was possible for the wood to tan, to get toasted—whether the poles would be any more golden when he came back to build the tents. He wondered whether Frances would come and help him with the construction.

Yasha had reserved Room 18 in Frances's name. Haldor had given it to her for the funeral night, and Yasha hoped she could have it a little longer—he swore the museum had more rooms than it had guests. He went to Haldor and begged. Frances could live in Room 18 as long as she worked for the museum, Haldor promised, up until the end of the season. Haldor had called Frances's cell phone, standing next to Yasha, who coveted the number. He could hear Frances's relieved voice through Haldor's flimsy Nokia. To finalize the arrangement, Haldor had requested Frances's shoulders-to-hips length in centimeters, for her new sack uniform.

The ponies were waiting for their dinner of old bread up at the farm, but he would visit them later, after he saw her. He expected her to arrive any minute. A tiny crab crawled out of the sand. Yasha kicked it and watched it fly into the surf. The top of the world lay out in the water, right there, washing in at him and his bare feet, and washing up to his father, in his box, farther down the beach. Yasha put on his socks and shoes. He climbed back into the driver's seat, and his shoes spilled sand around the pedals.

Each time he started the truck, Yasha knew that he might not be the one to turn it off, that they might wind up pulling him out of the fjord unconscious, the truck wrecked, the engine soaked. That Sigbjørn would unbuckle Yasha's drippy seat belt, lift him out, carry him into his smithy, and try to revive him by the warmth of his coals, with no luck. Yasha wanted to be buried beside his father, at Eggum. He wanted to make the same request. He started the engine. It was a good truck, he liked its red bulk around him, and he drove it back down the road toward the museum, to welcome her home.

. . .

"Please come," I said into the microphone.

"We're not coming," my mother said.

"Not a *chance!*" bellowed my father.

"You are breaking Sarah's heart," I said, knowing very well that broken hearts didn't scare them. Hard to say whether my parents considered their own hearts long since shattered, or whether they believed that people were more durable than all that.

"And she is breaking mine," my mother said, surprising me by taking up the expression.

I said, "I'm still going."

"And now *you* are breaking mine," my mother said.

"And you are breaking *mine*," I said.

"Enough of this," said my father.

There was a pause in the conversation, and I heard a knock at my door.

"Come in!" my mother shouted.

I went and opened the door. Yasha stood there, with sand all over his pants and in his hair and, oddly, in his eyebrows.

"What have you been doing?" I asked.

"Poles. How do you like the room?"

I thanked him for talking to Haldor. I would have kissed him right then, had my parents not been watching.

"Gregoriov!" my father called out. "Come in."

"We haven't seen you since the funeral," my mother said.

"It went well." Yasha walked up to the screen. "Frances helped."

"Oh did she?" said my father. "With what?"

"The blessing," said Yasha.

My mother looked incredulous.

"I said the Mourner's Kaddish," I told her. "Yasha's mother wanted someone to say it."

My mother took her glasses off, folded the arms in, and placed them down on her table. She leaned close to the camera, so that I could see the blood vessels in her eyes. I had never seen her look so tired. "A Jewish funeral," she said. I wasn't sure if she was thinking of her mother's, years ago, or her own, years from now, or about my sister's wedding.

The next thing my mother said was, "Marry our daughter."

I saw Yasha's chest inch backward, as if his lungs alone were trying to leave the room. He looked at me, then at the sand on the floor, and then his head fell to the side and he looked into the camera at a slant. He bunched his lips and his eyebrows semi-indignantly, as if someone had played a joke on him but he hadn't gotten it.

My mother must have been joking, but she was smiling the way she smiled when she was deathly serious, and she had begun waving her glasses around like a wand, very excited, with every word.

"She's just about your age, what are you, nineteen?" my mother said.

"Seventeen," said Yasha, "and I thought Frances was twenty-one."

"Sarah," my mother said, "Sarah." I gaped at the screen. "Sarah is twenty, and in some deranged rush, you see, to get married. So you see, she might as well marry you, if she's going to do it—I'd prefer that, I'd prefer your mother, sounds like, to Scott's, I'll tell you one thing," my mother said, now aiming the glasses directly at Yasha, "Scott Glenny's mother would never ask anybody to recite the Mourner's Kaddish. I'll tell you that right now."

Even my father looked embarrassed. He looked most like Harpo Marx when he was embarrassed—like Harpo caught with oranges down his pants. I loved it when my family's severity broke. It never happened to more than one of us at a time. When my parents yelled hideous things at each other, Sarah laughed. When Sarah touched the cow in the replica Corot hanging on our living room wall, my father slapped her hand, then my mother stroked it. When my mother told Yasha to marry Sarah, my father blushed and rubbed his ear.

"I understand if you want to leave," I said to Yasha. "You probably want to leave."

"Why should he?" said my mother.

"I have to call our landlord," Yasha managed to say into the camera. "He's been taking care of my cat."

"By all means," said my father. "Good to see you, Gregoriov."

"You can use my computer," I said.

"Not yet," said my mother. "We haven't gotten anywhere."

"I'm going to use the phone in the kitchen," Yasha said. He was already at my door. "Nice sack," he said, taking in my outfit from a distance.

"Think about it," my mother shouted, putting her glasses back on. "Will you?"

Yasha left. I bent down to the floor, partly to get away from the webcam, partly to clean up the sand. It was sunny, and each little grain was visible against my green floor. I wondered why the color green signified envy. I had never been jealous of my sister before: not when she French-kissed before I had ever held hands, not when she officially became Scott Glenny's girlfriend before I had ever called anyone my boyfriend, not when she got engaged the same day Robert dumped me. I was jealous now. My mother's ridiculous suggestion made the floor seem particularly green.

"Your sister is beautiful," my mother said, when I stood up. "And I love her. I love her more than I can bear."

"She's fine," I said. "She's not sick, or pregnant—"

"She's not *what*?" said my father.

"She's fine," I said. "She's happy."

"I'm so unhappy, I could combust," my mother said under her breath.

"Come to the wedding," I said. "It's the only thing you can do. You'll see her, she'll look more beautiful than you've ever seen her before. You'll see them together. Really *see* them. Take your glasses off and look at them. They're good." I wanted to say: They're better than you. They're choosing to stick together. They're better than you at love. Instead, I said, "Come with me."

"That was some lousy hell of a locker-room pep talk," my father said.

"Go find that Gregoriov boy and tell him I meant it," my mother said. "There's some way out. Who knows? It might not be him, it might be him, cute curly-haired Russian, who knows? In any case, I haven't given up."

"I have," I said. "Bye." I started looking for the button to hang up.

"Come home," my father said. Then he realized his mistake. He looked around at the apartment, full of boxes. I knew we were both thinking of something he'd once said: *There won't be a house for you anyway.*

．．．

Frida sat in the kitchen, breast-feeding her baby girl. Yasha came in and stopped short. Frida's enormous breast was hoisted up over her shirt's low neckline. It looked like the breast was about to rip the shirt. Her baby had blond hair, short and white just like Frida's. They were really something together. Frida, Mini-Frida. Breast, shirt, mouth, tiny baby hands. Yasha hadn't yet been discovered. Frida had her eyes closed, and could have been sleeping were it not for her nose, which flinched and flinched until she sneezed. Her eyes opened.

"I forgot your name," Frida said. "Hello."

"Yakov Vassiliovich Gregoriov," Yasha said. "Pardon me."

Yasha had forgotten why he'd come in, and Frida didn't ask him. The baby slurped, very audibly in the otherwise silent room, and Yasha listened, and watched, staring in the direction of Frida's nipple, which the baby's cheeks concealed. He had forgotten himself completely.

Kurt came in the back entrance and said, "Lunchtime!"

Yasha jumped and said, "Fine, so, yes, well, right, the phone."

"The phone?" said Frida. The baby went on. "It is on the wall."

Kurt pointed to the wall between two industrial refrigerators. Yasha retreated into the nook with relief. He dialed Mr. Dobson's number. The rings were long and there were many of them.

Mr. Dobson had just woken up. It was seven o'clock in the morning in Brooklyn, and did Yasha realize he was calling so early? And good morning, Gregoriov, and was Russia full of those, what are they, samovars? The whole boulevard wasn't right without its Gregoriovs, Mr. Dobson said. Yasha pressed the receiver hard against his ear and listened behind Dobson's voice for the sounds of a possible cat. He heard a television. Gregoriov, Mr. Dobson said, samovars?

Yasha wished he had written a script. There was a great deal of information to deliver, likely to be followed by questions he'd have to answer, and he hadn't adequately prepared. Frances's parents had startled him, rushed him out into the kitchen. Frida's breast had startled him. Kurt's *Lunchtime!* had startled him, rushed him right to the phone. It was seven o'clock in New York. Frances's parents were evidently early risers. Mr. Dobson was also awake and on the line.

"Hello," Yasha said. "It's just Yasha. My father isn't here anymore."

"Where has the grump gone," Dobson began, "hunting rabbits?" Dobson's voice was rough in the phone, not fully awake, and

Yasha was only half listening, half watching the baby's boneless jaw pump milk down her miniature throat. Frida was humming. Kurt was wiping down the stovetop. "Gregoriov," Dobson said, "where is the old grump? Can't go on with these empty shop windows forever," he said, and Yasha saw again the bakery windows, full of Danishes, full of light, full of the unusually visible sea wind, and the sea out there, not this arctic sea, the American Atlantic: larger, dirtier, hotter. "Said it was a vacation," Dobson said, "so, hello, enough. Time's up."

"My father passed away two weeks ago, Mr. Dobson," Yasha said. "Time is up."

Mr. Dobson's silence on the other end of the line gave Yasha a moment to watch Kurt rotate all the sausages. He looked at Yasha while he flipped them. Kurt had been participating in the phone call by way of a sympathetic pout, until Agnes came into the kitchen right then through the back entrance and stood behind Kurt and squeezed him around the waist. At least this man wouldn't compete with him for Frances, Yasha saw. Agnes lodged her head into the space between Kurt's shoulder blades. Her head faced left, where Frida was lifting the baby's bangs, tying the hair up until the baby looked like a spouting whale. The pink sides of the sausages went down, the charred sides faced up, and the steam and the smell made the baby squirm. In the corner of the grill, a pile of onions caramelized. Even in the silence, Yasha could not hear his cat.

Mr. Dobson was sorry. He couldn't believe—Vassily Gregoriov. Yasha could not quite stand Dobson's real and audible sadness. It intensified his own pain, pulled it up to the surface of his skin where the hurt became especially active, making sweat or tears drip out. Mr. Dobson had never been emotional. He had been brash and cheerful, and had shouted and sung, and even the one time his father had handed Dobson a challah fresh out of the oven and the crust had been hot, and Dobson's index finger and thumb had burned, Dobson hadn't minded any more than a loud shout and then it was over. He had been forgiving, friendly. *Good riddens.* Dobson couldn't say that anymore. Hadn't it come true? "I can't believe it," Mr. Dobson said, "that man."

"I need you to submit an obituary," Yasha said. "I want it in the Russian papers, and the *Times*. It can be short. It just needs to say that he lived, and we loved him, and he died."

"Yasha," Mr. Dobson said. "Yes," he said. "But—"

"I'm in Norway," Yasha said. "I don't know when I'm coming home—it depends on this girl."

Mr. Dobson said he didn't know a thing about girls, and he didn't know a thing about the *New York Times*.

"Ten words," Yasha said. "Send it over. They've got to have an obit department, no? Mail it in. Ten words. Vassily Gregoriov, beloved father, lived in Russia and Brooklyn, died in Russia, buried at the top of the world. I guess that's twenty words. Could be fifty if you add a few, Mr. Dobson," Yasha said. "You can mention the bread. I want it in the papers next week."

"I can do it," Mr. Dobson said. "Who will pay for it?"

"I will," Yasha said. Kurt had turned off the heat and was leaning against the edge of the counter, watching Yasha talk. Frida watched, and Agnes watched while she scrubbed a pair of crusty horseshoes. The baby reached for Frida's breast with both of her hands. Yasha reached into his pocket and felt a heavy coin worth twenty Norwegian kroner.

"One more thing," Yasha said. "I'm going to need my cat back."

"He's been living inside the bakery," Dobson said. "I can't get him to stay out. He sleeps up on the shelves. He's licked the floors clean. He doesn't eat the food I leave out for him. He drinks the water. He comes in and out of my house. Sleeps in the bakery. Meows like a living hell. He's lost weight. That red string's still around his neck."

"Take the string off—you want to choke him? Take the string off, and bolt up the cat flap on the bakery door. It's not good for him to be in there," Yasha said. "My father threw out all the food. Tell him my father died," Yasha said. "Okay? Make him a bed in your living room. He likes to sleep on butcher paper."

"What about the bakery?" Mr. Dobson wanted to know.

The nook where Yasha stood was about two feet wide. He held the phone up with his shoulder and reached his hands out to the sides. Each hand touched a refrigerator. He couldn't imagine ever needing a whole room again, ever filling a whole empty room. Couldn't he live in this gap, two feet wide by seven feet tall, in the shadow for most of the day, coming out into the lit kitchen once an hour for something to eat?

"Have to rent the bakery out," Dobson said. "No offense meant to the dearly departed."

"When?" said Yasha.

"First of January. End of a five-year lease. Been in the Gregoriov name for what, ten years exactly? First of January, I have to turn it over. First of the eleventh year."

Kurt opened the leftmost refrigerator and retrieved a large salmon.

"I would have liked it to be yours a lot longer," Mr. Dobson said. "I would have liked it to be his. I'm upset."

"I'll clean things up," Yasha said. "Send in the fifty words, please, Mr. Dobson. Bolt up the cat door. Take that string off his neck."

Mr. Dobson said, "Okay, Gregoriov."

Yasha returned the phone to its cradle on the wall and stepped out into the kitchen. Frida's shirt lay flat across her chest. Her baby was asleep in a bassinet. Frida handed chopped bits of carrot to Kurt and Agnes, who arranged them around the decapitated salmon on a serving platter. Yasha left the kitchen—everybody watched him go, except the sleeping baby—and walked out through the Ceremonial Hall.

Olyana sat playing the hall's baby grand, crooning "Kalinka" in angelic, falsetto Russian. The day's worth of visitors, over whom she'd proclaimed either death or victory, stood watching, bewitched, heeding the Russian as if it were the secret, original language of the Valkyries.

. . .

I sent a message to Nils. I used the most English-like words.

(Are) Er
(you) du
(there?) der?

I said it to myself: Er du der? Er du der? while I waited for my phone to beep with his reply. I sat on my bed. I hadn't been able to reach Nils for days. I'd sent a message every morning, and, unlike the days at the asylum when I could hear his phone beep, hear him shuffle to it, hear him sit down to thumb in each letter, and receive a reply in a moment—I'd heard nothing at all.

I wondered if both my English and my Norwegian had become incomprehensible.

My first message had said:

(No) Ingen
(sheep) sauer
(here.) her.
(Only) Bare
(pig.) gris.

I didn't know the word for *boar*. I missed the sheep from the colony's parking lot and their loud bells. They had been friends to me in a way the wild boar wasn't. The wild boar wasn't a friend to anyone. There was nobody at the Viking Museum, not even Yasha, whose harmony resembled Nils's. It seemed Nils had never lost anything—had never needed anything, had spent his life studying one color. That was all, and enough. I missed Nils's fish dinners, his green cans of beer, his brown shoes. I wanted to ask Nils whether sheep or pigs lived in the forest that surrounded his house. He'd said the forest was called Huppasskogen. He'd said it was superlarge, that it went all the way around the penin-sula where he lived, and protected the farmland from the fjord, which was called Lyngen. Lyngenfjord.

When he didn't reply, I blamed my Norwegian. I wrote my second message in English:

Did you make it home?

Hearing nothing in response to the English either, I tried again.

(I) Jeg
(am) er
(supertired.) kjempetrøtt.
(Time) Tid
(for) for
(wine) vin
(and) og
(brown cheese.) brunost.

Nothing. So that morning I wrote Er du der. Er du der er du der er du der? My phone lay silent. I had assumed, I think, that when someone as unlikely as Nils came into one's life, he stayed. That he'd appear in conjunction with the high moments: baby born, here is Uncle Nils. Who is Nils? This is Nils. We met a long time ago, in the Far North. A Friday night, some autumn: I am going to "The Color Yellow," Nils's first exhibit in the Norwegian National Gallery. This is the painting he began in the artist colony. Bringing my baby along to see the Oslofjord. Letters would be written and delivered to him wherever he lived, and delivered to me wherever I lived, wherever that would be. We would know each other, remember each other, anywhere.

The only thing I knew about Nils at this moment was his phone number. If he didn't answer, I had lost him. I could not find his house, unnumbered as it was, no address, no town name, at the foot of the Huppasskogen. I imagined Yasha driving me there to look for it in the red pickup. I looked out my window for a sign of Yasha anywhere. Only the wild boar, and the beach. I was more frightened then than I had been since arriving in Norway.

The waves rolling in asked: Why did you come here?

I had come to get out of the city, and away from the family to whom I belonged. I had found a country covered in sour blueberries, foxes, rocks, and one-lane roads that were drawn in the same shape as the shoreline. I had met Nils, Yasha, his mother, a few make-believe Vikings. I didn't belong to any of them, and they didn't belong to me. I looked out the window for Yasha again.

The waves rolling out said: Nothing here is yours to keep.

I imagined Yasha staying at the Viking Museum indefinitely, and my going home without him, and calling the museum, and Sigbjørn answering, and Haldor answering, and Yasha never coming to the phone. Yasha becoming another unreturned message. My phone sat blankly on the windowsill, its black screen reflecting the clouds. Yasha would be back at the lavvos by now. I went over to my second bed where he had once slept, near to me but not near enough, and found one of my necklaces tied up in the sheets. I put it on. I told the dangling ballerina: I will not lose Yasha. Maybe his mother had lost him, maybe his father had lost him, Brooklyn had lost him—not me. It wasn't a matter of somebody keeping him. It was a matter of my wanting him, wanting his face near my face.

A few curly hairs made the shape of an otter on his pillowcase. Yasha was human, a creature. Nils was harmony itself. Toward Nils, I felt different sort of longing. More like how one feels toward stars. Wanting their shine, their comfort in the dark, knowing full well how far they are—I picked up my phone to write another message. I wanted it to say *Please*. There was no such word. The only way to say it was:

(Be) Vær
(so) så
(kind.) snill.

Yasha kicked the tree sculpture as hard as he could, hoping to put a dent in it. Two weeks had passed since Frances had moved into the museum, but he'd failed to come any closer. Frances helped Kurt serve breakfast first thing in the morning; Yasha built lavvos in the afternoon; feasts and reenactments stretched through the evenings; they never came home at the same time. He'd spent nights with his ear to the wall between them, listening out for her, but she'd grown so quiet—she hadn't been completely well. Her parents' calls kept her busy, and miserable, and she seemed changed by Nils's absence. Sometimes, when her eyes rested on him one second too long, he could swear she wanted something from him, could swear she wanted *him*, but the outright invitation he required never came.

More difficult than overcoming his own nervousness was overcoming hers: she still looked at him with condolence in her eyes, attending to his comfort and speaking to him gently, when he wanted to be vigorously ungentle with her. He didn't know how to convince her that he was fully available, that he was more man than mourner.

The bronze of the tree trunk looked only shinier as Yasha's sneakers brushed dust from its bark finish, kick by kick. The four dwarves on the ceiling looked down at him, and Yasha wanted them to come down and fight him already, wanted to rip their little shirts from their bellies. The one thing Yasha could dent was the diagram, which was mounted on a thin piece of apparently pliable wire. He kicked the midpoint of the wire, and the whole plaque tipped over. Yasha saw himself and his mother reading the diagram's text aloud, his mother shouting about the universe. They would now have to turn their heads sideways to read from it. Yasha looked to the receptionist's desk. She hadn't yet returned from lunch.

He backed away from the tree. The receptionist was named Gunn, and she made him uncomfortable with her *"Hei hei!"* greeting and her constantly open mouth. When she came back, the two of them would have to walk to a supply closet, get a hammer, and straighten the thing. He sat down in one of the lobby's guest chairs and let his head fall back to the wall. One of his ears touched something cold. The low chair and the cold ear made Yasha think of getting a haircut. He wanted somebody to be rubbing his head, and dunking it into cold water. He turned to see what the cold was and saw a doorknob.

Maybe it was a coat hanger. The chair was flush against the wall; there wouldn't be a door behind it. He faced out again. The knob became less cold the longer his ear lay against it. He rubbed his own head, imagining the clipping sound of tiny scissors. Yefim's Barbershop had always played Simon & Garfunkel, and Yefim's hands had been strong enough to squeeze his head until the blood flow stopped and restarted. Yasha heard a *"Hei hei"* in the Ceremonial Hall and Gunn's plates clanking into the industrial dishwasher. He opened his eyes and saw the Yggdrasil diagram looking at him sideways, like a dog. He stood up and heard Haldor's voice speaking to Gunn. If Haldor came with her, Yasha started to think—the knob was unmistakably a doorknob. Moreover, a seam now appeared lightly dipped into the surface of the wall, and there, three feet apart from each other: two hinges.

The door was the same width as the chair. He pulled the chair away from the wall, stepped behind it, and pushed the door open.

Inside, there was only a staircase. Going down. Yasha closed the door behind him, and real darkness enveloped him for the first time in several weeks. No daylight cracking in between the futile window curtains. No sunrise or sunset, and none of the dawny, dusky thing the sky was always doing. Haldor and Gunn came into the lobby. Yasha stood silently behind the door, behind the chair. They were speaking in agitated Norwegian. Gunn's chipper footsteps rushed back into the Ceremonial Hall. Yasha couldn't hear Haldor anymore and took the first step down the stairs. The step didn't make any noise. He dropped his other leg down to the second step. No problem. He climbed down to the bottom, where a room opened up.

His mother had been right: there was a goat under the tree after all. Here it was. But she couldn't have known about this one. Yasha found himself standing directly under Yggdrasil, centered between its three roots, which had always seemed cut off by the lobby floor, but which extended, in the shape of long icicles, down another three or four feet into this basement. Where the roots ended, there stood a modest wooden table. It looked almost exactly like the bedside table in Yasha's room. It was covered with a sack, the kind Frances wore. The table had been placed under the shortest of the three roots, and on top of the table Yasha saw a model house, and on top of the house, a goat. The house was made of popsicle sticks and pebbles. The goat, though Yasha was not sure, looked like it was made of brown cheese.

"Mrs. Gregoriov," Haldor's voice said, suddenly audible. Yasha looked around, expecting to find his mother or Haldor down in the cave with him, or at least a walkie-talkie, some kind of source for Haldor's voice. There was no radio, and he sensed their weight directly above his head.

"Chief Haldor," his mother said. He hadn't spoken to his mother all day, perhaps not since the day before, and her voice, which had never become fully familiar to him after the long absence, and which was always so mellow and slick, leaked down to him. It wasn't coming through the floor. It was more directed, more funneled.

"There is something I have wanted to say," Haldor said, and Yasha saw that the metal roots were hollow and cut open at their tips. Open tubes. Haldor's voice moved down them efficiently, making Yasha think of piss moving down a drain. It fell right into his ears. "Do I get permission to say it?" Haldor said.

"My dear man," his mother said, "are you not the chief?"

"The blacksmith calls me chief," Haldor said. "Not you, necessarily."

Yasha didn't know where Haldor was going with this, but none of the possibilities were attractive, and he couldn't stop listening. This room he had crawled into was only slightly larger than the tree's circumference. He had no way out, unless he wanted to climb up the stairs and out from behind the chair and enter himself into the middle of their conversation—something he supposed he might have to do any minute, if it became necessary to interfere. Surely his mother could defend herself. Surely his mother could defend herself?

"Chief Haldor," she said, "go ahead."

"I am happy in you, Olyana," Haldor said. "I am glad in you."

Yasha and his mother were quiet, and he felt they were deciphering this statement together, one mind split by the floor. It was a romantic thing to say, though these were the words of a child. It offered something large, without asking for anything. His mother, generally quick at the draw, had not yet replied.

Yasha raced to formulate an answer, though he had no means of feeding a line to his mother—if he spoke into the open roots, would his voice shoot out of the branches?

Haldor said, "It can be that it goes too fast to ask for you. You are still sorry, surely, on your husband."

Yasha put his eye to the longest root. He could not see anything. He wanted to see what face she had made. He wanted to see how sorry.

His mother said, "Vassily has only just left us, yes . . . by the grace of your very good service."

Haldor grunted.

"Still," she said, lengthening the l's at the end of the word, "I left Vassily years ago. Vassily and my son."

Yasha had something to add to this conversation. Along the lines of: Correct. That is what you did. Yasha bent down and smelled what was definitely the stale brown cheese that made up the body of the goat figurine; he smelled the metal of the tree roots. He understood that the small amount of light that illuminated this cave, as opposed to the deep black staircase, came in through the root tips along with the sound. There must have been a hole in the trunk somewhere, if not in each of the branches. What had this basement been built for? It seemed designed for storage, but had been remodeled into something less practical, more wonderful. He wanted to show Frances this cave. He wanted to spend the rest of the summer with Frances in this cave.

"Your son is a good youth," Haldor said. "He continues to love you."

Wrong! Yasha very nearly shouted into the longest root.

"And I continue to love the man I love," his mother said.

"Olyana," Haldor said quietly.

"He is the one I will not leave, my dear chief," Olyana said. Yasha could hear the smile in her voice, and was certain that she had lifted her hand to her collarbone and was resting her fingers there, the way women like his mother did when they were feeling absolutely sure about something. "You heard my son at the funeral. The man I love lives in Tribeca. His name is Ian Strom."

"*Ja vel,*" Haldor said.

She said, "I have loved him for ten years."

Yasha stared at the model of Valhalla and saw a model bakery, its tiny cut-out windows facing a crowded, ocean-bleached boulevard. The cruller twist and the everything bagel made their pathetic "10" in the bakery window display. Mr. Dobson, the schoolchildren, and Dostoyevsky were all there, all miniature, walking in and out of Valhalla's many doors. There was Yasha, there was his father, inside the popsicle stick palace, rolling dough at the crack of dawn. They had gone on putting their babkas in the window the whole time she had been so in love. She had loved somebody, anybody, for those ten years.

"So it is," Haldor said.

"So it is," said his mother. She laughed lightly and shifted her weight. The ceiling over Yasha sighed as she moved.

She is the real chief, Yasha thought. Poor Haldor. The lobby had gone quiet, and Yasha put his ear to a root. Haldor's heavy steps moved, not toward the Ceremonial Hall but out of the museum. He heard the beach-side door open and shut. His mother's boots sounded down the hall, harder to hear, toward her room. A moment later, Gunn, who had likely been hiding behind the waffle table the whole time, scurried in and took back her desk. Yasha knew he would terrify her, climbing out of the wall.

He took a good look at the cheese goat. It was hand-carved, and someone had put a great deal of care into it. The goat had circles for eyes, oval nostrils, and an open mouth that sucked on one of the metal roots. Its hair had been carved as thin lines into the cheese, its tail was short and lifted with the pleasure of the sucking, and its hooves were smoother than its legs. What this was—who it was by—who it was for, Yasha couldn't say. But it had received the maker's full attention. The goat stood, as the plaque had said it would, on the roof of Valhalla. The model Valhalla, on the other hand, was empty inside. It really could have been a model of the Gregoriov Bakery. There should have been a miniature cat inside, curled up and sleeping alone in the dark. It made no sense, a brown cheese goat and an empty palace. It made no sense, a cat sleeping in an empty bakery.

Yasha dreaded his exit. He could hear Gunn getting to work again. There was no good way to explain himself, and what was worse, if Gunn had any inclination toward tattling, Haldor would be in the lobby in a minute, demanding to know how much Yasha had heard. Yasha looked again at the small myth on the table, and left it for the unlit staircase. He put one foot on the bottom step. He had missed this kind of darkness. If he and Frances were ever in a place this dark, he thought, wouldn't their bodies lose their outlines and combine automatically—mouths, hands, chest against chest? He climbed the staircase as quietly as he could, which, thanks to the sturdiness of the iron steps, was quietly enough. Yasha stood behind the door, behind the chair, which he had left a few inches out of place. *"Hei hei,"* he heard Gunn say into the phone. *"Hei hei,"* Yasha whispered back.

· · ·

I couldn't find Yasha on the beach. I had seen Sigbjørn having a cigarette, and a family from Sweden, all four of them wearing Swedish-flag baseball caps. I saw Haldor out by the water, looking uncharacteristically glum. The two old lavvos were visible at the end of the shore, and the three new ones hadn't yet been built. It was almost two o'clock. Yasha might have eaten slowly today, I thought, might be lingering at the lunch buffet. I decided to head out toward the lavvos, camp out under one of the built tents, and wait for him, if he wasn't in the Ceremonial Hall.

He wasn't in the Ceremonial Hall. Nobody was. Kurt's salmon platter lay almost untouched on the banquet table, and behind the kitchen door I could hear Frida singing her eerie Icelandic lullaby that always made me think of lava. A slow day. Gunn was at her desk, helping a caller book a room for the whale meat festival. I wanted to ask her if she'd seen Yasha. Gunn and I had hardly ever spoken. I left the hall and took a seat in her guest chair—another place Yasha might have been, but wasn't. The chair slid back until it hit the wall. Gunn looked up from her call.

"*Unnskyld,*" she said to the caller. "Can I help you, Frances?"

"I can wait," I said. She went back to the call. The room was nonsmoking, she said, and the beds were separate, but could be pushed together.

"*Frances,*" the wall said. "*Make Gunn move.*"

I sat up straight.

There was no question that the voice was Yasha's. There were plenty of other questions. I stood, took a good hard look at the wall, saw nothing, and approached Gunn's desk, grinning nervously. She held up the "one minute" finger. I rested my elbow casually against her countertop. I resisted looking back at the wall. I didn't know what to tell Gunn. *"Hei hei,"* she said, and hung up.

"It's tea time, Gunn," I said. Rightfully, she didn't know what I meant. "Let's have a cup of tea," I said, "before they clear out the hall."

Gunn's mouth, which had been hanging open, closed and smiled.

"Is that all you wanted?" she said.

I no longer needed her help in finding Yasha, and Yasha apparently had new needs of his own, so I said, "Isn't tea a good thing to want?"

Gunn picked up a mug from her desk and turned it upside down.

"Tomt," she said, which sounded like *tomb*, and meant "empty." I hadn't thought of checking Vassily's grave while looking for Yasha. I hadn't thought of his being inside the wall either. *Go find that Gregoriov boy*, my mother's voice rang in my head. I wondered if Yasha had been spending any time at Eggum, driving out to the grave in the truck. Gunn stood up and tied a sweater around her shoulders. She was blushing. I wondered if anybody, guest or employee, man or woman, had asked Gunn to tea before. She had a severe face and a squeaky voice and she breathed with her mouth open. I had never seen Kurt or Haldor be friendly toward her. She sat at her desk professionally, ate her lunch professionally, and went home at five o'clock.

We crossed the threshold into the Ceremonial Hall and while Gunn refilled her cup, I took one look back toward the lobby. The chair was moving forward. Then I saw Yasha dart out from behind it, take a moment's cover behind Yggdrasil's trunk, and run out through the museum's beach door.

"Earl Grey," Gunn said with delight.

"The best," I said, and took the tea bag she offered me. We both added milk, and Gunn emptied half of a packet of honey into her cup, the other half into mine. We each stirred with our own Thor's-hammer-handled spoons. Her phone rang. She made a guttural sound and tossed her spoon into the clearing bucket, nodded her head to me, and sipped her tea down. It didn't spill as she ran to the desk.

"*Hei hei,*" she said, slightly breathless. I caught up with her, nodded the way she had, and took my cup onto the beach. Yasha was right there. He was sitting cross-legged in the middle of the sand. He stood up when he saw me.

"There is something I need to show you," he said, with an earnestness I hadn't heard in his voice since the *I love you very much* he had said to his father's casket. "But I can't go back there right now," Yasha said, looking at Gunn through the lobby's back windows.

"Lucy," I said, "you've got some 'splaining to do."

"You watch *I Love Lucy*?" Yasha said.

"The best."

"Don't our beds remind you of theirs?"

I laughed. I thought about our beds, specifically his, and the necklace I'd found in his sheets. I was wearing it now, the ballerina dangling in the break of my collarbone. She kicked around in the wind, repeating back to me what I had told her this morning: I will not lose Yasha.

"I'm going to feed the ponies," Yasha said.

"May I come?"

"*Self certainly,*" Yasha said, in Haldor's voice. We both laughed until his face brightened into total seriousness and he said, "Haldor loves my mother."

"Excuse me?"

Yasha ran around to the back of the museum, to the kitchen entrance where they kept the pony food. For a few seconds I was alone on the north-facing beach. The pressure of the world's edge faced me—the horizon line was a finish line. Yasha and I had both come a rather far and strange way, toward either an end or a height. We were getting there. Love and geography had become synonyms, both meaning: move across a great space. Yasha emerged carrying a crate of bread loaves. We walked to the parking lot, dropped the crate onto the pickup bed, and started driving uphill.

I noticed that Yasha did not adjust any mirrors when he drove, or use turn signals, or reverse. His hands gripped the steering wheel so tightly that they shook, but this matched his speaking— he was trying to speak faster than his mouth allowed.

"Haldor said he was happy glad in her, really happy and glad— he said both those things. I don't know what he was saying, he was like, *I am happy in you, Olyana.*"

"That's what they say," I said. "That's how they say it."

"Say what?"

"I love you." Crisis. "I love you in Norwegian," I said, as fast as my mouth allowed. "Norwegians say, I am glad in you."

Yasha said nothing.

"Jeg er glad i deg," I said, *"glad* means glad."

"Haldor is glad in my mother," Yasha said, looking for the first time away from the road and right at me. Then his head snapped back to the road.

"Is your mother glad in him?"

"No," Yasha said, his grip on the wheel loosening. I waited for the next thing he would say, which I could see him pulling, with some difficulty, up his throat. "Ian," he said. "The man she left us for. She's loved him since she left us."

Seven ponies stood waiting for us with their necks stretching over the fence. Yasha stopped the truck, spent a moment checking around the steering wheel, pulled the key out, hesitated, and put it in his pocket. I knew a nondriving New Yorker when I saw one. But he had just mentioned his mother's leaving, and I could not mention the emergency brake.

"I didn't think she was capable of it," Yasha said, opening his door. We got out and walked around to the back of the truck. I poked one loaf—the crust chipped off under my finger like paint. "Real stale," Yasha said. "I hope it feels good on their teeth."

I hadn't considered their teeth. The ponies were white or black, with the signature Icelandic manes that made them look like Beatles. Their tails were as long as their short legs—they swept in a C from their butts to their hooves. The white ponies had gray tails; these looked like the ponytails of old women. When Yasha made his first toss into the pen, the nearest white pony spread its lips around the whole loaf and walked away with it, to a spot in the crabgrass where it could chew.

I threw another in. Two ponies chomped it neatly in half. They were cooperative, but hungry. I missed my sister, who would have known how to cut their hair, remove their ticks, clean their eyes. Yasha threw a third and fourth loaf into the pen. As I rested my hand between the eyes of one black pony, my phone rang. It was my sister.

"I was just thinking about you," I said.

Yasha looked up at me.

"Her," I said, pointing to the phone, and then felt cruel.

"I'm in a state," my sister said.

I walked away from the pen, toward the farmhouse. Behind me, thuds announced each of Yasha's subsequent throws. I could hear him thanking two ponies for sharing.

"I bet," I said. Her message had said that she'd call me when she stopped crying; it had been weeks. It was now the last day of July. Five weeks until the wedding, and the mother and father of the bride had made their early exit. I hoped Scott was outdoing himself. I hoped he was smothering her with care. I hoped my parents' absence felt like a twig thrown against his presence.

"I am coming," I said. I knew that I was not my sister's concern. She wanted news about them; she wanted to hear they'd changed their minds. All I could say of them was, "I told them that I'm coming."

"I'm scared," my sister said. "I don't feel well."

"What kind of well?"

"I'm dissolving."

My sister sounded small—the register of her voice triggered in my mind the symbols and dice of third-grade board games, the Persian rug that appeared when my parents' sofa bed folded away, her legs—which had always been longer than mine, even as toddlers—bending at the knees into large triangles while she sat listening to the game rules, my smaller triangles bouncing as I made up the rules. I imagined lowering this tiny version of my sister into a glass of water and watching her dissolve, as if she were sugar. I shouldn't have been so far from her. I shouldn't have been anywhere near ponies, or blacksmiths, or the Norwegian Sea. I should have been in Central Park. On my sister's octopus-print, waterproof picnic blanket. Cutting her hair, removing her ticks, cleaning her eyes.

"You are one solid, magnificent chunk," I said. "Where are you?"

"Gold's Deli," she said.

"Onion rings?"

"With eggs."

"Delicious. Now, listen," I said. "When are you flying out?"

My sister didn't answer, and I heard the three-hundred-pound man who owns Gold's asking her for exact change. I looked up. Yasha had thrown in all the bread and had crawled into the pen himself. He was standing sheepishly in an empty spot between the scattered, chewing ponies like a scarecrow, looking at me, and then at a pony, making sure the pony was eating. Onion rings would have felt good on their gums, I thought, looking at the animals flopping their lips around the hard rectangles. My sister came back.

"My ticket was with you," she said, "and Mom and Dad. Do you know if they've canceled them? Scott might be flying out early."

"Why would he do that?" I said.

"Scott doesn't feel well either."

I didn't know what kind of euphemism this was.

"Tell Scott I want to talk to him," I said.

"He isn't here," she said. "He's home."

I'd seen the word *home* explode before. It had happened to my downstairs neighbor Lily, the daughter of our building's superintendent, who'd grown up in a building where her father was king, only to move as a ten-year-old back to Slovenia, the country where her grandfather was dying. It had happened to Yasha, twice. First Russia, then the bakery. Both gone. Or not gone, but made foreign—through distance, through vacancy, through the permanent misalignment of then and now. When Sarah said *home*, I flipped through the wrong answers—she didn't mean our old apartment, or either of my parents' new apartments, or my Room 18—and I knew it had happened to us.

"Mom didn't mention the tickets," I said. "If they cancel them, you and I will buy our own." Haldor would have to find more work for me. Maybe he'd let me take on a couple of wool-dyeing shifts.

"I want them to come," she said. I did too. Besides, after the injury of their refusal, it seemed miraculously gracious of her to still want them there, and I wanted her to have anything she wanted.

"Sarah," I said, "you love him?"

"I do," she said. "Fuck, Frances, I shouldn't be saying those words before the wedding."

"International calls cancel out jinxes," I said.

She said, "I love him."

"Then the rest is cats," I said, "and apartments." I made the same hand movement Yasha's mother had made at the funeral.

"I have to go," my sister said. "Frances," she said, "it's going to be a small wedding. We didn't give ourselves much time to plan. We wanted it to be simple. I'm not having bridesmaids or center-pieces or any of that. But if Dad doesn't give me away," she said, "who should give me away?"

I didn't know. "We'll talk about that later."

"Maybe Scott's father would. We haven't told his parents yet about my parents."

"Maybe, but you don't need to know right now." My parents might turn around yet, I thought. Everybody had five weeks. "Go home," I said. "Go to bed. When you wake up, it will be a whole new month."

"Bye," she said. "Okay. Bye."

The ponies were alone in the pen, the bread all swallowed, and Yasha had returned to the driver's seat. He was twirling the key ring around his thumb. Sigbjørn's tractor had cut deep tracks into the mud around the farmhouse. I walked within one groove down to the truck, which was very red beside the black and white ponies. I got in, and Yasha locked our doors. Inside the small cabin, we couldn't hear the ponies stomping or batting their thick tails against the fence. Yasha put the key in the ignition, but didn't turn it. We sat still. He and I have since discussed that this was an unbearable stillness.

· · ·

Kurt assigned Frances to the pizza preparation shift, as soon as she and Yasha returned from the ponies. Kurt said they would need to roll out seventy crusts. Frances followed him into the kitchen gloomily. Yasha was glad at the time to escape the dough work—the smell of yeast would have made him very upset, he thought, and perhaps they all knew it and so had moved him out to the lavvos—but the lavvos were nearly impossible to build. They were too tall and too heavy. By the time he came in from the beach, Frances was asleep.

She had left her door open. Yasha moved around her room in a hush. He was grateful to be in that room again and desperate to wake her. But he didn't wake her, and he didn't brush his teeth, which would have woken her, and he fell asleep on her second bed. They slept turned away from each other, facing opposite walls.

In the morning, he was rabid. She had gotten up and out first. With irritating symmetry, she hadn't woken him up. He opened the door and stuck his head out into the hall. There were people everywhere. He closed the door. It was the first of August. It was the whale meat festival. It was the fucking whale meat festival. He put on the pants he'd left in a pile by the bed—puffy blue work pants Haldor had given him for lavvo-building. He looked like the Cookie Monster. A child outside his window was shouting "Pig! Pig! Pig!"

It would be impossible to open the door behind the guest chair. Visitors would be checking in with Gunn all day. Yasha stood between the two beds. He crouched and hooked his fingers under his bed's wire frame. He pulled it across the room. It made hideous sounds the whole way. When he had trapped himself between the two bed frames, he climbed over his mattress—he hadn't yet put on his sandy shoes—and pushed them, with both arms outstretched, together and against the wall. There.

He closed the door to her room behind him. In the lobby, the child who had been shouting *Pig!* was now with his parents at the reception desk. The boy's mother lifted him up to her chest. The family was from England. It was hard to understand what they wanted with Kurt's whale pizzas. It was hard to imagine being lifted to a mother's chest. The beds are separate, Gunn was telling them, but can be pushed together.

Yasha looked at Gunn, searching for a wink, any indication that she had heard his bed screeching across the floor—no. The total amount, she went on, would be charged in kroner. She pulled out a conversion chart for British pounds. Behind her, the Ceremonial Hall was full of fresh waffles. The pizzas wouldn't be ready until the evening—the whale meat had to be marinated, grilled, portioned—but the event was advertised as all-day, and the schedule began with breakfast, followed by nail-smithing in

Sigbjørn's hut. Frida supervised breakfast. She stood pressing waffles, each waffle composed of five heart-shaped sections. At the tables, guests dismantled their waffles heart by heart, biting the tips off first and dipping the curved tops into their bowls of sunberries.

Follow me, you sunberry, Yasha rehearsed as he approached the kitchen. Through this door, down these—

Frances opened the kitchen door. She was wearing her sack uniform, and it was splattered with tomato sauce.

"Hey," Yasha said.

"I don't know how you did this," Frances said. "If I look at another ball of dough, I'll throw up."

"I have somewhere you can hide," Yasha said.

"Give me eight minutes."

"What is the time?" Kurt said.

Frida said, "I am not making any more waffles."

Sigbjørn came in through the back entrance and said, "Time for fire?" He smiled at Frances. Yasha watched jealously. Here's Sigbjørn, with his arms and his leather apron, Yasha thought, and here I am, wearing Cookie Monster pants. Between him and me, wouldn't Frances pick him, if given the chance? And didn't it look like Sigbjørn, who was staring at Frances the way he stared at his burning lumps of coal, would happily give her the chance?

"Everybody out," Kurt said. "Sigbjørn," he said, "make the fire."

Frances beamed at Sigbjørn.

"Superfine," Sigbjørn said.

Yasha felt sick. This stream of strange-named men, all saying *super* whenever they pleased, would never end and he would have to battle all of them. Kurt pointed ahead, and the team started to move. Sigbjørn retrieved two handfuls of kindling from his pockets and crunched the twigs for Frances's amusement. Yasha watched her laugh. In the cave, he thought, his only competitor would be the goat.

Frida, followed by Sigbjørn, followed by Frances and Yasha, filed out through the kitchen door and into the center of the Ceremonial Hall.

"Ladies and gentlemen," Sigbjørn hollered, "it is our time!"

A few guests giggled. Everyone looked up.

"Follow me, please, to the smithy." Sigbjørn walked out to the lobby.

The guests shrugged and stood from their chairs—leaving their breakfasts, taking their jackets, pushing their kids along—and followed Sigbjørn toward the back door. The hall emptied. That was the first thing. The second thing would be harder: it was Gunn. The stream following Sigbjørn moved through the lobby, past Gunn's desk, and she looked at them all with her mouth open, delighted. Then, as if she too were part of Yasha's moment, she stood and followed them out onto the beach. The door slammed behind her. Yasha heard Sigbjørn giving directions, and the crowd moving farther down the shore, and Kurt in the kitchen, chopping. Frances stood beside him, waiting.

"Fast," Yasha said. He ran into the lobby, and Frances followed. He kicked the chair away from the wall, pushed the knob, ushered Frances in first, jumped in behind her, and slammed the door shut. It was true—the darkness changed their bodies. In the first moment, he could not see her, but he knew where she stood, from her heat, and her being denser than air, and an electric signal that all their fingers seemed to emit, irrepressibly. He had to choose between swallowing her whole, or finding her knuckle by knuckle—they were fully available to each other now, so conveniently invisible. Frances began to feel around behind her.

"Is . . . this . . . a closet?" she said.

"No!" Yasha said. He found the first step and started climbing down. Frances placed a hand on his shoulder and descended hesitantly.

Weak light dripped out of the open root tips, illuminating the palace and the goat. The goat stood in the same position, head thrown back, sucking on the shortest of the three roots. Nothing poured from the root into the goat's mouth, nothing except a bit of light, but the goat wore her contented expression, a happiness confirmed by her lifted tail. Yasha turned around to Frances. Her lips were parted, as if about to speak.

She looked at the sack that was covering the table, and then at her own. She touched the sack on the table. The palace teetered. She withdrew her hand, looked at Yasha, and clutched vaguely at her own uniform. Frances lifted her arms and dragged the sack up with them. She pulled it over her head. Underneath, she wore a black bra. She unfastened the bra. The darkness of the staircase behind her made her look like an apparition.

Apparitions: Frances's skin, the goat's open mouth, Frida's baby's open mouth, sucking, the gleaming grill top, the goat sucking on the root, Frances's outline. Yasha took one step forward, and bent his knees. His knees found the floor. He opened his mouth, and let one breast fill it. He placed one hand on each side of her waist. She rested her hands on his head. He felt the weight of her breast push his tongue down. He breathed in through his nose. She leaned forward, and he drew away from her, until his mouth was collected again, kissing her nipple. He stood.

When they kissed, Frances stood on her toes. She kept her hands around Yasha's head. He kept his hands around her waist. They kissed with their lips only touching, until their mouths fell open.

. . .

I threw my sauce-covered sack back on and we rushed out of the basement, just before Gunn returned. Yasha led us straight to the truck—we tore out of the parking lot and down Vikingveien. Neither of us felt prepared to speak. Yasha drove faster, as if to shorten the period of silence. He was grinning. We drove down the road toward Vassily's grave.

All five lavvos stood evenly spaced on the sand, each housing its own campfire. Yasha rolled down the windows, and thin smoke, having traveled the length of the shore, came in on the breeze. It smelled like wood and salt water. I leaned back on the headrest. As our speed increased, the air came in harder through the open windows. Yasha brushed something from his eye. I had just kissed that eye, I thought. Then Eggum came into view.

There was the head sculpture on its pedestal, looking especially bald from the pale spot the sun made on top. I think it was the head that made Yasha start speaking. He turned to me as we approached the radar station.

"Where are you going when you go home?" he asked.

"Good question," I said. "I don't know. Parents are moving, Sarah is moving. There's a painting program I want to do in the city, but I don't know where I'll stay. I think I have nine hundred left in my checking account. I'll use up a good portion on the trains back down." I pictured farms whizzing past the train windows. "You know," I said, "I have no idea."

"If—" he said loudly. We had arrived.

I turned to him, enjoyed the sight of his hair bouncing off the tops of his ears for a moment, saw him try to stop the truck, and saw him forget how. He looked at the keys, put his hand to them, and, in a moment of outright confusion, slammed his foot down on the gas. The truck accelerated into the pedestal. The sculpture dislodged and flew toward us as the pedestal fell away. The head dropped onto the hood of our truck and lodged in a small crater. The air bags inflated, throwing us back. Yasha's hands still gripped the wheel.

The sculpture's pedestal, which apparently extended deep into the sand, leaned only slightly toward the water. It had crumpled the truck's bumper.

"Are you okay?" I asked.

"Are you?" asked Yasha.

We both leaned back, away from the bags. What frightened us? The exposed metal spike, sticking up out of the pedestal, once fastened to the base of the head like a spine. The condition of our own spines. Our red truck, crammed against the pedestal, its redness now part of the disaster. The smoke, not a campfire's. The hissing the engine made. What soothed us? The hissing, and the airbags, which looked like clouds. The heat of the light on the beach. That we would eventually call somebody.

We fell asleep. This is the strangest part of the story when Yasha and I tell it. Sometimes we admit to the session in the cave that preceded it, which was the culmination of a great deal of nervous energy, and which had evidently relaxed and drained our bodies, once done. Sometimes Yasha will attribute it to the heavy lavvo poles he'd lifted the night before. I talk about my sister, and the sleeplessness her situation evoked in me those nights. It was really the wind that put us to sleep. It was really the sun on the beach, and our being so close to each other, and so stuck.

Sigbjørn opened my door, and I woke up. He looked at Yasha—Yasha was still asleep. Sigbjørn reached his arm over me and pinched Yasha's nose closed. Yasha woke up and screamed.

"What are you doing?" I said.

"To make sure he breathes!" Sigbjørn said.

"He breathes!" I found myself saying.

"You bleed!" Sigbjørn said.

I looked down and believed him for a moment. The sauce was primary red, and the splotch shapes were sloppy, natural. I didn't know how long we had been asleep. I remembered the crash, or rather, the crash reminded me about itself as I looked through the windshield. Yasha opened his door and stepped out of the truck to get away from Sigbjørn. I came to.

"It's sauce," I said to Sigbjørn, but he was lifting me, and the head sculpture, in his arms and out to his tractor. I looked back over Sigbjørn's shoulder and saw Yasha close behind us. The truck remained, burrowing its nose into the pedestal.

"Pizza sauce," I said, when the three of us were seated inside the tractor's cabin.

Sigbjørn wasn't listening. He gave me the marble head to hold, started driving, then began, "I was at the lavvos, and I thought, Yasha is good for nothing. Today is the festival, he knows the time, he knows we are waiting for him. I thought, He is surely kissing Frances."

I said, "You thought that?"

"I told the chief I would go find Yasha," Sigbjørn said.

Yasha was in the backseat, looking down.

"Nobody in Room Sixteen. Nobody in Room Eighteen. Nobody in Room Twenty. Kurt was in the kitchen, he had not seen you. Frida was cleaning the waffle iron, she had not seen you. Gunn had not seen you. When Gunn asked me where Frances was, then I knew, they are surely kissing."

We were halfway back to the museum now, and I think they had added the whale meat to the fires, because the smoke from the lavvos was darker, and rising higher.

"So I kept driving up the road. Ah! I thought." Sigbjørn pointed his finger up and hit a button that raised the tractor's plow. "He is visiting his father. So I forgave you. I drove up to Eggum." He lowered the plow with another button. "Then I saw the truck. Something was wrong. He is dead, I thought. So, now," Sigbjørn said. He didn't say more.

We pulled into the museum lot. Kurt was at the kitchen entrance, carrying the whale meat out one tray at a time and leaving the trays on the gravel. Sigbjørn stopped the tractor, got out, opened my door, picked me up again, and carried me over to Kurt.

"Yasha crashed her," Sigbjørn said. He deposited me into Kurt's meat-stained arms.

"Where is Yasha?" Kurt said.

"With me. He can walk. I take him to his mother, and you put Frances to bed. She bleeds."

Kurt looked at my sack.

"It's sauce," Kurt and I both said.

"Put her to bed," Sigbjørn repeated.

My door was unlocked, as I'd left it for Yasha, and when Kurt turned the knob his forearm twisted the skin on my neck. He put me down on my bed, and then stepped back, not pulling down the covers or removing the marble head from my hands.

"The meat is burning," Kurt said.

"Let me get out of this sack," I said, and remembered the cave, bashfully, and thought perhaps I should keep the sack on and stop flinging it everywhere. "I'll be out in just a minute. I can serve the honey mead," I said.

"You are not hurt?" Kurt said.

"Not that I know of," I said.

"It will be a long day," Kurt said.

"It will be a long month," I said. August, giving way without mercy to a sad September wedding. This month: birthdays, the first month in which Vassily would not live, a month for going home. A long month, a long way home.

Kurt centered his black chef's cap and thumped it down over his head until it stopped right above his eyebrows. He left.

He left me holding the head like a hot water bottle over my abdomen.

"Kurt!" I shouted after him.

He leaned back into the room.

"Send Haldor here, if he has a minute. He should know what to do with this."

Kurt looked at the head sculpture and made a *puh!* sound, which must have meant something in German. *"Ja,"* he said. At least this always meant "Yes."

"Thank you."

He closed the door. I sank into my pillow and wondered at what age a child would weigh this much—what kind of baby this marble head could have been. It pressed uncomfortably into my stomach. I kept holding it. What had we been saying, just before the crash? I thought myself back into the passenger seat. "If," Yasha was saying.

If.

If I take over the bakery, and need an assistant, would you assist?

I would.

If I have never had sex before—had he ever had sex before?—and we went to the cave again, would you—

Would I? Yasha had not yet told me which day in August would be his eighteenth birthday. Nor had he asked any of the questions that I now imagined him asking:

If we both go back to New York, will we be going back together? If your sister gets married, will you want to get married? If I am younger than you for the rest of my life, will you get older, and older, and older? If Nils was too old, am I too young? If you came to the Arctic to be alone, why did you take your sack off?

I stood up, placed the marble head on my pillow, and took my sack off. I opened my window and threw the sack as far as I could. It landed a foot outside the wild boar's pen. The boar waddled toward it, sniffing. It must have smelled like tomatoes. A tomato would have fit right in among the boar's red apples. I wondered if the boar would taste the difference, taste the salt—if the tomato would taste more like grass, the apples tasting more like water. I wondered if the boar knew that apples are sweet. He stuck his snout out under the bottom rung of the fence. The sack looked like an anthill in the grass.

There was a loud knock at my door; I was naked.

"It is only the chief," Haldor said, the knob already turning.

I wrapped myself in a white towel. Haldor was wearing his white tunic, and we looked like weird versions of each other, standing a foot apart, on the right side of my room. It was only then that I realized the beds had moved. Haldor realized it right away.

"Big-bed lady," he said. I laughed so hard I snorted. "Olyana has done it in the same way," Haldor said. "The ladies, they like the big beds."

"And you?"

"Certainly," Haldor said, "my bed is a different subject. Special made for the chief, so, superlarge. I have two ravens painted on my headboard." He smiled and said, "What has happened to you?"

I was a little bit high off the bed jokes, and the open window, and imagining Yasha—I hoped it had been Yasha—pushing his bed against mine, so I said, "We were down with the goat, and Gunn was walking around over us, and we climbed out when she left, and Yasha wanted to go to see his father, and when we got there, he couldn't stop the truck."

I expected Haldor to say something about the truck, or the grave, but he said, "My goat?"

"Your goat?" I said.

Haldor's cheeks grew as red as his beard, and for the first time it was easy to imagine him as a little boy. A large-bellied little boy, blushing.

"I made a goat," Haldor said. "I was not thinking anybody would see it."

I felt such affection for the chief just then, I wanted to try to wrap my arms around him—I knew I would not get all the way around, but I wanted to try to move his belt of teeth out of the way, lean my ear to his tunic, and hear his heart pound. He was three times as large as my father, who tended to look smaller and smaller as his hair grew outward. My father had more hair than body, just as my mother had more eyes than body. They both only barely existed. If I had ever hugged them together simultaneously, which I never had, and wanted to try, and imagined trying at my sister's wedding, if only they would come, they might have begun to add up to Haldor.

"What . . . what did you think? About the goat," Haldor said.

I felt I had said too much, and didn't know what to answer. After an uncomfortable pause, I said, "I loved it. I think they should sell replicas in the Viking Shop. I would buy one and take it home with me."

"Maybe Olyana would like it."

"You are glad in her," I said.

Haldor sat down on the side of my big bed, the side that had previously been Yasha's.

"I am glad in Yasha," I said. I had not said anything like this to anyone. My sister and I talked exclusively about the wedding. My parents never talked about love, the way they never talked about pop music, drugs, or sports.

"*Uff da*," Haldor said. I sat beside him. Haldor nodded his head up and down for a little while. "I hope it goes better with you," he said. "I hope you take Yasha home with you." A bird on my windowsill made a cry that sounded like a bell. I felt very awake. "I hope you take Olyana home with you also," he said. "She does not want to stay here with me."

What was this web, and who had woven it? Haldor, Yasha, his mother, his father, my mother, my father, my sister, Sigbjørn, the bird on my windowsill, the boar in its pen, Kurt, Frida, the baby, the head, the truck, and I were no longer unrelated. I looked over the gull's head and up toward the highest clouds, and the planet occurred to me as an eyeball, and this arctic island its iris, staring up at the other sky, the black sky, the cosmos. Haldor and I stared at the floor, out the window, in turns. We had become elements of the same web, and this relationship allowed for silence, and for a few moments of mutual understanding. We sat still for fear that if we shook, shook the way we wanted to, we would wreck the filaments connecting us to the others. We depended on our web as much as we wanted out of it. We were trying to move each other around. We were trying to stay still. We were trying to be here and elsewhere at once. We were trying to be alone in love.

"Brown cheese takes a long time to go bad," Haldor said.

"I won't eat your goat anyway," I said.

"Thank you," said Haldor.

I pulled my legs up onto the bed and turned to face him. "I am afraid of going home without Yasha," I said.

"And I am fearing staying here without Olyana, but what can I do? I can make more goats. Go down under the tree and call myself a troll. Sometimes I am feeling so much like a troll, I found that room under the tree and thought, I can use some time alone here, in the dark." He looked at his hands. "I get so tired of the sun," Haldor said. Then, "You are going to California, yes?"

"Yes, California," I said. "The wedding. It's going to be ugly."

Haldor looked up from his fingers, which he had been studying, bending them one at a time at the knuckle.

"Not my sister, not the flowers. My sister is beautiful." The chief put his hand on his knee and nodded and seemed to believe me. "The day itself will be ugly. My parents will not be there. I will be there, but that won't help much. I don't help anyone. Yasha knows how to help."

"What?"

"Yasha buried his father," I said, "and is trying to forgive his mother, and trying to learn how to drive a car. I will have to do all of those things eventually."

"I did not know that he does not drive," Haldor said. "Certainly I would not be giving him the truck. You neither? And your father," he said, "is he sick?"

"That's one way of putting it," I said.

"And your mother, is she bad?"

"No. My mother is very good. She is so good," I said. "She provides and provides and provides. She forgets to provide for herself. I don't know where she finds pleasure. I wish she would be pleased by my sister." I knew Haldor didn't follow this. "She finds pleasure in apples," I admitted. "My mother loves apples."

Haldor looked out my window to the pen, where the boar was, as if on cue, eating the apples that had been thrown to him, one bright red hemisphere perched in his mouth, making him look slaughtered and served for Christmas. I wondered if the boar still had his private parts, whether they had been cut from him—whether there was a sow, somewhere on this island, with whom he could save himself. The apple disappeared down his throat.

"I have never left Borg," Haldor said. "I thought, Here is a woman who puts fire in this place I have always been, maybe this is a place for her also. So I asked her and she said, *I love Ian Strom.*"

"Ian Strom?"

"Ian Strom."

"The man who lives in Tribeca," I said. These were the things Yasha had said at the funeral, I dimly recalled, in the confusion before the Mourner's Kaddish.

"What is Tribeca?" Haldor said.

In my mind, the image of West Broadway replaced the image of the funeral. Mothers wheeled ergonomic strollers past renovated warehouses, safe from the nearby rush of West Side Highway traffic, cooled by the breeze off the Hudson River. I said, "It's a place where people live."

He said, "Would you say this is a place where people live?"

I went to the window and could see the beach, all the way back to the white horizon. A child was running up and down the shore, flying a whale-shaped kite. The sky was blue and clear enough to turn the whale's flying into swimming. The shore was wide and bright enough to make the child look like a piece of candy.

"We should all live here," I said.

"You should all go back to where you came from," Haldor said. He stood up and straightened his belt of teeth so it made a diagonal across his chest. He looked at the marble head on my pillow, seized it, and went to the door. "So will I."

When Haldor walked out the door, I didn't know where he was going. It seemed he might walk straight over the sea to the North Pole itself, or back into the first Viking age, or home to his two-raven bed. The head had looked less strange in his arms than in mine, or it looked in safer hands, and I pictured him walking to Eggum and jamming the metal spine back up the head's neck. I wondered for a moment if he had carved the head himself, before or after his goat. My painting of the ox outside the asylum lay on its side at the foot of my bed. What did we want from these animals? Why did we re-create them? To bring them, and their innocence, and their meat, and their company, into our web?

Haldor's goodbye had shone some light on my way out: I had to go home—I knew this—and if I could follow his instructions and take Yasha home with me, back to the place where he too was from, then we could make New York a place where people lived again. My sister would marry and move away. My parents would divorce and move apart. The north would fade further and further into itself, into our memory of it. New York City would be left to us. Yet, Yasha wasn't really from New York, not originally. Besides a left-behind cat I knew Yasha loved, the city had no immediate claim on him, nor did I.

· · ·

Olyana had tested the rotation of Yasha's wrists, knees, and ankles. She assured Sigbjørn they were not broken. She touched Yasha's neck and Yasha flicked her hand away.

"I'm fine," Yasha said.

"Little man," said Olyana. "You very nearly ruined the surprise. Do me a kindness, if you're *fine*—follow me."

She took one step forward, and Yasha noticed her shoes. They were clear hard plastic, the shape of Dorothy's red slippers, but completely transparent, showing her unpainted toenails. Olyana hooked her arm around Yasha's elbow, which he had not offered her. He could not imagine where she found things like these slippers, how she paid for them, why she packed them, why she wore them, today or ever. He stood up straight, in an effort to gain any height over her. In her heels, she matched him to the inch. Yasha felt so related to her he could hardly stand it.

"My good Gunn," his mother said as they passed reception.

Yasha looked at the doorknob behind the guest chair. Gunn bowed her head ceremoniously to Yasha and his mother as they passed, while the British family perused the festival's activity schedule. His mother did not leave the lobby until Yasha pushed the door open for her. Olyana walked through, retaking Yasha's elbow when they'd both come out onto the sand. They walked toward the archery targets. Olyana had to pull her clear heel out of the sand each time she stepped.

Yasha said, "Why did you buy those shoes?" This was not the first question he'd intended. He'd actually wanted to ask her about love. For the first time, she seemed capable of it, even filled with it. The speech she'd made to Haldor was the most generous expression of love Yasha had heard from her. He entertained the gross, exhilarating idea of his mother being a talented lover. Physically. He wanted to inherit some of her talent. He looked at his mother's arms. They seemed to declare that they knew how to hold, how to be held, even if she had been holding someone other than him these ten years. Yasha thought: She has something to give back to me now.

"The shoes were a gift," she said.

Yasha said, "What else does he pay for?"

His mother said, "Oh." She lifted her skirt up to her knees. "You wouldn't believe. For one thing," she said, "your father."

"He paid for my father?"

"So generously."

His mother had a way of frightening him with the most pleasant words. In the parking lot, at the far side of the archery fields, Yasha saw the damaged red pickup hitched at an angle to Sigbjørn's tractor. There was a black car parked beside the tractor.

Why had Yasha wanted to bring Frances to the grave site? To hush his father's Why nots. To tell him, Done, done, done. To show him Frances. He didn't know if his father had been buried wearing his glasses. Probably not, Yasha thought. Surely his father's sight had been restored to him. Surely that was a benefit of death.

"To move a body across international borders," his mother said, "terribly expensive. Far more expensive than these shoes. He didn't flinch," she said, her cheeks jumping, as they often did, up toward her eyes.

Yasha had never considered this expense, and was profoundly embarrassed. Nobody had at any point asked him to pay. Why had they asked her new man? And why did her new man do it? Daniil had paid for Yasha's plane tickets: Moscow, Stockholm, Oslo. Yasha had paid for his own train ticket north, exchanging the last Russian bills his father had given as pocket money for five hundred Norwegian kroner, using two hundred on the train ticket, twenty on a Coca-Cola, twenty on a *Go'morgen* yogurt when he woke up twelve hours later still on the train steadily approaching the Arctic, sixty on a cheese sandwich, and the last two hundred on the ferry from Bodø, across the cold fjord to Borg.

Had his father died in Brooklyn, it would have meant more borders. His father's body would have needed to cross an ocean, not to mention the dozen Western countries, on the way up to the top of the world, the place where Vassily wanted to die, or truer, the place where he wanted to live after he died. Mostly ice. Real peace, his father had said. Yasha looked at the red and white rings of the targets, mounted on easels just behind the place where he and his mother had stopped. This was not the top of the world. This was very close to it. This was the Viking Museum at Borg. This was the solution they had found. It had all been made so generously possible.

"Why did he do it?" Yasha said.

"Die?" his mother said.

"Pay," Yasha said. "Your friend."

"Ask him!" she said.

She laughed. She looked wilder and merrier then than Yasha had ever seen her. She began to flatten her dress over her stomach. Yasha understood nothing other than that her dress was the same red as the bull's-eye. Where was she looking? No longer at her slippers, or at him. Up, over the tops of the targets, toward the parking lot. Yasha looked in the same direction and saw a bearded man getting out of the black car. When he opened the driver's-side door, it slammed into Sigbjørn's tractor. The man closed the car's door, gave the tractor a pat, and walked toward them. When he came onto the sand, he removed his boots. His jeans were already rolled up. With both boots in one hand, he ran between two targets and straight to Olyana, who engulfed him in open arms.

When the embrace ended, Olyana said, "Here he is."

"Here who is?" Dostoyevsky said. He seized Olyana's hand.

Yasha took a step backward. Here who was? His first irrational thought: My father has sent a messenger. His second irrational thought: Septimos told this man where to find me. Third: It's not him. Fourth: It is him. Fifth: I have no bread to sell him. The Dostoyevsky guy had a beard, and a straight nose, and combed hair. He had always worn leather boots, rolled-up jeans, with musical instruments hanging off his shoulder. He came on Fridays. He read from his paperbacks. He made Yasha furious. The reward for remembering this man was that in the memory, his father was standing at the adjacent register, and the dinging of the register buttons in the memory meant that his father's fingers were moving, meant that his father still moved.

"Alyosha," Dostoyevsky said. "It's been ages."

Why was it possible for this man to speak, if his father could no longer open the cash drawer and charge him $2.50?

"I always refused to tell him your real name," his mother said, giggling. "He calls you Alyosha."

Yasha felt he could hear his own voice speaking from a distance. *Doesn't mean I am Alyosha, for fuck's sake*, it said. His father had laughed.

His mother said, "Came home all the time with his sourdough and a book, saying he had read to you, saying you were taller every week, saying how well the bakery smelled. Saying what an idiot I had been to leave the two of you, saying he wasn't worth the sacrifice. And I would say, Don't you worry about my sacrifice."

I'm right here, Yasha thought. Your sacrifice.

"We used to have the strangest arguments," his mother said.

"We never have any arguments," the man said. He kissed Olyana on the lips. I'm right here, Yasha thought again. One of Olyana's knees bent and her foot flicked up behind her, the way Yasha had only seen happen in cartoons, and her other leg sank deeper, with all her weight now on it, heel-first, into the sand. The slipper hung off her floating foot. Yasha grabbed it. He walked it up to the nearest target and punctured the bull's-eye with the stiletto. The rest of the clear slipper hung out of the target like drool from an open mouth. When Yasha turned back toward his mother, the kiss had not yet ended.

. . .

I called my parents. Small car crash, I told them, no injury, just shock. They were upset. They were upset for their own reasons.

My father had gotten hired to illustrate a report documenting the effect of cell-phone use on human thumbs, and he'd stabbed his own thumb with an X-Acto knife. The skin between the thumb and index finger, he informed me, was called the *thenar space*. It was this skin my father had punctured, and actually infected (his knife generally lay out on his desk uncovered, dusty, inky, covered in his shed hairs). It was now stitched up, but the infection needed monitoring. Thankfully, my mother said, they had Dr. Cordon.

I asked him how he was feeling. He started saying something about "motherfucking fingernails." If he had tried to distract himself, by way of injury, from his everyday distress—it hadn't worked. I wondered what he would have to do to himself to succeed, to distract himself from the endless stream of clinical studies and cow's-eye dissection kits that needed their materials illustrated. I hoped my mother would be around to stop him from doing it. I guessed she wouldn't be, now. Our leaving each other had become dangerous—I had left them alone when I went north; they were leaving my sister alone to give herself away; they were leaving each other alone now to who knows what result. I wondered if my father would ever draw again. If I am lucky enough, I thought, someday to make a painting for the cover of a toy helicopter user's manual, I will not be outraged, because the painting is the thing itself, the fulfilling thing. Illustrations had long since ceased fulfilling my father.

His illustrations filled a corner of a page. He wanted something larger for himself, and why shouldn't he? He wanted to make his own work. The difference between drawing and illustrating, he said, is that you draw for yourself and you illustrate for some schmo who can't draw. He'd wanted to contribute something significant, something fine, to the profession. The professionals had made his work feel like marginalia. I looked at the blueberries Agnes had gifted me on her Princess Mette-Marit plate. My father could have drawn their blue guts exactly, could have drawn the difference between the berries' skin and their flesh. He could have drawn consummate fingernails. But as the industry paid less attention to him, he had lost the joy in paying attention.

"For a bunch of holier-than-thou orthopedists," he was saying in conclusion.

My mother looked intently at my father. Behind them, the apartment was emptier than ever. All my father's drawings had been taken off the wall, and my mother's vases no longer lined the countertops. Where had they moved these things? Where were they going, and how far from each other could it possibly be? They had lived in our tiny apartment for thirty years. They had no more obvious place to go, I thought, than I did. Than Yasha did, for that matter. All of us were reentering New York, our former home, as though we'd never lived there. My sister was the only one of us who knew where she was going. Who thought she did, at least.

My father's left hand and wrist were mittened in white bandages.

"One more thing we won't need to explain at the wedding," my mother said, pointing at the gauze. "And a good thing too. Imagine the questions."

"Did you stab yourself because your daughter is throwing away her life? No! I stabbed myself because thirty years later my best audience is nine-year-old schoolchildren. Not to mention my own nine-year-old marrying herself off like a child courtesan—"

"Dad," I said to cut him off, "have you told Sarah about your hand?"

"Sarah doesn't speak to us," my mother said.

"I sometimes wonder why I do," I said.

"Don't you turn against us now," she said. "Who's going to schlep these boxes?" She pointed behind her. There were the vases: in a box labeled *Vases* with my mother's porcelain hand-writing. "We're both counting on you for the heavy lifting, in case you didn't know. You can take turns. One day my boxes, one day his. I'll tip, your father won't."

It was strange how they still said *us* and *we* and *both*. The walls behind them had never looked whiter, and my father's enormous yellow hair looked like a halo painted onto a canvas. My mother's skin was the same white as the walls, her eyes especially dark by contrast. My mother and father both looked younger, as if the blank walls brightened their faces, reflecting light into lines where shadows had built up over time.

Kurt came back to my room as I was looking at them. He needed help with the festival's honey mead.

"Are you well enough?" Kurt asked.

"Of course." I turned back to the computer. "I have to go."

My father waved his white paw.

I spent the evening serving honey mead to three French broth-ers. One was twenty-six, one was twenty, and one was nine. They stuck around after the official activities had ended and sat with us in the staff lavvo well into the night. The littlest didn't speak English and spent the night grinning shyly at his brothers. With perfect grace they paid no special attention to any of us, neglected none of us, wrestled their littlest brother, and roasted their dinners. Even Sigbjørn was moved by their elegance: he offered them all his beers, and when they didn't drink any, Sigbjørn followed their example and put the cans away.

A dog ran laps around the bonfire. Every couple of laps, Sigbjørn would catch the dog by its collar and hold it still a moment. The dog would look up, examining his captor, and Sigbjørn would say, *"Jo."* It was my favorite Norwegian word. It was pronounced *you*. It meant "But yes," or, "Yes, even though you say no," or, "Yes after all." Sigbjørn squeezed the dog's jaws shut with one hand, scratched its ears with the other, and moaned his long *"Joooo." Youuuu.* The dog, looking up, said, I am not a dog, and Sigbjørn answered again and again, But yes, you are. Yes after all.

The dog sat by Sigbjørn for the rest of the night. I spoke my high school French to the little boy and taught him how to make his hands into a flute and how to put his feet in ballet positions. I had two weeks until I had to go home. My flight would depart on my birthday. The French brothers said they were staying on the island for some time. I could have asked to see them again. Their presence would have been soothing. But I wanted to be light like them and pass in and out lightly, so I said goodnight knowing I would not see them again.

Sigbjørn offered to drive them home. The oldest said they'd set up camp on Utakleiv Beach. Sigbjørn told them they'd chosen well—the winds would be moderate overnight, and they'd wake to a great view. He lifted the sleeping youngest brother and led the others to the tractor. Yasha promised to put out the fire. I promised to clean up the trash and stack the benches.

They left. We stood still and listened to the tractor driving off until we could no longer hear it. I looked at Yasha and I did not want to pass lightly. I did not want any more light.

. . .

To be free, Yasha thought, to be free to be free to be free. He kissed her. The fire had weakened, but a few logs still hissed. Yasha stepped away from her and saw Sigbjørn's empty cooling bucket; he picked it up, took Frances's hand, and walked out onto the beach to fill it. All the red and orange had left the sky and it was almost dark—the blue-gray felt luxurious. Frances took off her shoes and walked into the water. It was hilariously cold. Yasha bent over and made imprints of his palms in the wet sand. A wave came and filled them. Frances kissed him. Here was his relief, his rest.

Frances stacked the benches in pairs, and picked bits of tinfoil from the ground around the bonfire. Yasha put out the fire and found Frances's hand in the dark. Walking down the road toward the museum, they watched how still the fjord kept and how fast the sky moved. Here was the living world. Yasha felt the air sink through him as he breathed.

In her room, the beds lay pushed together. Yasha smiled sheepishly. Frances turned off the lights. He removed her shoes, her necklace. She removed his glasses. They undressed.

Yasha opened his eyes and saw a streak of green across Frances's floor—a stripe of light coming in between the curtains. There were famous versions of this morning in a boy's life. Yasha had imagined eagles landing on his shoulders and invisible fountains erupting from under the fields. He had not imagined his mother in a floor-length gown playing the Cheburashka birthday song. She played loudly enough to wake up the whole museum. Yasha walked into the Ceremonial Hall. His mother sat erect on the piano bench, her fingers curled over the keys like talons.

"Our little man has arrived," she said. She played a two-note drumroll with her left hand. Ian clapped his hands beside the piano.

"Good morning, Yasha," Frida said, holding out a fresh waffle topped with a baseball-sized dollop of sour cream.

Our little mourning man, Yasha thought. These were the right words. Incredible, he thought, to be no longer merely *his*: his son Yasha, the Gregoriov boy, his assistant, his window display maker, his boy, his company, his substitute wife. He had not been *our* anything before. If he tried, he could remember living in the same Russian house as his mother and father; even then, he had never been called *our son*. He was his modest father's son, and his flaming mother's son. They hadn't shared him. They had each claimed him separately, and wholly.

Now I belong to many people, Yasha thought with immense satisfaction, as his mother picked out high notes with her pinkie finger and nobody rushed him to answer.

Kurt left to feed the leftover whale meat to the boar. Haldor went out to start taking down the five lavvos, pole by pole. The festival was over and left in its wake traces of grease on the archery targets, firecracker husks in the grass, and stomped blueberries all along the path from the smithy to the boats. Frances had been assigned to clean the berries and cardboard pieces out from the gravel pathways and the fields. Haldor had assigned Yasha the cleaning of the Ceremonial Hall, the easiest task.

Frances came into the hall. She wore an orange shirt, yellow shorts, and red sneakers. Her hair sat on the top of her head in the same baseball-sized clump as the sour cream. Yasha beamed at her with his teeth showing.

Frances squinted, and nodded questioningly, and Yasha nodded back with utter confidence.

"Just checking," Frances said, and she turned around and walked back to her room.

"Give me that waffle," Yasha said to Frida.

"Anything you want," Frida said.

"Anything I want," said Yasha.

"Ja byl kogda-to strannojj," sang his mother, with feeling.

Sigbjørn was sitting at a window-side table, having his own breakfast. Kurt had prepared a sausage he claimed would cure any hangover. "Hey, birthday," Sigbjørn called out. "What was that about?" He bucked his chin toward Frances's room. "What happened last night?"

"I guess she thought it might have been a dream," Yasha said. He took the seat across from Sigbjørn, and unwrapped a knife and fork from within a rolled-up paper napkin. The napkin, once unfolded and placed in his lap, read GRATULERER MED DAGEN.

"Granule med dragon?" Yasha said.

"Congratulations with the day," Sigbjørn said. "What dream?"

Yasha wondered if Kurt had set the whole Ceremonial Hall with birthday napkins. He saw Frances leave her room again and go outside to begin her work. Not since his last Friday in Brighton Beach, a couple of hours before his mother had appeared, the last ordinary hours of his life, when he'd come home to his father, full of pizza, singing American songs—not since then had Yasha felt the sum of energy around him collect so obviously in his favor.

. . .

I was on my hands and knees flinging ants into the bushes, clean-ing up the blueberries, thinking about virginity. It was one of the things—they seemed to be accumulating—that didn't come back. Three things had vanished, had fallen off this upper edge of the world: Vassily, in his beach grave; Nils, in his forest; and then this thing I had taken from Yasha, in our double bed, in Room 18. He would have to go on without it. I hoped I had taken it kindly. I hoped he didn't want it back.

Now it was eleven o'clock, a blue sky again. A brighter blue than the berries. They were mashed, and everywhere, and I had cleared all the trash from the Viking ships—the festival guests and their berries had stained a good deal of very old wood—and I was making my way, clearing this little path, toward the smithy. Of course, the path reminded me of Nils. It was the one we had run down, my first time here, sweating, to the boats. I hadn't heard anything more from him, in any language.

I gathered the stomped berries in a bucket, as if restoring them, as if calling Nils back. No magic happened, and I knew I would feed the stomped berries to the boar. I thought about Yasha's back, and how I'd flattened my hands over it the whole gray morning. How warm he was.

Which algebra would be solved, I wondered, if he came to my sister's wedding? Without his mother, without my mother. Without his father, without my father. Yasha could give my sister away. And I could sit in the front row, weeping, pretending my hair was as long as my mother's, pretending my legs were as long as my mother's, pretending Yasha was my husband, and my sister our beloved child. For a moment there seemed no other way for the wedding to go on. I had a thought that Nils was sick some-where. I looked at Yasha and practiced asking him to come with me. Just then Yasha and Sigbjørn walked past me, heading toward the smithy.

· · ·

"What do you think of Tribeca?" Sigbjørn asked Yasha.

"Ian?"

"You approve?" Sigbjørn said.

Yasha wasn't sure. He dug a line with his foot in the smithy's gravel floor. He put both his feet on the right side of the line, and thought: He knew my father; he paid for my father's body; he knows my mother better than I do; he came here; he is here. He put his feet on the left side, and thought: He has a beard; he is not my father; he likes the sound of his own voice; he likes the look of his own shoes; he likes my mother; and screw him.

"I don't know," Yasha said.

"Lots of loving," Sigbjørn said. Yasha looked up. "Everybody is coming here this summer to love. Not me," Sigbjørn said. "Frances comes, I am interested in her, she is interested in you," Sigbjørn said. "Your mother comes, I am interested in her, I think she is interested in Haldor, really she likes Tribeca. Now Tribeca is here and I will have to watch them making kisses. The summer is almost over," he said. "You know what happens to me? Goodbye, ladies. Hello, my grandmother. Superfine."

To change the subject, Yasha said, "So you start with two pieces of iron?"

Sigbjørn laughed. *"Ja,"* he said, "clumps." He reached away and when his arm returned, his hand opened, showing two silver nuggets. Yasha imagined them changing shape in the fire. Sigbjørn stopped pumping, took one nugget in each hand, and then slammed them together. "Kiss kiss kiss kiss kiss," Sigbjørn said, twisting each nugget separately, pressing them against each other with force.

Frances walked in. She was carrying two buckets, one full of berries, one full of trash. Her knees were dirty.

"Sky and sea," Sigbjørn said, "look who it is."

Yasha stood up.

"Who was that man with your mother?" Frances asked.

"Ian Strom," Yasha said. "Her boyfriend."

"Ian Strom," Frances said. She put the buckets down and sat on the stool where Yasha had been.

"Wasn't me with your mother!" Sigbjørn said. "The answer is never me." The nuggets were no longer kissing, and he clutched one of them in his tongs. He plunged the tongs into the depth of the coal pile. The iron as it melted made a sound like wind blowing. A few lumps of coals cracked in half from their own heat.

"What does that mean?" Frances said.

"Do you think I ever know what my mother means?" Yasha said.

"Right," said Frances. "Do you know how long he's staying?"

"No."

"Do you know how long you're staying?"

"Why?"

"Because I was wondering—"

"Hey, lovemakers!" Sigbjørn said. "What is this, a smithy or a hotel?"

Frances stood up. "I'd like to invite you to my sister's wedding," she said. "September, in California, you can use my father's plane ticket. He stabbed himself in the hand. He wasn't going anyway. That's all. Sorry, Sigbjørn. I mean it, Yasha." He had never seen her so nervous. "I don't know how to go if you don't come. So. Before you go off with your mother and her friend, consider coming with me." She left the smithy and turned right; a moment later she crossed back and went left. Her head hung low on her neck, as if the buckets were pulling it down.

Yasha expected Sigbjørn to make a joke. Instead, he handed Yasha a hammer. Sigbjørn withdrew the combined nuggets—the iron had assumed the exact red of the coals—placed the glowing clump on an anvil. "Go!" Sigbjørn said. Yasha swung the hammer down onto the iron as hard as he could. If Frances hadn't left, he thought, she might have heard these bangs as some kind of answer. They sounded more decisive than anything in Yasha's mind.

While Sigbjørn cooled the iron, he asked Yasha, "What shall you tell her?"

Yasha had always understood the association of sex and marriage in the historical, even biblical tradition. Still, he had not expected the one to lead so quickly to the other. It's not my wedding, he told himself. It's not Frances's wedding. All the same, the image of Frances's sister, who in his mind was identical to Frances, puffed up in a wedding dress, walking down an aisle, confused him.

"She sounded like she wanted you," Sigbjørn said.

That was the heart of it. She sounded like she wanted him. He could not have performed so badly the night before, after all. And it would not be Frances in the white dress. It would be Frances in a pink dress, or a blue dress, any kind of dress in the world, and he would wear a tie to match. Sigbjørn lay the new bar of iron out on a leather sheet. Yasha came close to him and peered over his shoulder.

"I would like to learn what you do with iron," Yasha said.

"I would like to learn what you do with girls," Sigbjørn said.

Yasha remembered the breast-sucking he had done the day before. "What do I . . ." Yasha fished, "do with them?"

"I don't know," Sigbjørn said. "You make them love you so easy." He inspected Yasha's hammering. "Run and tell her you're coming," he said. "I have to fix your bad work." Sigbjørn got the fire going again. Yasha walked out of the smithy humiliated, triumphant, in a kind of trance.

On the beach, the birds were out fishing. The wind came from the direction of the museum and struck Yasha in the face. He liked to feel the wind catch on his chest before it blew past. Yasha studied a gull and imagined the gull's wide wings growing out from under his own shoulder blades—one wing stretching up toward the archery targets, one stretching out toward the water.

As he walked, the wings he'd grown caught more and more of the wind. In his mind they were grotesque and fringed—long white feathers formed a wall behind him, from his head to the sand. He could almost feel their tips dragging, getting dirtier, slowing him down. He knew these were not flying wings. His wings were the kind that beasts like griffins and sphinxes grew when they became royal, signifying majesty and decadence, never enough to lift their animal weight. He walked slowly, and let his wings drag in the sand.

When he reached the parking lot, the wings drew up and collected behind him, then dissipated. Only his body again. Gunn was on the phone. The Ceremonial Hall had not been cleaned—that was his job. First, Frances. He walked down the hallway past his own room and toward hers. When he arrived, the door to Room 20 opened and his mother stepped into the hall. She had put on her Valkyrie costume, and her wings, Yasha saw, were sturdily set on her back, clean, finer than his had been. "Come in," she said, "how did you know we were waiting?"

She put her hand to the small of his back and led him into the room, where Ian sat on the foot of her pushed-together bed. The wrong double bed. The wrong room. The wrong man. The wrong woman.

"Alyosha, birthday boy," Ian said, as his mother closed the door behind them.

. . .

I was on my bed being very nervous. I had made a fool of myself, and I had no more paint. I needed at least to paint while I waited for Yasha's answer. To make one more painting before going home. Nils's work had been so bright; the new season called for different colors, now that the night had become visible again. Blacks and blues. Haldor, in telling me that he was tired of the sun, then asking me about California, had made the connection I had long ago assumed: California was taking the sun back from Norway. Everything seemed to depend on everything else. I heard footsteps in the hall that stopped in front of my room. I sat up and brushed my hair off my face. I heard Olyana's voice. I heard her door close.

. . .

"We have a present for you," his mother said.

"It's a country," said Ian.

"Can we talk about this in a few minutes?" Yasha said. "I have to make a stop next door."

His mother turned to Ian. "He has a girlfriend."

"Atta boy," said Ian.

"Excuse me?" said Yasha. His mother came around and sat on the bed beside Ian, crumpling the lower tips of her wings. Yasha took a step away from them, toward the door. "You and I don't make sense outside the Gregoriov Bakery," Yasha said, looking at Ian's beard. "If I don't have any bread to sell you, I don't have anything to say to you."

"Easy, Alyosha," Ian said.

"Bye," Yasha said, and he opened the door.

"We are moving to Zurich," his mother said behind him. Yasha closed the door again.

"And we've bought you a ticket," Ian said. "Window seat. First class. Whole shebang."

When Yasha turned back around, Ian was holding out the ticket. At once, Yasha was seven years old. He was going to America. Or was he seventeen? Going to Russia? Was he standing by his crib or by the oven? Where was everyone always taking him?

His mother stood and snuck toward him while he was remembering. All at once, her hands fell onto his shoulders. When Yasha looked up, he looked into her face.

"This time I keep you," she said. She spoke directly to him, not to the whole room, not to an audience. "This time, when you fly away, it is not away from me."

He could see a centimeter of gray at the roots of her hair, before the red began. She had been younger in Russia, the first time he said goodbye to her. They had both gotten a lot older.

"Yakov," Olyana said, "do you hear? Not away from me."

"What's in Zurich?"

"A music school," Ian said. "I'm the new children's educator."

"Why Zurich?"

"They wanted me," said Ian.

Yasha heard Frances's sink turn on from the other side of the wall. The sound was interrupted by what must have been her hands—he could imagine it, the way she washed her face, so much like a rabbit. They wanted me, Yasha thought.

"And I wanted him," his mother said, "and I wanted you too. So forgive me. I want a lot."

"It's really you," Ian said. "You will make this make sense. I have been telling Olyana for a long time—you are what is missing. We know it."

Yasha thought: My father is what is missing. Frances's faucet turned off. He wanted to catch her before she left her room. What if I am going to Zurich, he thought. What about California? What if, for once, I am not going anywhere?

Ian's things were scattered over his mother's bedside table. Yasha grabbed a car key by its big plastic fob. "Let me think about it," he said, and left the room. The hallway was shockingly quiet. *"Frances,"* he yelled. Frances came right out. "Let's go," he said.

The key opened the door to the black car parked beside Sigbjørn's tractor.

"Can you do this?" Frances said.

"Aren't I doing it?" said Yasha.

"Go ahead," said Frances, buckling up.

. . .

"Go ahead," I said. *Why a seat belt?* I heard Agnes's voice shouting as I buckled myself in. *Are you scared?* I heard the engine start. I saw Yasha look down, get the pedals straight. We drove the first five kilometers in silence. We were approaching Skjerpvatnet Lake.

"I'm not going to Switzerland," was the first thing Yasha said.

"The wedding is in California," I said.

"I'm not going to California," Yasha said.

It hit me three times: Yasha's refusal, becoming my parents' refusal, becoming my sister's departure. "Where are you going?" I said.

"Nowhere. I'm staying. I'm not going anywhere this time."

We were driving at 138 kilometers per hour down the E10 highway. I looked out the window. Purple *geitrams* grew down the side of the road.

"I don't understand," I said, touching my seat belt with both hands.

"I keep getting on planes," Yasha said. "Hurry, to America. Hurry, to Russia. Hurry, to the end of the earth. Each time, I leave my mother."

"I thought your mother left you."

"We all left each other," he said, and I knew exactly what he meant. "But if I leave here, I leave my father," he said to the steering wheel. "So I can't be done here. Papa isn't done."

"No," I said vaguely, in agreement.

"No Zurich. No San Francisco," Yasha said. He was unraveling. He mumbled, "Opposite directions."

"What does Switzerland have to do with this?"

Yasha didn't answer. When we had passed the lake, he said, "Sigbjørn says I know how to make a girl love me." I looked at him. "I don't know if I do. I mean, I don't know if you do. Sigbjørn

233

doesn't know that I love you," he said—he looked at me a moment too long, the car drifted, a car behind us honked, and he looked straight ahead again. His profile looked like Caravaggio's *Boy with a Basket of Fruit*. I wanted to be the basket he carried. He said, "I have to stay here."

I found I couldn't look at him any longer, so I turned to the window. Signs for Leknes started popping up. I wanted to get out of the car; I knew the asylum wasn't far, and I knew if I walked along the highway, on the other side of the *geitrams*, I could make it there without getting hit.

"Let me out," I said.

"No way," said Yasha. "Did you hear me? I said I love you. All I'm saying is I can't follow you home."

"That's fine," I said. "Completely." I didn't know what I was saying. "Let me out," I tried again.

The asylum, in all its seven shades of blue, with its open lot where only Nils had ever parked, where sheep now chewed the weeds at the side of the building, flew toward and then fell away behind our car.

"We passed it," I said.

"We're almost there," Yasha said, turning in toward Leknes center.

The grocery store's parking lot was full. I couldn't understand where any of these people lived. Yasha and I had not been nearly so alone on this island as it had always seemed. It felt, once again, like we were climbing out from under Yggdrasil. Our lovemaking had its place, which was nontransferable, nonassociative, not an answer to other questions.

When the car was parked, Yasha said, "I have to stay here through the winter."

I still didn't know where *here* was. The museum would close in September.

"I don't know where I'll live," Yasha said, apparently having the same thought. "It doesn't matter. Somewhere close enough to Eggum. I've heard about the winter storms," Yasha said, turning to me with the eyes of a very young person. "I want to make sure the grave makes it. The beach was my father's idea. It wasn't, I don't think, a good one," he said.

What could I say? I told him I loved him. I told him I wanted to go to the supermarket.

I was crying when I asked the REMA 1000 cashier for paint. Of course they didn't have paint. I really just wanted to see their dear milk aisle, beer aisle, bread aisle, toilet paper.

"Har du maling?" I asked.

Å *male*. To paint. The same as: Å *male*. To purr.

Maling. Paint. *Maling*. Purring.

The cashier said, *"Hva?"*

I was thinking about cats by then.

I said all I knew how to say: A cat named Rambo rescued another cat at a farm last evening near Tangstad.

. . .

Ian was waiting for Yasha in the parking lot when the car rolled in. Frances got out and excused herself.

"Is that her?" Ian said.

"Your keys," said Yasha. "Thank you." Yasha dropped the car keys into Ian's open palm.

"You scared us," Ian said.

"My mother doesn't get scared," Yasha said. "Sorry for scaring you."

"Yasha," Ian said. "What is that short for?"

"You can call me the Subharmonic Thundergrowl of the West," Yasha said, "and I have a favor to ask." Ian laughed. "Go to Zurich without me," Yasha said. He leaned toward Ian, who was no longer laughing, and spoke quietly. "I used to like the way your guitars sounded when they slammed into the bakery door. You must be talented. They'll love you over there." He started walking Ian toward the museum door. "But I don't want the ticket. Thanks anyway. I want Tribeca," Yasha said. Ian didn't respond. Yasha put it more formally. "Please give me the keys to your Tribeca apartment," he said, "for while you are in Zurich."

Ian let out a long breath and starting cracking his right hand's knuckles. Yasha waited while he cracked the left hand. "Wanted to have you over to that apartment a million times." Ian put his hands back in his pockets. "Had spare pillows for you," he said, "You know, in case you ever wanted to come over and crash after school. Not far from your school, my place. Your mother would never let me—"

"How do you know where I went to school?"

"Didn't your mom pick you up for lunch? The one time? I heard all about your playdate."

Yasha wasn't familiar with playdates. Playdates were for younger kids. Not seven-year-olds who had just come over from Russia and had no friends on hand. Yasha could only think about dates, real dates, the kind this man had been going on with his mother.

"What's she like?" Yasha asked.

"Who?"

"My mother."

"A barrel of monkeys," Ian said. "You know, I thought she was a lunatic—my fingers nearly bled, first week of lessons."

Lessons, Yasha remembered. Everybody had been his mother's student. His father had been. This man too, with his boots and his beard—his mother had probably taught this man how to grow his beard. His mother was everyone's teacher.

Ian kept talking. *"Practice your octaves, practice your octaves,"* he said. "I thought, I should give up. Then, of course, I couldn't give her up."

Yasha thought: Have I given her up?

"How did you get her to America?" Yasha asked. "It didn't work with us, when we tried. The first time."

"I hate that," Ian said, "I hate all of that. The whole story. I keep thinking she's going to bail on me too, any minute. And I keep thinking that I'm a lout."

"You are a lout," Yasha said. He didn't know what *lout* meant. He hoped it was a kind of insect. Yasha tried to crack his own knuckles, but they made no sound.

"What can anyone do?" Ian said. "I try to hang on to her."

"Hard work," Yasha said.

"It's gone all right. So far. I'm grateful." Ian looked at Yasha as if they were cousins or old friends. "Because when she's there, it's good. You know? And she keeps being there, so far."

Yasha pitied him in his innocence—Ian didn't know who he was dealing with, hadn't seen his mother at her worst. Yasha had never seen his mother at her best.

"We'll see how it goes in Switzerland, I guess," Ian said. "I wish that you would join us."

"I can't," Yasha said. "Next best thing is to give me your keys."

Ian exhaled again. He reached into the back pocket of his rolled-up jeans and retrieved a key ring. It held three keys and a monogrammed pendant.

"I didn't think you'd come with us," Ian said, holding the keys up, letting the pendant turn in the air. "Alyosha sticks." His manner had lifted into something Yasha could identify as charming. He reminded Yasha of his mother. They made a powerful pair. "My upright bass will get your window seat," Ian said.

There was a second in which Yasha wanted to take the place that had been offered to him—wanted the window view, wanted the Alps coming into sight when the plane got low enough, a little more time with this strangely admirable man and the redheaded woman who wanted her son again.

Ian placed the keys in Yasha's hand and said, "Water my plants."

Olyana came out through the front entrance.

"Where have the men gone?" she asked.

"We're here," Ian said.

"And?" she said. She looked at Yasha. She looked at Ian. "Ian is happy, I can see you have made him happy. You're coming with me," she said.

"You're going with him," Yasha said. His mother hesitated. "You're very right," Yasha said. "No more leaving behind—" he didn't want to say *Mother*, or *Olyana*; he looked at her wings, and said, "—Valkyrie. We're not sneaking away from each other. It's all out in the open this time. This time we're both innocent." Yasha could see the word appeal to her. At the back of her mind, scales were balancing. Their tilt had surely been an inconvenience to her, Yasha thought, all these years.

Through the Ceremonial Hall windows, Yasha saw Gunn cleaning up the festival mess. She had collected all the teacups in a stack that rose six inches higher than her head. She bent down for one more cup.

"I've been awful today," Yasha said. He went in to see what he could do.

. . .

By the time I was packed and bound for California, the sun set in the evenings and stayed down all night. Yasha didn't sleep in my room anymore. It happened wordlessly, the change, one day in the corridor. Yasha, his mother, Ian, and I left the Ceremonial Hall together after Haldor's last staff dinner, walked past Yggdrasil to our rooms, and there they were—our three different doors: Room 16, Room 18, Room 20. I don't know whether it was mere propriety that made Yasha say goodnight, nodding to his mother, then to Ian, then to me. Opening his door, going in, staying in. Propriety, or else it was the first move in his new direction—his middle path, straight through the emptiness his father had opened.

My room was dark. A new dark, as complete as the light had been. It made me shiver and sleep.

The changing of the seasons couldn't be helped. Yasha had found a way to help, to help that grave, and I felt my old uselessness creeping in with the sunsets, earlier every night. It was important to come closer to my father again, who needed to be surrounded; to my sister, who needed to be supported; to my mother, whose needs I never knew. I would go back to school, a graduate course in painting, and pay my hardest attention. I had failed to get all the sun's information, hadn't paid it the attention Nils had. I knew this summer's endless day had kept a few secrets from me. Secrets about color, and veils, and how to make a thing glow. Secrets about the innumerable species of darkness.

My sister had landed in California.

Yasha was quiet on his side of the wall. I listened, and knew he was there, but could not hear him. I wanted to fill my hands with him. Pale night light bounced off the edge of my tiny sink.

Who knows where the moon had been? I hadn't seen it for months. Now it hung in my window. The wild boar had become invisible, being night-colored. Terrifying how black the fjordwater was then, the white sky receding, and the moon taking its place.

CODA

As it happened, Sarah asked our father one more time to give her away. As it always happened, in my parents' mouse-sized apartment, what was said to one was heard by the other.

"Is this how it will be? When we are *separate entities*?" my mother said to my father. "Our daughters will turn to you? To you, and not to me?" It was the reverse of the answer one is supposed to give the Wicked Child on Passover: "This is because of what the Lord did for me, for me and not for you, when he freed me from my bondage." It was to be neither of them, my mother said to my sister, or both.

That was how my father came to sit on the bride's side, front row, with nobody else on the bench next to him. How my mother—in a gesture of defiance so total it defied her own wishes—sat with the groom's family, beside Mrs. Glenny. Mrs. Glenny, in a large hat and sunglasses, was dressed for Easter. My mother was dressed in black. She attended on the condition that nobody—neither she nor my father—did anything "special." It was left to me to give Sarah away.

You could have expected that Sarah would be lovely: cap sleeves, ranunculus bouquet, lace gloves that ran up and over her elbows. You could not have expected the color her cheeks would turn that morning: a color I had come to associate with a particular distance of the sun from the horizon, a carmine color that meant both sunset and sunrise. As a bride, she looked particularly tall. It seemed the weight of her body had rearranged itself, and hung higher, making her shoulders heavy, her stomach light, her knees heavy, her feet light. She had my mother's height and dark hair, my father's blue eyes, and my arm to hold, walking over the footbridge and into the Glenny backyard.

In gratitude for my parents' attendance, Sarah had crafted a makeshift chuppah from the poles of Scott's soccer goal. Scott wore a yarmulke. When my mother saw this, she pointed at it and said to Scott's mother, "Your hat sure beats his." Mrs. Glenny said, "Scott's told us all about the Yamaha, Mirela. We couldn't be more delighted." My mother referred to yarmulkes as Yamahas for the next two years, until Scott left Sarah, and Sarah asked her to stop.

But that day, Sarah and I thought that we had won. It was foggy, and cold, and the wind that came in off the San Francisco Bay blew through all of our hair—Scott's wires, Sarah's coiled braids, my thin curls, my father's·halo, my mother's drapery. The only thing anybody could later say, and never deny, and never divorce, was that we were there; we came as we were asked. Yasha hadn't come, but something else had been asked of him.

Scott married Sarah at three in the afternoon on the patio of the Glenny house, on a September day in San Francisco that had been erroneously forecasted as sunny. The bride and groom looked anemic, gangly, both of them, although noticeably amazed at each other—at the ceremony, at the splendor they hadn't seemed to expect. At their first dance, in the middle of the great white tent, Scott held my sister so tightly I thought she'd squeak. They weren't right about each other, it turned out. It turned out they had been too young all along. But before the solution became divergence it was, for this evening, a very physical togetherness, in which Sarah and Scott clung to each other, and the party twirled on around them.

At the party, my father drank. My mother drank absolutely nothing. Neither sat down and neither danced—they wandered around the dance floor apologizing to guests for stepping on their feet and nodding at Sarah's girlfriends. "Do you want this?" my father went around asking the girls. "Is this what you want for yourself?"

I sat down on the floor when my father started clinking his glass. There wasn't enough time to find a chair, and I wanted to be low to the ground. His smile and even the butter knife he used to clink his glass seemed unspeakably dangerous. He stood in the middle of the dance floor. My mother stood at the far right of the tent, near the band. Scott and Sarah sat at the bridal table, having just begun their dinners. My father threw his hands in the air.

"We're so picky!" he began. "Picky picky picky." He began to sing. "'Pick-a-little-talk-a-little-pick-a-little-talk-a-little-cheep-cheep-cheep-talk-a-lot-pick-a-little-more.'"

It was the housewives' song from *The Music Man*. It was Sarah's old favorite. There was an unused trumpet on the floor of the band stage, and my mother rested her hand on it, as if to keep herself from falling down. Had she too wound up on the floor, I could have crawled over and joined her. She stayed upright, clutching the trumpet.

"My name is Saul," he said, "I'm Sarah's father." He pointed at Sarah with his knife. "My daughter is making a *decision*," my father said, spreading his arms out on the last word. He turned around in a slow circle, to see who all was listening, and everyone was listening. When he faced the bride and groom again he said, "Would I pick what she is picking? I would not! No, sir, I would not!" A friend of Scott's who didn't know my father, and who was in a great mood, cheered, "Me neither!" Someone put a hand over his mouth. "You pick the love you want," my father went on seamlessly. "You pick. The love. You want. Okay. I picked—"

This was where I thought it would break down. Again, the familiar sensation of my father's hair growing while we watched, away from his head in every direction—he was marvelous, and even holding the glass of rosé I knew was his tenth, he was precise.

"I. Picked. Wrong. Didn't I?" Both my mother and my sister were crying. I was enthralled.

"I am the angriest person I know. Also the most entertaining. Wouldn't you say?" The young man whose mouth was still covered clapped his hands in appreciation. "Thank you," my father said. "Now. In case you don't know my work—and believe me, you don't know my work—I spend my days drawing swollen submax-illary glands so that tenth-grade biology students can learn the diff—" This was the one word he slurred. *Difference.* "The diffrenz between mucus and saliva." He looked hard into the eyes of the guy who had cheered for him and said, "You have never seen wrists like the wrists I drew for the pamphlet on carpal tunnel syndrome." This quieted even that guy. "Do I love this work? Actually, yes. At least I *did*, in the beginning. I knew what I loved and I picked it, for better or worse."

There was a pause, and a few people drank from their glasses.

He said, "Sarah is picking her love. Aren't you?" Sarah was still holding the fork she had raised to her mouth just before my father started speaking. Her eyes and his eyes said Blue Blue Blue Blue to each other. "And I congratulate her. For the picking itself. Because that is hard to do. Few people ever do it. The most of us," he said, "something picks us. Or we pick nothing. Take what we get. My Sarah said, 'Daddy'—no, she never calls me Daddy—she said, 'Dad, I pick him.' And we said no. And she picked him anyway. And she got him." When I think of this speech, it's this line that most makes me wish that Sarah and Scott had kept each other. This part about Sarah wanting him, and getting him.

"The next job, Sarah," my father said, "is to remember down the line that nobody picked this but you." For the first time since clinking the glass, he lowered his knife. "What you'll have, what you'll lack—all your fault. Your misery? Your fault. Your happiness? Up to you. The only thing that ever made me less scared of my misery was my wife. There she is, by the band." My father gestured. My mother did not wave to the crowd now looking at her; she held on to the trumpet. "Forgive me," he said. "I've lost track of things."

And that was it. He left the dance floor and took a seat at an empty table, where nobody came to comfort him, and the trumpet player eventually lifted the trumpet out from under my mother's hand, and the band started to play, relatively quietly, until the party was in swing again.

To Scott's credit, he comforted my sister through her hysteria for the better part of two hours. My mother composed herself—even took a seat at my father's table. They didn't speak, but they sat together. I kissed my sister's head and left the tent for a short walk.

· · ·

Stretched out along the house's corridor wall, the gifts looked like fish in an aquarium. Most of the wrapping was silver, gold, or light blue. The ribbons were voluminous—they looked like foam. One of the gifts was perfectly spherical. They were so intensely silent, these objects, I half expected they would release a burst of song when opened, following my father's example. The spherical gift was silver. The cube was gold. A set of three white-wrapped gifts was tied up with a turquoise ribbon. Beside it lay a padded envelope. I looked at the envelope because by comparison it was so unattractive.

The envelope hadn't been wrapped and the shipment label was peeling off. Written into the recipient box was my name and the address of the Glenny house. Written into the return address box was *480 Leonard Street, New York, NY 10013*. The postage stamp was fifty-six kroner.

Seeing as the package was addressed to me, I opened it. When I try to remember what I was thinking as I opened it, I can only recall feeling surrounded by silver and gold fish, and the sound of my father singing *Cheep cheep cheep*. The envelope contained a key ring. On the ring hung three Mul-T-Lock keys and a silver medallion. The medallion was embossed with IS.

IS.

Is, I thought. Is. It is. Is what?

It is it.

There are photographs from the rest of the party in which I am dancing. In all the photographs, I am holding the envelope. You can see the corner of it behind my sister's arm in the picture where we have our arms around each other. You can see it in my left hand in the picture where my father and I are drinking glasses of water. As far as I remember, nobody asked me about it. Everyone had, by that point, lost track of things.

When I got back to New York and moved into the apartment at 480 Leonard Street, my parents didn't give it much thought. They had gotten used to my being out of the house, and my graduate program had started, and for all they knew I was living in a dorm. They hadn't yet vacated their apartment. It was completely empty, and they were living in it that way, with some thrill, it seemed, as if they were squatting.

The apartment above the Gregoriov Bakery needed to be emptied. The phone at Ian's apartment rang one day with a Mr. Dobson, who had gotten the number from a Yasha Gregoriov, who wanted to know if I could please pack up his and his father's belongings.

When I arrived at Brighton Beach that morning at the end of September, Mr. Dobson greeted me at the bakery door. He had two things to tell me. Bad news first, he said: Yasha's cat had been run over. It was the first time the cat had left the bakery in two weeks, and he hadn't eaten in as long—he walked through the cat door onto Oriental Boulevard, and stood weakly in the center of the road. "All my fault," Mr. Dobson said. He hadn't closed the cat door as Yasha asked. The good news was that as of January, the Gregoriov Bakery would reopen as the Ladisov Bakery, and that the Ladisov family would keep all the old ovens. I walked upstairs and saw the two rooms in which Yasha had grown into himself. A sweet, dusty place. At the center of everything I'd come to learn about Yasha, these two rooms would remain empty, a blueprint of what I'd missed: his first life, watching bread rise, with his father. I packed their things into two thick garbage bags I found in the lower level. The bags sat on either side of me as I rode the B train over the Manhattan Bridge.

In October, Sarah and Scott had their first big fight. Sarah was so startled, she took a red-eye one Thursday night and spent a few days on Leonard Street with me. We talked through it—I was of the opinion that the relationship was salvageable at that point— and when silence fell and we both reached for our phones, I thought of my father's thumb assignment. He'd turned it down. He told me he was now working on something else. He wouldn't say what. I wrote a letter to the Viking Museum, addressed to Yasha, saying his cat had died. I painted Sarah in the nude. That painting has since gotten Sarah a few dates, but we'll see where they lead. I heard that Robert was still in Japan. I heard that he was reporting directly to the Secretary of State.

I didn't hear back from Yasha until the end of November. His father's grave had withstood its second major storm, and Yasha was half confident that it would remain stable. This, alongside Septimos's death, he wrote, marked the end of an era. The era was his life so far. He hadn't heard a peep from his mother, and that was fine. Haldor had left on his Baltic cruise, and Yasha was living with Sigbjørn and Sigbjørn's grandmother. He had starting eating and liking fish for the first time, the way Sigbjørn's grand-mother prepared it, with butter. The bread Sigbjørn's grand-mother baked was as fresh when it came out of the oven as his father's had been. It is bread's nature to be warm, he wrote. I got his letter a few days before Thanksgiving, and when I called my mother to pass along Yasha's regards, she was shredding apples

for applesauce. I asked her what the applesauce was for. She said
Thanksgiving. She shared the applesauce with my father, my
father put ketchup on it, and that was all they ate. My mother
had begun to decorate the apartment again from scratch. I visited
them for the holidays and found three sketches of my mother's
face tacked to the bathroom wall.

When the sun stopped rising in Eggum, Yasha said he was ready
to leave. He said the sky turned purple at eleven in the morning,
pink at noon, purple at one, then black for twenty-one hours.
He said the mountains turned the same colors as the sky. He
said the fjords never froze. He said the Icelandic ponies stayed
out all winter and their manes grew over their eyes. He said the
storm winds were so strong, they made the trees shake so
humanly, he'd had a long dream, filling the dark hours, in which
all trees walked away. He said the blue that settled over the fields
before the black was the most erotic color he'd ever seen. He said
he'd been drinking goat milk. He said that one morning when the
sky was purple he'd seen a bit of grass through the snow, that
some of the snow had melted, that he wanted to get out before
the next storm, that it all depended on the boats—when they
ran, how rough the fjord was on any particular night. He said he
was leaving everything where it was and coming back to
everything. He said he was taking nothing with him. It would be
eighteen hours down from the Arctic, he said, then due west.

NOTES

Yasha hears an excerpt from Richard Pevear and Larissa Volokhonsky's translation of *The Brothers Karamazov* (New York: Farrar, Straus, & Giroux, 2002).

Haldor reads from I. A. Blackwells's 1906 translation of *The Younger Eddas of Snorre Sturleson* and from Jean I. Young's 1954 translation of *The Prose Edda*.

Olyana reads aloud Jesse L. Byock's description of the Yggdrasil tree, as found in *The Prose Edda* (New York: Penguin Classics, 2005), page xxvii.

Nils and Frances listen to Oliver Stallybrass's translation of Knut Hamsun's *Victoria* (Toronto: Hushion House, 1994).

The Viking Museum, as portrayed in this book, is a fictitious institution and is not meant to resemble the LOFOTR Viking Museum of Lofoten. I extend deep thanks to LOFOTR for its inspiring example, and to Lofoten Golf Links for teaching me how to build a lavvo.

ACKNOWLEDGMENTS

I am joyfully indebted to Jenni Ferrari-Adler; Lea Beresford, George Gibson, Nancy Miller, Cristina Gilbert, Marie Coolman, Theresa Collier, Lily Yengle, Gleni Bartels, Laura Keefe, Derek Stordahl, Patti Ratchford, Alona Fryman, Megan Ernst, Alexandra Pringle, Alexa von Hirschberg, Kathleen Farrar, Lynsey Sutherland, Madeleine Feeny, and all of Bloomsbury; Sally Wofford-Girand, Sam Fox, and all of Union Literary; the extraordinary writers, faculty, staff, and director of the NYU M.F.A. program; the Rona Jaffe Foundation Graduate Fellowship; the Yale English department; the New York State Summer Writers Institute; the National Library of Norway; *Kunstkvarteret Lofoten*; Reidar Nedrebø and Anne Grete Honerød of *Baroniet Rosendal*; Christian Kjelstrup and all of *Aschehoug Forlag*; Jon Gray; Louise Glück; Jessica Strand; Alice Quinn; Mark Strand; Graham Duncan; Lill-Anita and Bjørn-Erik Svendsen; Eric Bulson and Mika Efros; Julie Buntin and Julia Pierpont; Aaron Parks; Noah Warren; Laura Bennett; Rachel Brotman; Lizzie Fulton; Liz Fusco; Annie Galvin; Meggie Green; Halley Gross; Ingrid Schibsted Jacobsen; Signe Kårstad; Diana Mellon; Cassie Mitchell; Annette Orre; Rachel Rose; Alexandra Schwartz; Ingeborg Sommerfeldt; Alex Trow; Zach Bjork; my loving family: Lia and Jim, Jon and Becky, Max, Michael, Bob and Marti, Lea and Bruce, Shmuel and Lee, Eitan, Goldie, and my heroic late grandparents.